MURDER,

MURDER, MURDER IN

Gilded Central Park

❦━━━━━━━━━━━❦

CECELIA TICHI

Murder, Murder, Murder in Gilded Central Park

ISBN 978-1-68524-815-4

Chapter One

New York City, 1898

"VELVET? WHERE IS SHE?"

"We haven't seen the dog this morning, ma'am. We're on the lookout for her."

"She hasn't barked? You didn't hear her bark?"

"No ma'am."

A dumb question because our French bulldog rarely made a sound, except to snore during naps. The dogs I knew as a girl herded livestock or guarded camps near the silver mines out West where I grew up. They barked or bayed at the moon.

Not our "Frenchie," the rescue dog that greeted my husband and me at breakfast every morning in this chateau that was built by my husband's parents eleven years ago in 1887. The East Side of Central Park was now my home as Mrs.

Roderick Windham DeVere, but the bevy of servants still felt awkward to a western mountain "bride" of three years.

Suppose our dog was lost in this maze of rooms? Her bowls brimmed with water and feed. Where was my husband?

I let the footman hold my chair, nodded "yes" to coffee, and eyed the half-dozen newspapers fanned on the table.

Park Police Baffled...Third Victim... Clothing Ripped Asunder...

My coffee cup snapped down. The New York papers outdid themselves for headline drama, but this was beyond ghoulish. I flipped them over. Time enough for the gruesome details after breakfast. Barely had I seen the headlines, when a warm hand touched my shoulder.

"Roddy...and Velvet in your arms...."

"Good morning, my dear Valentine DeVere," My husband's kiss and the dog's pink tongue against my cheek were tonics. "She came sniffing while Norbert shaved me," Roddy said, "and I thought you'd prefer breakfast with a clean-shaven gentleman." He gently set the dog down, and we watched her spring for the food bowl."

"I was getting worried," I said.

"Blame it on my whiskers." My husband's valet, Norbert, had shaved his ruddy face and tamed his sideburns. "The usual, Bronson," he said to the footman and sat down across from me. "Val, will you have your western mix?"

I said yes to the beans-and-bacon "Chuck Wagon" hash reminiscent of my girlhood in Colorado and Nevada, when the breakfast table was often a smooth flat rock, the sourdough biscuits tangy, and the campfire coffee strong and dark. In my married life on Fifth Avenue, New York City, the toast needed jam, and the pale brown liquid in the Royal Doulton cup was, at least, hot.

Roddy looked fit in his blue paisley dressing gown, while I faced him in a silk sacque and feathery slippers that signaled my new station in life. My husband had met with an alumni group last evening to consult about a cocktail honoring their college and was not home by the time I turned in.

The footman hovered with silver tongs, ready to pincer a slice of toast onto wafer-thin breakfast plates.

"Your tea, sir?"

Roddy nodded. Before I could stop him, the "helpful" footman flipped the newspapers face-up to show *The New York World*—

Central Park Strangler Strikes Again!!!

"Good god...." Roddy pulled the paper toward him. "That vile nickname will stick. Olmsted and Vaux will turn in their graves."

I recognized the Central Park planners' names, Frederick Olmsted and Calvert Vaux.

"From now on," Roddy said, "the killer will be known as 'The Strangler.'"

His eggs and my hash appeared but got cold as we read. My husband's bitterness burst in every syllable. He pushed back the light brown, roguish wave of hair that often dipped over his broad forehead and never failed to charm, including this moment.

"'October eleventh,'" he read aloud, "'third young womanly life crushed in darkest night... demonic brute....'"

"No suspect is named, Roddy."

"'Demonic brute' means that police haven't a clue—or else they are tight-lipped and saying nothing. Every paper will bray about 'The Strangler.' And newsies on every corner cry, 'Read all about it...two cents...Strangler Invades Central Park for Third Time!'" He lifted his teacup and drank deeply. "And by the way, the moon is almost full, so 'darkest night' only boosts the newspaper's morning sales."

"Last night was cloudless, wasn't it?"

"Not a cloud," said Roddy. "The killer struck in bright moonlight."

"Brazen."

I shivered, and we grew silent. The first two recent murders had everyone on edge, and today's news would double the shock. Until this year, homicide was unheard of in Central park. A fifth-generation New Yorker, Roddy had said that robbery and "picking pockets" did happen, as did misbehavior such as sleeping on benches.

But Murder? Never once.

Roddy leaned forward with arms folded on the table. His deep blue eyes had narrowed, meaning that I was about to hear something of great importance to him. "Val," he said, "Whoever is killing these young women, the police must find him fast. As of this third attack, the killer is now in our part of the park."

"Our part?" Central Park was open to everyone, the so-called "Lungs of the City" free for one and all. Somehow, the park reminded me of the free spaces of the West. Was "our part" the nearby zoo? The music pavilion? Or perhaps the boathouse?

"Our part of the park," Roddy repeated, his tone stern. "The East Drive," he added, "…near the Pergola, where you and I and our friends drive and ride. The young woman's body was found near the bridle path…where you rode Comet yesterday."

"And you rode Justice. Roddy, suppose we passed her body on the bridle path yesterday?"

"Doubtful. The killer struck at night. Of course, he might have lurked in the daytime to plan his attack." He pushed away his plate.

I poked at the hash and gave it up. We had been vacationing in late August when the press reported a young woman's strangled body discovered in Central Park by an oak tree in the Ramble. She was thought to have been about nineteen or twenty years of age. The news had spread just as we prepared to depart from our summer cottage in Newport, Rhode Island, and return to the city.

A month later, we were barely unpacked when another young woman was found dead, her neck purpled and broken under the Trefoil, one of the park's many bridges. Co-workers had identified each body. The first victim was formerly employed by a milliner, trimming ladies' hats, and the second had worked in a steam laundry far downtown. Neither had reason to be in the park, as far as anyone knew, and neither was connected to the households that bordered the park.

Both were laid to rest at city expense because neither victim's family came forward to claim her body.

This third victim, like the first two, was an unidentified young woman, her body found by the Pergola where we rode several times weekly and within a short walk to the Pond, where I often walked our dog in the daytime.

The killer's pattern was emerging. So was the timing. By crude calculation, a young woman was choked to death at night in Central Park at the rate of one victim per month. "Roddy," I said, "If he is not stopped, another young woman—"

"—this time next month," he said.

"Mid-November, almost Thanksgiving," I said.

"Horse Show month," he replied.

A calendar slip-up on my part, for New York Society cherished its mid-November Horse Show at Madison Square Garden, which opened the fall and winter season of parties, balls and the theatre. Society took boxes at the Garden for Horse Show Week, when premier equestrian skills were displayed for days—though not the skills I valued, the bronco busting and calf roping of cowboys and ranchers two thousand miles away from New York.

Would a fourth murder be next month's frontpage news? The days were growing shorter. And December—?

We dived deeper into newspaper accounts and soon reached the same conclusion. The third victim, like the others, was probably a wageworker and apparently alone when attacked.

Questions swirled. Did she know where she was in the hundreds of acres of Central Park with its hills and dales, its little forests of trees and winding pathways? Was the young woman lost? Her purpose—or purposes—in the park were mysteries. Had she intended to meet someone, perhaps the killer?

"Only young women have been attacked thus far," Roddy said. "No man...and not one lady."

"The last point, my dear, is hardly relevant."

Roddy's glance said "touché." In our social set, every lady had gentlemen escorts and the protection of coachmen and grooms who ferried us uptown or down at any time of day or evening, who patiently manned the carriages at curbside at the end of every Broadway play or late-night dinner at Delmonico's. In short, none of us went outdoors on foot after dark, and never alone.

For a young woman employed in the service of the households bordering Central Park, however, conditions were vastly different. Scores of young Irish and other immigrant women worked "in service" six days per week, from early morning to late evening as housemaids, parlor maids, or as kitchen sculleries. They assisted nurses or nannies in nurseries filled with infants and children.

The latest victim was perhaps a newcomer from Ireland who now lived in the topmost floor of a great house that lined Fifth or Madison Avenues, like the young women from Kilkenny in our household. In the daytime, the young women might go on errands, usually in twos, and Sunday mornings found them on their way to Mass at St. Patrick's Cathedral.

Whatever the season, an ironclad "bright light" of every servant was a guaranteed weekly "evening off." On that one evening, she was free to go wherever she wished throughout the city and its boroughs.

Which raised the urgent question: Would this mid-November bring another death to the park in the depths of the night...one of our young women?

Roddy put down the *Times* and the *Herald*. "Ironic," he said, "that the servants were safer at the summer resorts."

"Protected by the social calendar," I said, for New York houses routinely "closed" from the first of June to October, including ours at the corner of Fifth Avenue and 62nd Street. When families vacationed at Newport's palatial summer "cottages," their servants came too. As they did at Bar Harbor, Maine, or the Hudson Valley or afloat in the Mediterranean aboard an ocean-going yacht.

Roddy put a finger across his lips. "How many young women servants work in homes around Central Park nowadays, Val?"

"No idea."

"Take a guess."

I tightened my sash. "The richer the family," I said, "the more servants to prove the point. In this part of the city, I'd guess the high hundreds."

"And every single one is now at risk of her life."

"On her evening off, yes." Sudden memories flooded my thoughts. "It could have been a young woman like my own mother, Roddy. A different generation, but the same journey." My voice mixed sadness and lament. "She came from Ireland, an immigrant girl. If she hadn't married Papa and gone West...two Irish immigrants in America for a better life."

He clasped my hands in his. "...if only she had lived to know her daughter, Valentine, how very lovely, how smart... and how fortunate that you, the daughter of the dearly departed Kathleen Louise Mackle, agreed to be my love, my life."

"Roddy...."

"My dear Val...."

His eyes teared, as did mine. We held hands and gave ourselves the moment, recalling the improbable event that brought us together in a silver mining town in Nevada. It was love at first sight. It was.

Roddy's tenor voice lowered as he bent forward, kissed my fingertips, and sat back. "For the sake of your late mother and today's young women, we cannot be idle. Mayor Van Wyck must weigh in. We need a proclamation pledging all resources and a reward for tips leading to capture and conviction. Our neighborhood must do its part. Everyone who enjoys the park deserves safe recreation. Everyone."

His fervor filled me with pride. By "our neighborhood," Roddy meant the wealthy must also press officials for the safety of the workers' families who enjoyed Sundays in the park. (Hadn't Roderick DeVere courted me with the promise that Central Park would show "the spirit of equality" as in the West?)

Not that I mistook the park's trees and paths for the Rocky Mountains or the tawny stretches of Nevada's sky-line, but the park felt good when I walked Velvet or gazed from our front windows at the parade of horse-drawn carts, bicyclists, and people of every stripe coming and going on the pathways.

This was now my life, and I worked hard to make it my home. Was I naïve? The West had its outlaws, cattle rustlers, train robbers, and "tin star" marshals who worked both sides of the law. My papa dealt with claim jumpers in the mining camps.

Those crimes seemed somehow aboveboard. The Central Park "Strangler" felt menacing in a different way.

Roddy's jawline tightened. "I'll call at Tammany Hall and City Hall, and police headquarters too...and the court-house. Others must join me."

My husband rubbed his rock-hard jaw. No one would guess that this gentleman at breakfast in a dressing gown spent a good deal of time in the city's saloons and taverns gathering evidence against temperance crusaders. My law school-trained husband could be found often in the notorious "Tweed" courthouse defending the "oases" of spirits and brews against hordes of well-meaning vigilantes. Few knew that, to this day, Roddy's past and present mixed in legal moves and a sideline consulting about cocktails in our "Golden Age of Cocktails." Soon after we met, he had confided his refusal to be trapped in a life of the idle rich. As a teenager intrigued by the solo performance of a celebrated bartender, Roddy determined to master the secrets of the bar—while law school fitted him for life as a barrister.

Not that my husband championed breweries or distilleries as such. He deplored drunkenness and believed that many who surrendered to alcohol were afflicted by illness. But he loathed the self-righteous mobs bent on forcing their ideas on everybody else. "One day," he had said many times, "the temperance vigilantes will clamp down, drinks will be ruled illegal, and criminals will rule our cities." It sounded far-fetched, but I didn't argue.

"The city police must take charge and put their best men on the Central Park case," Roddy continued. "The park police are out of their depth. If it's a runaway horse or a noisy drunkard, park police are best, no question, but this is beyond them. Let's hope the Lexow hearings cleared that nest of 'crooked cops.'" He added, "Finally."

The Lexow matter was four years ago, before our wedding, but the topic of police corruption in the city threaded its way through conversations about bribes and payoffs, extortion, thuggery, and a mysterious "third-degree."

Our wall clock struck the hour, and Velvet leaped for shelter at my ankles while the gong banged like a creature in our midst. Roddy's mother, Eleanor, had brought the clock from Vienna as a gift and proclaimed it "a Junghans German gong wall clock…perfect for your morning room, dear Valentine." My mother-in-law always spoke my full name, Valentine, in tones suggesting an early frost. I chose not to protest the ornate clock. My papa—may he rest in peace—always said, pick your fights.

"Nine a.m. already," Roddy drained the last of his tea. "Busy day," he said. "…the Dewey committee, then the mayor's office at City Hall and a stop at police headquarters… and midafternoon on Chambers Street."

"The courtroom…."

Roddy nodded. "The temperance posse has targeted the St. James Hotel bar. They claim the bartender serves whisky to newsboys, which is absurd. Billy Patterson would never do such a thing. I'll defend Billy and the hotel. Judge O'Toole is a good man. We'll see…."

He pushed back his chair, and the day splintered when my husband asked, "And what is on the agenda for you today, my dear?"

I did not reply. My day yawned vacantly ahead. I stood. Roddy stood. And the gulf that split a gentleman's day from a lady's gaped wide open when my husband repeated, "Once again, what is on the agenda for you today, my dear?"

I murmured about walking our dog and spending a few hours in my workroom, where some books awaited new bindings in Morocco leather. In truth, nothing "popped" on my calendar as a lady-by-marriage in Society. Three years into my new life as Mrs. Roderick DeVere, and following a Newport summer that crackled with surprising adventure, I suddenly found myself with little to do—and no purpose.

As the day unfolded, however, I need not have fretted, for unforeseen events were underway to bring a challenge to Roddy's and my doorsteps—literally speaking, to the dozen limestone front steps that had been imported from the Loire Valley for this Fifth Avenue French Gothic chateau in New York City. By the evening hours, that is, Roddy and I would find ourselves faced with a critical decision that we could not have foreseen.

Chapter Two

MY HUSBAND LEFT, AND I walked Velvet and busied myself in my second-floor workroom, when two huge horses thundered down Fifth Avenue pulling a fire patrol wagon. The clanging bell drew me to the open window—to see the fire crew abruptly halt here at the corner of 62nd Street. In minutes, three helmeted men clutching fire axes burst upstairs into my workroom, where they found me standing open-mouthed beside a table stacked with books, papers, leather, and an open gluepot that gave off a smoky stench.

Several servants peered in from the hallway to watch the fire patrolmen gawk at my rawhide apron, my tied-back hair, my leather work gloves.

"You—" a short patrolman with a crescent scar on his cheek barked at me, "move aside or get into the hall."

I stood in place.

"I said, move it. Make it snappy. Are you deaf?"

I sputtered my name. The fireman's partner threatened to shove but halted when my voice rose like a shout into Colorado's canyons.

"You are...not a servant?"

I stood my ground. Stone-faced, I said, "I am Mrs. DeVere."

The patrolmen stewed in their mistake and grasped the fact of a false alarm.

"So sorry, ma'am...a call from this address...."

Who had called the fire patrol? Someone outdoors who caught a whiff of the glue wafting from my open window? Or perhaps housekeeper, Mrs. Thwaite, making mischief?

Mrs. Thwaite, an overbearing woman we had "inherited" from my in-laws, bristled at every order from her Wild West "cowgirl" mistress. I hoped she would soon find a new position and depart. She ruled with a keyring that dangled from her belt like handcuffs.

Did she call the fire patrol to put me in this awkward corner with a squad of helmeted men with gleaming fire axes?

The next exchange was short. The patrolmen apologized, and I thanked them and praised the modern East 90th Street firehouse. I also promised to find out who among our household staff had used the new telephone to report a fire (though Mrs. Thwaite was among the young housemaids clustered in the hall).

I assured the men that Mr. DeVere would join me to instruct our staff about casual alarms. The red-whiskered patrol leader with the crescent scar stepped toward the glue pot, bent down, and sniffed.

At the time, I thought nothing of it.

By early afternoon, once again in the workroom up to my elbows in bookbinding thread, large needles, Moroccan leather, scissors, and the rank glue, I was surprised when my maid Calista brought a calling card on a silver tray into the workroom. "Shall I read the card for you, ma'am?"

I nodded, and Calista lifted the card and read, "Colin Finlay, Detective Sergeant, New York Police Department."

"A detective? He's downstairs?"

"In the foyer, ma'am. He asks whether you might be at home. He requests a brief interview."

"What on earth for?"

"I wouldn't know."

She replaced the card on the tray, holding its edges with her trim fingernails. I relied on Calista's judgment in many ways. Her former job as a stewardess on a coastal steamer taught her everything a woman needed to know about timing and subtlety. A few years older than the Irish servants, she had come to America from an island in Greece. "What sort of interview?" I repeated.

"He said 'brief.'"

Calista avoided staring at my worktable, though her opinion of my amateur bookbinding was hardly a secret. Every lady in Society must claim a special interest. Some favored needlework, others flower arrangements. Still others collected teacups. Eleanor DeVere had presented my "starter piece" of Sèvres porcelain, hoping that a vase with handles shaped like ladies' high-heeled slippers would inspire a collection to civilize her daughter-in-law from the "Wild West."

"Shall I inform him that you are not at home? Not receiving today? Or perhaps he might call when Mr. DeVere is present?"

That did it. My papa did not raise his daughter to be a "little lady," and Roddy did not wed a shrinking violet. I would speak for myself. "I will meet with the detective, Calista. Have him shown to the Corinthian drawing room."

Capping the noxious glue, I stripped the gloves, untied the apron, and hastened across our carpeted hallway to my boudoir suite to select an indigo woolen skirt, white shirtwaist, and a short jacket with severe lapels. With hair pinned up, I descended the staircase, wishing for a downstairs room that was furnished with simple chairs and a pine table. Instead, I proceeded to the "classical" room that was done in my in-laws' taste for anything old and European.

The detective's visit, I assumed, was meant to seek information about the latest murder. He would ask, had we seen anything unusual? Any suspicious person near the bridle path? I would probe about the police investigation. This visit might answer some of the questions from the morning.

"Mr. Finlay?"

"Mrs. DeVere, good afternoon."

Hat in hand, a lanky figure in a shiny black business suit sprang forward from a spindly chair in a far corner. At first glance, he seemed awfully young, with narrow shoulders, long arms, and a smooth, boyish pallor. At closer range, it was clear that he was older, his corn-colored hair lightened with white streaks and a narrow face etched with fine lines under gray eyes. He was, I would guess, approaching his late thirties or early forties. From a vest pocket he drew a badge and a letter certifying his official position, which I read and returned.

"Detective Sergeant Finlay," I said, "do sit down." We moved to a tufted Louis XV loveseat and matching chair.

He set his black bowler hat over one knee. "I appreciate your time, Mrs. DeVere. I am detailed by the chief of police to perform investigative duties."

"Which surely consume all your time these days," I said, "when Central Park is plagued with tragic deaths." He barely nodded. "So, I trust that you seek a word with those of us whose homes face the park...for information?"

He did not respond. "Just for the record," he said, "might I jot down a few notes?"

Tempted to insist on notes of my own, I nodded while he plucked out a notebook and pencil stub that was sharpened with a blade, not the new mechanical sharpener that everyone liked.

Menswear these days called for a tight fit and short suit jackets, and I scanned his coat, vest, and trousers for the telltale bump of a gun. No bump was in sight, though an ankle holster might conceal a small pistol, perhaps a Derringer. My papa's Colt .44 "Peacemaker" lay in an upstairs drawer. I told Roddy, "Just in case."

The profile of our butler, Mr. Sands, hovering just beyond the sitting room Corinthian columns was annoying, as if he prepared to intervene on my behalf.

As if I could not fend for myself.

"How might I be of assistance, Mr. Finlay?"

"This house—is it framed in timbers?"

"Timbers?"

"Beams...," he said, "like ships timbers?"

I hesitated.

"Sailing ships," he said.

What was he driving at? "The building material of this house is mainly stone, I believe," I replied. "And the roof is slate."

"Slate," he echoed.

Was this a prelude to other crimes? Were thieves scaling the outdoor walls along Fifth Avenue? Rooftop burglars on the prowl? If so, I must load my Colt.

"And the interior—?" He looked around. "Wood panels, fabrics, plaster..."

Bewildered, I said, "Actually, Mr. Finlay, my husband's parents built this house eleven years ago. If this visit concerns building materials, you might request an interview with them. They could tell you about its construction."

He made a note but did not respond.

"My husband's parents are close by," I continued, "Mr. and Mrs. Rufus DeVere have an apartment suite at the south side of the house. It formerly was my husband's lodgings... before our marriage." He made another note, which was disappointing and odd.

Should I say more?

Not to the detective, though the domestic reversal had been a surprise to Roddy and me. My in-laws abruptly insisted on moving into the part of the house that was once Roddy's bachelor quarters. The senior DeVeres now enjoyed a separate entrance on 62nd Street, while we newlyweds— Roderick and Valentine (née Valentine Louise Mackle of Virginia City, Nevada, and the Colorado Rockies) were the master and mistress of this three-story chateau with a basement kitchen and servants' rooms in the fourth-floor attic.

No need to voice the bare truth of the domestic turn-around. Rufus was a proud man, and Eleanor held her head high. The fact was, my papa's big silver strike in Nevada and the Mackle fortune rescued the senior DeVeres' own sinking fortunes and paved the way for my wedding to their beloved son-and-heir—and the love of my life.

Detective Finlay made another note, set his pencil aside, and faced me. "Mrs. DeVere, the Fire Patrol and the police are separate organizations, but whenever necessary, we communicate because certain crimes involve fire."

"Arson," I said.

"So we must investigate. And such crime often involves ignitable liquids...."

"Kerosene," I said, "or paraffin...." Feeling quizzed and cornered, I stopped. "Mr. Finlay, do you suspect that arson might be planned for this house?" I added, "Or from within this house? Is that the purpose of this interview?"

His pale cheeks flared bright pink. "We must investigate credible leads."

"From the Fire Patrol? The patrol that responded to a false alarm at this house this morning?" His cheeks were florid. "Because one member of the patrol reported his suspicions?"

"Sergeant," he murmured.

"A man with...?" It was vulgar to say *scar*. "...with a mark on his cheek, a crescent?"

Another nod, and the detective looked miserable, though his jawline tightened to stubborn resolve. He had a job to do, and he must do it despite the posh chateau, the oriental rugs, the Corinthian columns and Louis XV furniture. Or simply because, as a New York Police detective, his jurisdiction was Fifth Avenue.

If he had information about the murders in the park, this was my moment to try to learn whatever the police might know. This was no time to belittle an officer who had risen to the rank of detective.

I sat back and managed a small smile. "Mr. Finlay, let me explain...our butler will assist." I raised my voice. "Sands, if you will...." Our butler, a model of British dignity, was unfazed by my request to retrieve the gluepot from the upstairs workroom.

True to the servants' hierarchy, the crock of glue was brought by the footman, Bronson, who placed it on a nearby table as requested. I urged Detective Finlay to lift the top.

Which he did, releasing foul vapors that smothered the sweet gardenia from a nearby vase. "Smoke," he muttered, sneezed twice, and reached for a handkerchief.

Coughing, I reached to cap the crock, then explained about the awful glue, the workroom, and bookbinding. "I grew up in the West," I said. "I collect western books." He stared. "I am binding them in Morocco leather so they look attractive upstairs on the library shelf." He looked perplexed. "It's a hobby."

He seemed relieved at "hobby," mopped his forehead, opened his notebook and gripped the pencil—which might have ended the interview if the point on his lead pencil had not broken off with a hard *snap*.

He patted his pockets. In seconds he would take his leave, though the knife marks on his pencil stub prompted a thought.

"Quickly—" I called again to Sands, "bring the little folding knife from my dressing table. Calista knows where...."

Staying seated, I managed to hold the detective in place for a few moments until the knife was delivered to my hand. "Mr. Finlay, won't you please sharpen your pencil with my Barlow knife?"

Startled, he watched me easily open the jackknife as I had done from girlhood. "The knife was my late Papa's," I said. "We used it for everything...gutting game, small repairs. It's my letter opener now. The haft is elk bone."

The detective looked bemused.

"Growing up in the West," I said, "I cherish a few mementoes. To me, New York is rather new, quite recent... and these deaths in Central Park are terrifying. We fear for our young women household staff...and for ourselves."

I swallowed and touched my throat to signal distress about the park. "It does me good to see my papa's knife used for a good purpose," I said. "Everyone in the West whittles. Don't worry about the shavings."

He drew the blade against the pencil, and the point surfaced as he caught the wood bits in his hat. "I hope the Police Department investigation is going well," I said. "The newspapers are terrifying.... Perhaps you wish to offer advice...something we ought to look out for?"

He shaved the tip to a point.

"We could help if you tell us what to do. Those of us who often ride and drive in the park could be like the deputies in the West."

He stopped whittling, closed the knife, slipped it into my outstretched palm, blew on the pencil point, and made a few notes. Pocketing the notebook, he paused to look directly into my eyes. "Have you heard of the Lexow Committee, Mrs. DeVere?"

"Something about police reform?" I murmured.

"Reform," he said, "is like a hornet. It stings once, and it's gone." He blinked but held his gaze. "Some of us take our duties very seriously. I assure you that we are dedicated to our work. Organized gangs are a serious problem in the city, and gambling is an infestation. Both must be fought by law enforcement." He hesitated, as if reluctant to say more. "The newspapers will not report this, Mrs. Devere," he said, "but as of late last night, we have an important lead in the case."

He stood, and I rose as Sands came forward to see him to the door. At the Corinthian columns, Mr. Colin Finlay turned, holding his hat like a basin. Killers," he said, "always become careless, and when they do, the New York Police Department is ready to make its move."

Chapter Three

THAT EVENING RODDY AND I sat in matching plump Bergere chairs while two footmen lighted the logs in the black granite fireplace in our sitting room on the second floor. The mantle clock struck five o'clock, and we sat quietly until the fire flickered and the footmen withdrew.

"Your letter opener did the trick?"

"My papa's Barlow knife, Roddy...always razor sharp. A good luck charm this afternoon—of sorts. The police have a lead in the case, but the detective wouldn't give specifics."

"I'd be surprised if he had, Val. Police procedure restricts publicity. Let's talk, but first, shall I mix us our favorite cocktail of the autumn?"

"An old fashioned?"

Roddy stepped to the breakfront cabinet for glasses and bottles. The footmen kept ice and fruit on hand in the rooms we enjoyed. I kept a journal of the drink recipes, and soon heard the clink of ice in crystal glassware.

The Old Fashioned

Ingredients

- 2 oz. rye or bourbon
- 2 dashes Angostura bitters
- 1 sugar cube
- Maraschino cherry
- Selzer or club soda

Directions

1. Place the sugar cube in an Old Fashioned glass.
2. Wet it down with Angostura bitters and a short splash of club soda.
3. Crush the sugar with a wooden muddler, then rotate the glass so that the sugar grains and bitters give it a liquid lining.
4. Add Maraschino cherry.
5. Add large ice cube or cubes.
6. Pour in the whiskey.
7. Add selzer (soda) water.
8. Garnish with an orange twist, and serve with a stirring rod if desired.

We raised our glasses, and Roddy said, "Here's to the light and warmth of an open fire, a gift of autumn…and to the day, mine and yours."

We sipped and savored, and Roddy loosened his collar and cravat. "In sum," he said, "the court finds in favor of the St. James Hotel bar, which reopens immediately with Billy Patterson behind the bar. The temperance posse will be fined if another act of their 'hooliganism' occurs. Judge O'Toole spoke firmly, and the trial lasted about half an hour."

Roddy put his glass on the table between our chairs. "About the Central Park emergency, the Mayor proclaims that the park will be safeguarded by 'New York's Finest,' and a reward will be announced in every newspaper at dawn tomorrow." His tone turned wry. "The killer ought to be worth five thousand dollars in gold, don't you think" It will be known as a 'private donation,' but the mayor's office agreed."

We both sipped, and Roddy rose to poke at a log, sat back down, and took a deep breath. "My visit to police head-quarters was brief," he said, "and the decrepit old building on Mulberry Street will do for another year, but the place is choked with brass-buttoned uniforms coming and going. Smells bad too." He sipped. "I managed a word with the new chief, William Devery—'Big Bill' to his friends."

"And?"

"And everyone remembers his favorite command to the squad when he was Captain Devery some years ago. To quote, 'If there's any grafting to be done, I'll do it. Leave it to me.'"

"He wasn't joking?"

"I'm afraid not, Val. We all wish Roosevelt were still the police commissioner instead of campaigning for governor. Some think he'll be the President one day. Anyway, Devery said all the right things, promised an officer at every rock and grove in the park."

He shifted closer to me, his broad shoulders needing no padding by a tailor. "Now, what happened here today? Sands seemed perturbed. What's this about the fire patrol and a detective?"

My summary was short and pointed. "At least, Roddy, we know the police have a lead, a break in the case. The detective seemed confident. And I hope you'll think better of my 'hobby.' Detective Finlay liked 'hobby.' And he understood about that foul glue."

Roddy sipped his drink, stood, and used the poker. Sparks flew, and the flames flashed. Seated once again, he said, "Val, your glue has done its work. I trust you will now turn to a professional book bindery."

I stiffened. My workroom was an irritant between us. Roddy's mother had given me *The Decoration of Houses* by Edith Wharton and underscored such lines as "good editions in good bindings form an expanse of warm, lustrous color."

My effort to achieve "warm, lustrous color" had run afoul of Eleanor DeVere's idea of worthy books. Her favorite poetess was no match for my women's memoirs of pioneering courage in the West. *A Lady's Life in the Rocky Mountains* was on my worktable, and so was *A Trip Across the Plains in an Ox Cart.* The authors deserved fine bindings.

So did *Crooked Trails* by Frederic Remington, and *Roughing It* by Mark Twain, with its vivid portraits of my hometown, Virginia City, Nevada, where the young Twain had been a reporter for the *Territorial Enterprise* and got "smitten with silver fever." Twain's mining went bust, but storytelling became his Big Lode, and *Roughing It* filled me with nostalgia.

So did my western women, Helen Carpenter and Isabella Bird, standing tall beside the men in the DeVere home library. Miss Bird spoke for me, pitting the luxury of a simple log cabin against a "uselessly conventional life" cluttered with "a house and servants." Mounting her horse after breakfast to gallop "when the sun was high and the air intoxicating," she felt "tireless" and celebrated the western air as life's "elixir."

My kind of woman!

Isabella Bird, however, never became another person's life partner, which creates a world of difference. As I was learning.

If only I had better bookbinding skills. The Moroccan leather scraps and broken needles (and jabbed fingers) mocked my efforts, and one whiff of the noxious glue always sent our little dog speeding to the farthest drawing room even though I kept the window open. The "warm lustrous color" was nowhere in sight.

"Val," Roddy said, "You know I support your western library. It's not about the books. It's—"

"—Roddy, must I say it again? I cannot pretend to enjoy porcelain vases, and I will not paint flowers on dishware in my all-too-plentiful spare time. I must have something to do."

"But you don't seem to enjoy your workroom, Val. A hobby should be a pleasure. Case in point, my stamp collection, hours poring over bits of colored postage…. No fun at all. Maybe bookbinding isn't for you."

He had a point but struck a nerve. "Nevertheless," I said, "the facts of daytime life let you freely go about the city, appear in court, pay a call on the Mayor and the chief of police, attend a meeting, talk to a bartender, mix a new drink—and perhaps inspect our stable to make sure the horses are properly cared for…. By chance, did you stop at our stable this afternoon?"

My husband looked sheepish. "Not by chance."

Roddy and I shared a private stable with our friends, Cassie and Dudley Forster, and my husband knew of my special interest in the horses.

"I decided to take a quick look," Roddy said. "You know the stories about horses not groomed and watered, the men smoking…and the fires. My father never lets a stable fire go unmentioned."

It was true. Rufus DeVere had become fixated on the fires in the city's many stables when hay lofts caught fire and horses died. "Apollo and Atlas are well cared for by grooms at the club," Roddy said, "so we needn't worry. Our private stable with the Forsters is another matter."

Roddy pushed on. "You always want Comet to be fed and watered and brushed. You insist that the leather and brass be spotless, polished…."

"Which I would gladly do myself, as I did in Nevada, where a woman inside a stable isn't a candidate for Mr. Barnum's freak show."

"Val—"

"It's true. A 'lady' in the city must not brush her own horse, let alone lift her saddle or clean the leather or…." I stopped before the list expanded. "A 'lady,'" I finally hissed, "is hemmed in more ways than I can count."

I grabbed a poker and shoved a log. The flames crackled, and we drank our Old Fashioneds in silence. The atmosphere felt hot and cold, and the sitting room darker as a footman drew the heavy draperies and announced dinner, which meant going to the dining room after dressing for dinner, Roddy in a silk tuxedo and me in a gown that Calista would have laid out for me. More needless costuming, in my opinion. The ladies in Virginia City, Nevada, always looked smart without changing their clothes six times a day.

Before dressing for dinner, Roddy and I attempted a pleasant conversation about the servants' misuse of the telephone for "emergency" purposes. "The entire staff ought to be summoned to hear us issue new instructions," I said. "We are the householders. They ought to hear it directly from us."

Roddy, however, recommended that Sands and Mrs. Thwaite be put in charge of the task, that we gather the servants only in a catastrophic event, such as an outbreak of war or plague.

"Only on the rarest occasions, Val. Otherwise, our authority could be lessened"

We left it at that and went to our separate suites to prepare for dinner. Roddy's valet, Norbert, would assist with shirt studs, just as Calista fastened the hooks of the blue tulle gown she had selected for me, along with a sapphire necklace from Roddy's late grandmother.

The evening stretched before us, so I thought. We had no plans beyond the evening meal, a light soup, the fish, and a *jardinière* fillet of beef with little balls of carrots and turnips. I refused the buttered cauliflower, a favorite of Roddy's. In truth, we were too glum to enjoy the meal or the warm candelabra lighting.

We had nearly finished a fruit compote dessert when Sands appeared with a soft knock and steps so swift that he was at Roddy's ear in seconds. "Sir, if I may...highly unusual...."

Roddy said, "But of course" and the butler retreated, leaving Roddy staring at his dessert spoon.

Had I committed a blunder this evening? Did we have guests? More than once, the demanding social calendar had left me dispatching apologetic notes and flowers for having missed a reception or tea dance. Roddy was always forgiving, but he cared about social rituals.

"Roddy..." I began.

He looked up. "No worries, Val." He paused. "Do you remember the Philbricks?"

"Philbricks?

"The dinner at Beechwood last summer—Mrs. Astor's dinner?"

Thirty or forty guests on a warm summer evening in Newport. "The lady with very white hair...a cloud of white hair?"

"Yes, that's Mrs. Victor Philbrick...Gladys. I don't believe you were introduced to her or her husband."

I was not. Roddy leaned close, his voice low. "The Philbricks have requested a visit here this evening. Highly unusual, but I took the liberty of extending a welcome."

I seemed to recall that the Philbricks were longtime family friends of the senior DeVeres, something about mutual business interests. "Perhaps they intend to visit your parents?"

"No. They want to see us. Sands was quite clear." He added, "It's been a trying day, Val, so if you'd rather be excused...."

His voice held an olive branch to end our quarrel. "Of course, I'll join you, Roddy."

He smiled and took my hand. "I'll have Bronson light a fire in the smaller reception room."

A room I actually liked with its soft cream walls and paintings of pastured sheep in distant meadows. A fire would be cheering. "You have no idea why this sudden visit?"

"None." He pushed his chair back. "I do know the Philbricks have had their struggles. They have raised their grandson after young Clayton Philbrick's parents drowned when the *City of Brussels* sank in a fog in 'eighty-three. The boy was...I think six or seven at the time."

"Horrid."

Roddy nodded. "But fortunate to have loving grandparents. They doted on Clayton. He must be about...twenty, twenty-one years of age, out of school, a young man on the town...clubs, sport, fast horses...."

If Roddy felt wistful for bachelor days, he did not show it as we rose from the table and prepared to welcome Mr. and Mrs. Philbrick into a cozy room with overripe sofas and chairs that were ideal for a book or conversation. Or a doze. One glance at the elderly couple who were ushered into the room on the dot of eight o'clock told us no one would nod off tonight.

Chapter Four

WITH HER SNOWY COIFFEUR, Gladys Philbrick
stood inches taller than her husband in a high-necked,
long-sleeved pearl gray gown that seemed chosen to cover
every inch of flesh, as if for protection.

She entered on the arm of a portly, stoop-shouldered
man with a fringe of gray hair, bushy dark brows and sad,
sunken eyes. His evening suit was rumpled, his shirtfront
smudged. She walked stiffly while her husband shuffled
despite his stout walking cane.

"So kind of you to see us, Roderick...Mrs. DeVere,"
she said.

I urged her to call me Valentine and added how pleased
to make acquaintance. The Philbricks seated themselves
side by side on a sofa, while Roddy and I chose armchairs.
The couple declined refreshments.

Roddy saved the moment from turning awkward. "You have graced this house as a guest of my parents on so many occasions," he said.

Victor Philbrick nodded, and Gladys attempted a smile. "And many earlier times when we all lived in townhouses on Washington Square," she said, "before these Fifth Avenue years." She sounded mournful. The moment sagged.

"You're certain that we cannot tempt you with a bit of plum cake?" I asked.

"Thank you, no," said Mr. Philbrick. "We have come on an errand." He fell silent. Roddy and I sat like birds on a wire.

Roddy gently asked, "How may we be of help?"

"Roderick, you were several years older than our Clayton," said Gladys. "You two were not boyhood friends."

"Sadly, no," said Roddy. "But perhaps we can renew acquaintance if he'll join the Bicycle Tea later this month?"

The Philbricks looked uncertain.

Victor said, "Eli Fryer said something of the sort a few days ago when we saw him at Sherry's. That booming voice of his…. 'Looking for that grandson of yours on his bicycle.'" Victor looked doleful.

"That's Eli…." Roddy smiled gently. "We all know that he is devoted to the Bicycle Tea. Some say it's more important to him than Mrs. Astor's ball."

The annual outdoor event, quite simply, enlisted gentlemen and ladies of Society to pedal bicycles all afternoon in Central Park and celebrate at the finish with drinks and little cakes outdoors.

"Surely Clayton enjoys a bicycle," Roddy said. "All New York rides on two wheels these days."

Roddy's attempt at cheer failed. The couple looked downcast.

Gladys clasped her hands together. "The truth be told," she said, "our Clayton likes his comfort. He's never been one for exercise. 'Why walk when I can ride, Mimi?' he'd say. 'Let's always ride.'" She smiled. "He calls me Mimi."

"Clayton reached his majority some months ago," Victor Philbrick hastened to say. "He has now come into all that has awaited his twenty-first birthday."

We nodded. Society seldom spoke directly about money, but Clayton Philbrick's "all" meant substantial wealth was now the young man's inheritance to use as he pleased.

"I trust that your grandson will continue to benefit from your loving care," said Roddy.

The couple exchanged glances. "Thank you. We must believe so," said Gladys, "because we have received a shock."

"Shock?"

"Our Clayton enjoys the life of many young men of his set," Victor said. "He has friends, sports...the freedom of a young man who was well brought up."

He straightened his shoulders. "Our Clayton sang tenor in the St. Bartholomew Church choir...the choirmaster called his tenor range a rare gift." He touched his necktie. "His recent conduct has been...not always irreproachable, perhaps. He likes the ladies, but what red-blooded young man does not? Still, his conduct has been well within... within...." He left off.

Gladys Philbrick looked intently from me to Roddy and back again. "Late last night," she said, "our butler awakened Victor. A police detective appeared at our door, looking for Clayton. He had a document...."

"A warrant." Victor Philbrick reached for a pocket handkerchief and rubbed at his eyes. The vocal tremor was audible. "...a warrant for Clayton's arrest."

Gladys tugged a handkerchief from her sleeve and squeezed it in both hands.

"That young woman in the park..." Victor went on. "The woman in the newspapers...." We nodded. "It's a mistake, of course.... Our Clayton would never...."

Time felt stopped. "So, the detective believes that your grandson was possibly in Central Park last night?" Roddy asked. The couple nodded to my husband. "And was Clayton with you last night? At your home?"

"No," said Victor. "The detective asked when we expected him, but Clayton keeps his own hours.

"His own calendar," said Gladys. "Whole days pass...."

"My wife means that we have not seen our grandson for several days," said Victor. "Upwards of a week and more."

"We couldn't exactly say when..." said Gladys.

"A young bachelor living his own life, as bachelors will do," said Roddy. His words seemed to steady the Philbricks, a tactic he has honed from law school training. "May I ask," he continued, "the reason the police are interested in talking to your grandson?"

Merely "talking?" I thought. Didn't a warrant mean arrest and interrogation?

The Philbricks clasped one another's hands. "Something was found..." Gladys began. "Something near the young woman."

"Did the detective describe the young woman?"

"He did not," said Victor.

"Or the 'something?'"

The Philbricks exchanged a glance, and Gladys nodded. Her husband pocketed his handkerchief. "A gold cigarette case was found," he said. "It bore the insignia of a club... our grandson is a member." He wet his lips. "The Templars Club," he said, and the engraved initials—C.R.P."

"Clayton—"

"Clayton Rogers Philbrick," said Gladys in a hush.

"Did you see it?"

"It was described to us."

Silence followed. Roddy assured the Philbricks that the police would soon clear up the confusion. He cautioned them to expect a few difficult days while the investigation proceeded.

"The detective," I asked, "do you recall his name?" They did not. "His appearance," I continued, "could you describe him?"

"It was dark," Victor huffed, "well after midnight."

"But perhaps he made an impression?"

Victor folded his arms across his chest, as if my pointed question was not to be answered. At Gladys's touch, he dropped his arms, and said, "At first, he seemed very young."

"But then—?"

"Our butler brought a lamp, and I got a better look. He was a pale fellow, hair going white. The document in one hand...his arm hung halfway to his knee."

"Long arms," I said.

He nodded. "I don't see that it matters. What matters is—"

"—is the resolution of this painful matter," Roddy said. "And promptly." The waning fire needed another log, but Roddy folded his hands and continued. "It may be some comfort to know a reward will be offered, and the city is committed to solve the crime and restore confidence in Central Park."

My husband paused. "But you spoke of an 'errand' that brings you here this evening...or was I mistaken?"

The Philbricks exchanged a lingering glance. Gladys touched her hair, and said, "An errand, yes...and a personal favor."

"Please...."

"Last summer in Newport," Victor said, "there was a certain investigation ...a crime that was committed in our set...in Society."

"Deadly poisoning." Gladys spoke the words with a tremor. Roddy and I nodded. "It was no secret among our circle that you DeVeres had a hand in the crime—"

"—solving the crime," Victor said.

"We assisted," said Roddy.

"Please do not dissemble, Roderick. This is no time for false modesty." Victor Philbrick's plea surged from depths of fear.

It was our turn to exchange glances. "What might we do for you?" Roddy asked in his calmest voice.

"Look into the matter. Help us."

"Please," said Gladys.

"But the police..." I began. "The detectives...."

Victor waved a trembling hand at my face. "If you had grown up in the city, Mrs. DeVere—"

"—Valentine...."

"You would know the dark side of the New York police... ask your Roderick. Ask your father-in-law."

"Your mother-in-law," said Gladys.

Fireplace embers sputtered, and Victor spoke in constrained tones. "This visit has not been made lightly. Our grandson did not return at all last night. We have not seen him today...or any day this month. Our inquiries about Clayton's whereabouts have not been fruitful. To be blunt, his friends do not know where he is at this time. This matter of the cigarette case and the young woman...well, it must be cleared up at once...."

"As soon as possible," Gladys said. Her voice was plaintive. "So, will you help us? For the sake of friendship...."

Friendship, I thought, but what about the truth? If we agreed to help, was this couple prepared for whatever we might find?

Chapter Five

EARLY THE NEXT MORNING, Roddy suggested
we ride to the Pergola where the latest victim was found.
"We'll ride to the Wisteria Percola, dismount, and look
around," he said.

The new day was fresh and cool, perfect for an hour
in the saddle. The new groom saddled our horses, and
my husband felt both bridles for fit. He had doubts about
the new groom, a third cousin of our coachman, Noland,
who assured us all was well. With reins in hand and my
left foot in the stirrup, I vaulted up and over my quarter
horse, Comet—and into the very saddle that had caused
a scandal when I insisted on straddling my horse in New
York, as I had in the West. My McClellan saddle was nothing like that terrifying invention known as a lady's side
saddle, which I had tried in the city and nearly pitched,
headfirst, into a ditch.

On the bridle paths of New York, I was content to be the eccentric lady in a saddle that was the standard issue of the US Army cavalry and named for US General George McClellan. The stirrups hung long enough for a person to mount without a block or a human hoist, though Roddy always offered a hand and waited for me to be seated first. (My horse, Comet, was another tidbit for the gossip mills, for the buckskin quarter horse was bred for ranch work, not the equestrian show ring.)

The groom's cupped hands assisted Roddy onto the slip of a saddle that I thought best for featherweight jockeys, not my husband. Out West, we called such saddles "pancakes," though Roddy cut a fine figure in his britches and boots, a waistcoat and derby. His chestnut Arabian gelding, Justice, had a high tail and an elegant arched neck, a contrast to my mare with her muscular neck, her little ears and wide-set eyes. I too wore a waistcoat, a derby, and the boots that were proper for the bridle path. My skirt, however, was adapted from my bicycling outfit, a culotte that let me straddle my horse in comfort, never mind treacherous female equine etiquette.

We set off at a smart clip through the Scholar's Gate at Fifty-ninth Street and northwest along the drive. Few carts or carriages were out on this thirteenth of October just before eight a.m., which was our idea—to visit the site where the third young woman's body had been found two nights age, and without drawing attention to ourselves.

This jaunt was solely exploratory. We made no commitment to the Philbricks.

Two riders cantered past, and Roddy and I checked our horses, both eager to give chase, both responsive to our handling. Crossing over the transverse road, we curved east and abruptly west toward the Casino Concourse, where we dismounted, led the horses up a narrow hilly path, and tied the reins to an iron railing at the Wisteria Pergola. The allée was lined with empty park benches—no, not entirely empty.

At the farthest bench lay a figure at rest...lying down. Roddy softly walked in that direction, stopped, and retraced his steps. "Asleep," he whispered. "Let him be."

We scanned the thick creeping vines that weeks ago produced blossoms for the season. Autumn's sere leaves had curled and dropped, and the arbor's bare rafters and posts looked skeletal.

"Do you see anything?"

Roddy pointed to a place where the leaves had been swept, about ten yards from the entrance path. Apparently, someone had swept only that one spot in the last couple of days. We walked toward it and stood before a cleared space that was swept almost clean—roughly double the size of a human body.

"Here—?" I asked in a whisper. "Could this be the place? Could she have come here with her killer? Or did a stranger attack from...from where?"

Roddy squinted. "From the Mall or the Music Pavilion... closed for the season, of course...or the broad green lawn.... or the Casino Concourse."

I imagined the struggle.

We peered at the cleared space, where a small broom's strokes were visible on the dusty walkway. Otherwise, the allée was littered with leaves.

"What about the cigarette case?" I asked. "Was it here? Nearby?" The fallen leaves appeared undisturbed.

"Let's look closer." Roddy bent on one knee to examine the cleared spot. I joined him and peered closely at the dust when a shadow fell on the path, and a booming voice—

"What are you doing? What are you up to, you two?"

We looked up to see a uniformed policeman hulking over us, his helmet in one hand. A dead leaf stuck to his coat at the shoulder. Where had he come from?

"What is your business here?" He pointed at our horses and touched the nightstick at his belt. "No horses allowed at the Pergola," he boomed, brushing away the leaf. One cheek looked reddened from the park bench slats. So, he was the figure asleep on the bench moments ago. He glowered but looked confused as well, facing a couple in riding attire but crouched in the dust.

Roddy said, "We can explain, officer...." He turned to me. "Your lost gemstone, dear...."

I took my cue. "A family diamond," I said, "an heirloom lost from its setting weeks ago, and I have looked everywhere. I thought perhaps the stone had loosened during a visit here when the weather was warmer...but wherever the jewel might be, it seems gone forever."

If only I could have forced a tear.

"...and insisted on escorting my wife, officer," said Roddy. "I'm sure you understand."

The policeman looked less than persuaded, though Roddy turned the tables in the next seconds. "If I'm not mistaken, sir," he said, "you are not with the park police. Your badge would say 'Department of Public Parks.'"

His helmet now on his head, the officer fingered his badge as if to conceal it.

"The park police do not carry nightsticks," Roddy continued, "so you must be with the New York City Police Department...'New York's Finest.'" My husband said it with a flourish.

We had our truce. The police officer puffed up his ample chest and stood straight. He would not press us further about the reason for our visit, nor would we ask why a city policeman was stationed at the Wisteria Pergola in the early morning of the thirteenth of October. Nor would we hint that, by napping, he had been derelict in duty and was subject to discipline if reported. We parted with a pleasant "Good day."

Moments later, we were once again on horseback, having got the information we sought. The very presence of the city policeman assigned to duty in the Pergola verified the fact that we had indeed seen the place where the third young woman had been strangled to death.

Chapter Six

WE WENT FOR LUNCH at Delmonico's café, where we
planned to share thoughts about the morning, the Philbricks,
and ourselves. "A cheerful place," I said, picturing deft wait-
ers instead of footmen tiptoeing across heavy carpets.

We had worked up appetites after an extra hour on
horseback in the park. A fast trot helped clear out the grim
scene of early morning. Delmonico's would be just the place,
and we quickly changed and were seated by noon in the
newest "Del's" at Fifth Avenue and Forty-fourth Street.
The café on the ground floor was my favorite with its tile
flooring and bustling air. Roddy requested a quiet table,
and the maître d' led us to the perfect spot.

"Wine, my dear?"

"I think soda water, Roddy."

"Two soda waters," he said, adding lobster salad for the
lady and grilled beefsteak for himself.

The room was filling. "Bright and cheery," I said.

"The frost and festivity of October" Roddy answered, "but our 'festivity' is in question, isn't it?"

"Especially after last evening," I said. "Those poor Philbricks…. Victor looked almost ill. I can't imagine they got much sleep."

"How could they? Not until their grandson comes home and the police clear up the mistake." Roddy added, "—if it is a mistake."

The *if* hung between us. "Roddy, do you know anything about Clayton Philbrick?"

"Not really. He's not a member of my clubs…but then, my memberships are not for dudes or dandies." He cleared his throat. "The topic of clubs is sensitive, Val. Some say the Union and Union League Clubs are for…for the stuffy and stodgy…even the cocktails too orthodox. Some members suggest expanding the menu beyond whisky-and-soda, but others resist."

"Roddy," I replied, "I never resist with you…." I lowered my voice and leaned across the table. "And our boudoir fun needs no bottled spirits…because we are spirited as—"

His hand abruptly took mine under the table, squeezed, and let go. He had peered over my shoulder and saluted with two fingers. "Theodore… Theodore Bulkeley…."

"Why, Theo…hello." I turned to see the familiar tall, slender gentleman in a houndstooth jacket, trailed by a waiter who looked desperate to find him a table.

"Luncheon in the café, my dear DeVeres?" Theo Bulkeley's familiar pale blue eyes twinkled as he surveyed the room. "So, dear Valentine and Roderick," he said, "has your cook's midday mistake driven you to Del's?"

"Our cook gave us permission," Roddy quipped. "And won't you join us?"

"Please do, Theo."

"Actually, Theodore," Roddy said, "we will put you to work if you're willing to break bread with us. Or does our Bostonian friend prefer his baked beans?"

"Codfish cakes, Roderick. To remind you, the Bulkeley ancestry flourished from stern Puritan sermons and the very profitable cod fishery."

A relieved waiter held a chair, and we became a threesome.

More than a casual friend, Theo was a confirmed bachelor and my escort whenever Roddy's consultations about cocktails called him away for a day or a night. Our friend's sharp wit was a live wire that I relied on for news of the goings-on in the city. He and I were bonded as Society's "stepchildren," one from New England and the other from the West. Theo, however, had been adopted for his pristine Boston Brahmin ancestry, whereas my Irish background spelled *immigrant*.

Theo eyed our mineral water and frowned. "No glass of wine today, Valentine?"

Our friend had touched a nerve. Society offered ladies wine upon request, but distilled spirits were off limits. We imbibed privately, but I planned to be one of the first to put my calfskin boot on a brass railing and order a drink.

"And no luncheon cocktail for you today, DeVere?" Theo continued. "Mineral water for Society's alchemist of the bar?"

"Not today, my friend." Roddy did not blink at "alchemist," though he was often chided about his *bon-vivant* sideline. It was known in our circle that my husband consulted with resorts, hotels, and other businesses seeking new heights of popularity with unique cocktails.

The waiter stood by. "Maestro DeVere..." said Theo, "... if you might make a suggestion? Nothing too sweet."

Roddy said to the waiter, "The gentleman will have a martini with driest vermouth...the olive not pitted...stirred, not shaken."

Theo was about to enjoy the drink that Roddy and I often savored.

The Martini
Ingredients
- 1 ½ ounces gin.
- ½ teaspoon dry vermouth (or to taste)
- 1 green olive (not pitted)
- Ice cubes

Directions
1. Fill mixing glass with ice cubes.
2. Add gin.

3. Add vermouth.
4. Stir.
5. Strain into chilled martini glass.
6. Add olive and serve.

The martini arrived, and Theo sipped and said, "Beyond delicious," then glanced at the menu and ordered an omelet "...with ham." He turned to us with a smile. "Roderick and Valentine, you are just the friends to give me advice. Next spring is my cue to 'Go West, Young Man,' and Yellowstone Park sounds perfect...geysers shooting boiling water, sapphire peaks.... You two are experts on the West. Your met... where, Oklahoma?

"Nevada, Theo," I said. "Virginia City, Nevada."

"Is it near Yellowstone?"

Roddy sipped his water and said, "Theo, we New Yorkers relish ignorance of whatever lies beyond the Hudson River, but I can personally testify that Virginia City and Yellowstone Park are not in the same vicinity...not even as the crow flies."

I smiled. Every American schoolroom featured a map that pulled down like a window blind to show the states and territories, but not the rutted roads and dusty trails over plains, deserts, and craggy mountains. Not the mining camps, the skunks and grizzlies, the blue-black canyons and blizzards of my girlhood before Papa struck his Big Lode and moved the two of us to Virginia City where I was enrolled in school and tutored in becoming a lady.

Theo sipped his martini and grinned. "I forget, DeVere, about your brief exile in…the US Sahara, was it?"

We laughed. My husband knew about the West because his parents had quarantined him in a whitewashed adobe hacienda in the Arizona desert for a year. Rufus and Eleanor had found a copy of *How to Mix Drinks* in Roddy's room and feared their son-and-heir had surrendered to alcoholic cravings. They ignored his pleas about civilized sips when they hurried to the desert where he would "dry out."

We met that year. Roddy's father caught silver "fever" and hustled to Virginia City to reap millions from the mines—so he thought. As it happened, the visiting DeVeres dined at the Silver Queen Hotel & Saloon where Papa and I often enjoyed our dinner. Roddy and I caught sight of one another while Papa warned Rufus against investing in the defunct silver mines. To his parents' horror, Roddy showed off with a cocktail that involved lighted whisky poured from mug to mug. The Blue Blazer, he said, was invented by a revered bartender who had worked in Virginia City and in New York near the P.T. Barnum museum. He explained that cocktails caught his attention in teen years when he found that a bar near the museum offered "exhibits" far more intriguing than Mr. Barnum's mummies or whales' teeth. He credited our newfound romance to his parents' delusion about his "romance" with cocktails.

"The Northern Pacific would be my rail line west," Theo said. "What do you think?"

Roddy and I exchanged a certain look, and I gave my husband a nod. "Theo," he said, "if you want to see Yellowstone, let us offer you the *Louisa*.

"Your private rail car?"

"The very one."

Our friend closed his eyes. "The wonders of Yellowstone and your car too...." His swoon was both theatrical and sincere.

"The car ought to be enjoyed more often," I said. "We're pleased to send it West. The Northern Pacific will hitch the car to its westward train, and off you go."

Roddy and I had not yet traveled in the rail car that formerly belonged to the senior DeVeres. Our marriage had prevented its loss in a forced sale or auction when Rufus and Eleanor teetered on the brink of financial ruin because Roddy's father ignored my papa's advice and squandered the DeVere fortune on worthless silver mines. Named for my late mother, the rechristened *Louisa* now boasted a "soaking" bathtub sheathed in mahogany, onyx washstands, and silver fixtures. At some point, Roddy and I planned to hitch the car to a Central Pacific train and travel west. Steaming along, we will enjoy the passing scene, private dinners—and our own warm soaks. Together.

"*Bifteck* and *Salade de Homard*... and an omelet *à jambon*..." The plates were before us. "And will there be anything—?"

"—champagne," said Theo, "for three."

The familiar popping cork, and the toasts to Yellowstone and the *Louisa*, and then sips and savory bites—all in a moment's pause.

His fork poised, Theo suddenly murmured, "Why, look who's just coming in for lunch...everybody smile and wave."

We looked to the left to see a tall, corpulent figure leading his party of four to a reserved table by the far wall. He had doffed his top hat, glanced in our direction, and offered a flashy salute. We waved back.

"Eli Fryer," Theo said. "Probably sniffing for properties to buy...at bargain prices. If we all don't watch out, he'll be our landlord in a few years' time. Sometimes I think Fryer tries to outdo Old New York Knickerbockers with his zeal for property in the city. And who's that foursome with him in the derby hats? They look sketchy. I can't picture them on bicycles at Eli's Tea."

Roddy did not recognize the men, and neither did I. A sideways glance showed them all huddling, setting menus aside, and settling in for serious talk.

"Never mind," I said. "Let's enjoy ourselves."

"Yes, let's—and enough about my travels," Theo said. "He looked at Roddy. "What's this about putting me to work?"

"Nothing taxing, Theodore, but you are a man on the town. These days, you might know more about clubs than I do." Roddy paused. "What do you know about the Templars?"

"Ah, the Templars...." Theo put down his fork and reached for his wine. "Don't tell me you're thinking of joining the Templars, Roderick."

"I'm inquiring on behalf of an acquaintance."

"Good thing." Theo drank, and the waiter refilled his glass. "I'll says this: if your fellow is a loyal married man, he will be in the minority in the Templars."

"Bachelors...?"

"—bachelors of a certain sort. They're mainly younger men, the type mothers warn their daughters to avoid...thus, the daughters are all the more attracted...delicate moths to the flame."

We nodded.

"And those blades are thick as flies at stage doors when the shows end and the actresses and chorus girls step outside." Theo lowered his voice. "The Templars are in over their heads, so please do warn your acquaintance the club probably wants his initiation fee and dues. They've been recruiting new members to shore up their funds. They didn't listen to wiser heads when they overpaid for their building and furnishings and stocked a wine cellar worthy of Chateau Lafite Rothschild."

Our friend looked about at the neighboring tables and spoke at a near whisper. "Rumor has it their clubhouse is heavily mortgaged, and the club might fail...yet another defunct New York club, like the Arcadian and the Standard. They say the Lotus is shaky too.

"I like to quote old Francis Fairfield," Theo said, and his voice rose to a thin falsetto—'There is no knowing when a club, manifesting all signs of prosperity, both in appurtenances and reports, may collapse.'" He added, "The Templars, however, do not seem worried. They're errant knights, those fellows."

"Knights?" I asked.

"Sir Lancelots, Sir Galahads...like the Templar knights who fought the infidels in the Middle Ages...the Crusaders." Theo's voice thickened with disgust. "Self-proclaimed nobleman, so the fellows imagine. They have a contest going among the members. The winner is the man most often ticketed for 'fast driving' in Central Park. They decided their club neckties were not distinguished enough, so they ordered insignia jewelry cast solely for the members. Available at Black, Starr, and Frost."

I recognized the name of the premier men's jeweler. Several sets of Roddy's cufflinks came from Black, Starr, and Frost.

"I value the fellowship of our clubs, as I'm sure you do, Roderick. A New York gentleman's club ought to be his second home, bachelors and married men alike."

I ate my salad while Theo rhapsodized about the men's clubs, their comfortable sofas and chairs, their dining rooms, their breakfasts and dinners, their libraries, and squash courts. The Union League, he proclaimed, featured the utmost "elegant epicureanism," and I bit my tongue because ladies had no such resort in the city. My last bite of lobster, from the claw, came with a vow: when the ladies of Society decided to launch a women's club, I would be a charter member. And we would boast a cocktail menu.

Luncheon over, we thanked Theo, who insisted that this delightful occasion be charged to his Delmonico's account. The Eli Fryer group was deep in conversation as we departed, so farewell gestures were unnecessary.

"Hoping to see you both very soon," Theo said as we paused outside on the sidewalk. Relishing the golden afternoon sunshine, we were taken aback by Theo Bulkeley's sudden off key—in fact, chilling—failed attempt at his usual on-target humor. The friend whose wit is reliably welcome pointed his pigskin-gloved hand uptown and left us with, "You take very special care, you denizens of Fifth Avenue."

"Yes? And why 'special?'"

"You know why."

"But we don't."

"Don't tease us, Theodore."

His eyes twinkled, but his brows lowered into a frown. "Because your Central Park front 'garden,'" Theo said at last, "is now the greensward of America's Jack-the-Ripper."

Chapter Seven

WE TRIED TO RELAX in the glassed-in conservatory with potted palms and lemon trees. A little waterfall plashed into a marble seashell basin, and two Greek goddess pillars presided at the doorway, stone sisters who watched over the space that I had loved at the first visit to the chateau that was to be my home.

"Theo didn't intend to frighten us," I said.

"Nor insult us," Roddy replied.

"And his apology was heartfelt. Once he saw how upset we were…. Nevertheless," I said, "the fact is…Theo had a point. What do you think?"

"I think these wicker chairs are punishing." Velvet had filled Roddy's lap and fallen fast asleep, her front paws draped over his knees. We sat a moment longer listening to our dog's soft snores. "Roddy, I said at last, "What do we know about Jack the…."

Finger to his lips, Roddy signaled, *hush*. "It was ten years ago, Val. His victims were young women from the London slums. He mutilated their bodies, and he has never been caught."

"You don't suppose the 'strangler' could be...could be....?"

"No, I do not." Roddy rubbed his cheek and seemed to focus on a ripening lemon on the little tree in a cedar planter. "Val," he said at last, "I've been thinking about the situation...about my parents, and about you." He tried to take my hand without waking the dog, who shifted, yawned, and fell back to sleep.

"The Philbricks have been the DeVeres' friends for three generations, Val. The men had business dealings before the Civil War, the Philbricks in rock quarries, the DeVeres in shipping. My memory is hazy, and it doesn't really matter. The point is, Victor and Gladys dine often with my parents. They play bridge together. These last few years, the Philbricks have visited my folks at Bar Harbor in the summer."

I nodded. Since our wedding three years ago, Rufus and Eleanor DeVere have avoided Newport, I suspected because they felt mortified that their new daughter-in-law saved them from bankruptcy. Yielding the twenty-room Newport "cottage" to Roddy and me, they announced their new preference for coastal Maine. My husband and I now occupied the "cottage," Drumcliffe, for the six-week summer "season."

"They're all getting older," Roddy continued, "fixed in their ways. My father sold his last horse and hires hansom cabs these days, but he's obsessed with newspaper reports of stable fires. And mother...she complains that electric light bulbs are Edison's plot to add years to her face."

I kept quiet. Eleanor DeVere's complaints spanned modern life from electric lights to her daughter-in-law. On rare occasions when we two were unavoidably together, she quoted Society's revered queen, Mrs. Astor. "'Valentine, my dear,' she says, 'you must heed the wise words of our own Mrs. Astor—'When our girls marry, they are in love with their husbands and devoted to their interests.'" The words sounded carmelized.

"And the Philbricks..." Roddy continued. "You saw Victor. He used to be a strapping six feet tall with the stride of a grenadier. Gladys is holding up, but for how long before a nervous breakdown?"

"Roddy," I asked, "what are you saying?"

He lifted Velvet from his lap and set her gently on the rug at our feet. "For the sake of my parents' friendship with the Philbricks," he said, "I must try to assist. But you need not be involved, Val. This is a favor to my parents' friends... and my parents as well."

"Roddy, your 'favor' is my promise to be your partner in this...this...." I faltered. "What exactly do you have in mind? To find Clayton Philbrick?"

"And clear his name...if possible," he said. Once again, the *if* hung between us as the fountain burbled and our dog awoke and sniffed at a palm frond.

"Perhaps the police will widen their investigation," I said, "when the young woman victim is identified."

"If she is." Another *if.* "Right now," said Roddy, "our concern is helping the Philbricks find their grandson. The Central Park killer is a matter best left to the police." He fingered a leaf on a ficus tree.

"The Templars Club should be a first stop," Roddy continued. "The cigarette case with the insignia gave the police their lead, but it seems the young 'knights' all claim to have no idea—none at all—where brother Clayton might be keeping himself."

"...meaning that club members might shield their own from 'New York's Finest' in a uniform...or the coat and necktie of a detective."

My husband nodded. "But suppose Mr. Roderick DeVere were to pay a call on the Templars and—"

"—and in the spirit of one clubman to another, perhaps be taken into confidence?"

"Precisely. But a gentleman cannot simply knock at the door of a club and gain entrance. One must have references... associates...friends of friends."

"Surely Theo—" I started to say, then stopped. "This is strictly confidential, isn't it? Between us?"

"Right now, yes."

Stalled, we sat while footman Bronson appeared with a small bowl on a tray. "Sir," he said, "the sautéed minced livers you requested." The bowl was set down, and Velvet lunged at her feast, the little pointy black "bat" ears going back and forth. We had welcomed this "orphaned" dog just weeks ago, and she charmed us every day.

"Another of her thirty-second dinners," Roddy quipped as Velvet licked the bowl."

"Spanking clean," I said. "If only liver didn't smell like... liver."

Another moment, and Roddy said, "One of us ought to visit Black, Starr, and Frost, Jewelers. This isn't a coin toss, Val."

I understood. To gather information, count on a lady at the jewelry salon. "I'm the one," I said.

"And I will call on the Philbricks," said Roddy. "The police are certain to revisit them and ask any number of questions about their grandson. I will tell Gladys and Victor that we agree to make inquiries of our own."

His face was stern. "And they must promise to let us know what the police say—and whatever the Philbricks tell them in return. They must agree to our terms. They must."

Chapter Eight

THE MORNING THREATENED RAIN when Noland stopped our brougham and helped me to the sidewalk at Fifth Avenue and 28th Street. The treasures of Black, Starr, and Frost were not displayed through plate glass windows. This was not Macy's.

"Good morning, madam."

I was ushered inside by a portly man whose graying moustache was trimmed at the lip. The store's interior reminded me of an outsized opera box, paneled in dark velvet to display lustrous gems and precious metals in sanctified quiet. At the moment I was the only customer in the store.

"If you please, may we take your coat?"

I had prepared for the visit (and the weather) in a fur-collared military Macintosh, new this season, over a sky-blue day dress. Calista had suggested "important" jewelry and selected my Russian aquamarine necklace in a rose gold setting. Slipping off the coat and tugging at my gloves, I flashed my emerald-cut "rock" of an engagement diamond and the circlet of diamonds added for good measure. There must be no question about my fitness for the mission.

"Please, do be seated... and how may we be of assistance? I am Mr. Joffrey, a vice-president of our firm, at your service." He pointed to an arrangement of plush sofas, chairs, and tables suitable for display. I took a seat.

"My husband, Mr. Roderick DeVere," I said, "has been a patron of Black, Starr, and Frost, and the cufflinks he has selected are most pleasing."

"And would you be interested in a new selection of cufflinks, madam?" His voice crooned with authority and servility.

"Just now," I said, "I am interested in a gift for a young man...a friend of the family. The young gentleman is a member of the Templars Club." He showed no emotion at the reference. "I hope to surprise him on a special occasion," I said. "I understand that Black, Starr, and Frost offers such accessories as cigarette cases bearing the insignia of the club."

"Ah yes, the bas-relief of the visored knight...Camelot and the Crusades nicely melded. We offer signet rings and cufflinks, and time-pieces as well. The gentlemen of the Templars seem most pleased by our design. And of course, each piece bears our mark... the B.S.&F. initials and the incised eagle ready to take flight. And would you be thinking of silver or gold?"

"Most probably gold," I said, "although I do love silver."

"Of course. And the gentleman's name?"

I held my breath, hoping that no word about Clayton Philbrick's disappearance had reached the jeweler, let alone the discovery of the cigarette case in Central Park. "Clayton Philbrick," I said at last.

Such relief to see the moustache rise in a smile. "Ah yes, I believe Mr. Philbrick has selected several of our pieces. I can review his account. It would not do to select a duplicate, now would it?"

"By no means."

"If you'll excuse me for a moment…." Mr. Joffrey left me gazing at pedestals of monumental sterling silver that was fashioned into teapots and punch bowls encircled with birds and serpents, dolphins and King Neptune, all gleaming like Aladdin's cave.

I felt a sudden, tremendous pride and longing, for everything surrounding me was the achievement of my papa. His discovery of the silver Big Lode and his skill in the mines and mills—his genius and his work made all this possible. He turned raw, dirt-like ore into shining silver bars. Papa's Irish eyes would smile to see me here.

These thoughts nearly undid me. Reverie can be fatal to a task. My mind had wandered, leaving me stupefied when the jeweler reported that Clayton Philbrick owned a Templars cigarette case, two sets of cufflinks and a signet ring.

"And so, Mrs. DeVere, let us proceed. What might you have in mind?"

Nothing was in mind. I had lost track of why I was here: to get Templars' names for Roddy—negotiable names.

"For an utmost special occasion," the jeweler crooned, "perhaps a time piece...." He grew expansive. "And the special occasion in the offing? It might be helpful to know—"

"A dinner," I blurted. "A dinner at...at the Waldorf. The young man's several friends. Six gentlemen friends, I do believe. Yes, six."

"Then you might also consider mementoes for the gentlemen. The Horse Show next month.... We feature sterling stirrup cups."

"Stirrup cups," I echoed, my thoughts racing. "I ought to know the names of Mr. Philbrick's dinner guests," I said. "Perhaps he shopped here with fellow club members...and you assisted them at the time? I believe I would recognize the names if I could see a listing."

"Apologies, madam, but a club membership is confidential. Names must not be bandied about. I'm sure you understand."

If only my close friend, Cassie, were with me, she would know exactly how to charm the jeweler into compliance. Lifelong, Cassie (Cassandra Van Schylar Fox Forster) had dealt with tradesmen, servants, yacht crewmen—the human scaffolding of our Gilded Age. Sensitive and intuitive, she coached me at every turn. If only....

"I'm sure you understand?" He awaited my 'of course.'

"Is there a William?" I asked. "Or a John? I'm sure I recall a John." Spinning the most favored men's names, I fluttered my eyelids and touched my throat, as Cassie might have done. "Or a Richard?"

Damsel near distress.

"Highly irregular," he said.

Did I hear a plaintive tone? I stayed silent, hoping his fear of losing the sale might worm its way into the man's thoughts. Hold the silence, I told myself. Cassie would have approved.

"Just this once...this once," In moments, a calfskin ledger was opened before me, double pages of a very long alphabetized list in impeccable penmanship.

Memorization was never my strong suit. The recitation of Shakespeare was required in the Fourth Ward School in Virginia City, and I barely got through it.

To remember a half-dozen names from a list until I could write them down on the drive home—a *must*.

The jeweler tried to help, pointing with nails that were buffed to a high gloss. "Here's John T. Atkinson...and John C. Barber...John Braxner IV." The moustache seemed to expand. "Are these familiar to you, Mrs. DeVere? Here is William Newfield Constance...William Cunningham, Jr... John Phillips Elmond...."

The many Williams and Johns danced before my eyes, and so they did to the final exit from the salon, then the brougham, and finally coachman Noland driving the matched Hackneys, Apollo and Atlas, to my home at 640 Sixty-second Street, New York City.

Chapter Nine

"YOU ORDERED SEVEN STIRRUP cups?"

"Six for the friends, Roddy, and a seventh for the host."

I had joined Roddy in his paneled den with a Turkish tribal rug, law books, an ice box, and a cabinet filled with glasses, liquors, bitters bottles, and barware. This was the "laboratory of libation foundations" that let my husband experiment with new blends. Our footmen kept the ice box stocked and bowls of fresh fruit at hand.

"You would have approved, Roddy," I said, "but don't press me about the stirrup cups. I trust you will concoct a new stirrup cup beverage.

My husband's face showed pity—for me. "Val, the cups are filled with port or claret and served to riders at the end of a hunt. It's traditional," he added, "after a fox hunt."

"In the red coats."

"Pink...they're called pink."

I felt hot tears. "Out west," I said, "we hunt for food. And don't talk about big game heads on the walls."

A handkerchief appeared in Roddy's fingers. "Let me, please...." He dabbed at my tears. "I didn't mean...."

"It was a hard morning...thoughts of my papa, how I miss him, and...the stirrup cups...."

"Not to worry. You got the names."

I had scribbled them while Noland drove slowly, all Templars in good standing. I stopped sniffling. "Now it's your turn."

"My turn." Roddy paused. "Let me show you something. No, don't ask, just come downstairs with me." Seeming both merry and somber, he led me down the spiral staircase with its Caen stone railing—pleasing to the eye but treacherous.

We entered an ochre reception room with a George III Pembroke table, the name familiar since Roddy's mother drilled me in the vocabulary of antique furniture. We stood before a surface spread with newspapers that looked ragged and damp. It hadn't rained. "Did these get wet?"

"In a manner of speaking."

The bite marks told the story. "Velvet," I said.

He grinned. "She got hold of the morning papers and had herself quite a time. Bronson has taken her for a walk. Sands was irked, and Mrs. Thwaite had a fit."

I silently enjoyed this latest about our housekeeper, but Roddy looked serious. "See here, Val, this torn *Times* front page...."

Pieced together, the torn and bitten pages of the *Times* and *World* bannered the identity of the latest victim of the Central Park strangler.

"Actress... Dancer... cruel exposure ...

"She was an actress?"

Light of Life Extinguished.... Friend crazed with grief... LaRue doomed...."

"Is that her name?" I asked.

"Apparently, 'LaRue,'" Roddy said. "Roxie.... It looks like 'Roxie LaRue' was an actress and a dancer."

The newspaper collage had also spelled out two words that offered relief, *dancer* and *actress*. "Roddy, the third murdered woman was not a servant from a house near the park. Is it selfish to give thanks?"

He kissed my cheek. "We give thanks when we can." He slid an inky black image to the table's edge in front of me.

"Is that her?" I asked.

"Or perhaps the 'friend' who is reported 'crazed.'"

We couldn't decide. "One point," Roddy said, "this third victim was on the stage...different from the others."

I recalled the wage-work of the first two murdered women. The steam laundry and the hat workshop were far from theatrical footlights.

"Look here," Roddy said, "there's something about a show." He pinched a sodden sheet between two fingers, then nearly gasped, "Oh, no. Surely not."

"Not what?"

"The Knickerbocker Theatre," he said, "...another revival of *The Black Crook*."

The reference meant nothing to me. "Are you laughing? Tell me you aren't laughing."

But he was. "Shocking," I said. "The woman is dead, and her friend is grieving...and you find it funny?"

"Sorry, Val. It's the show. *The Black Crook* was notorious. The Crook was a villain in black ballet leggings, half-devil and half court jester. But the real attraction was a corps of...a hundred young ladies in skin-colored tights. It was the first stateside show with chorus girls. My grandfather talked about it. Thirty years ago it was shocking, New York's Sodom and Gomorrah. It made a fortune, broke all records." His grin looked sly. "I'll wager that a traveling company staged it in your Silver City."

"—Virginia City, Mr. Roderick Windham DeVere, as you well know." Roddy liked to tease about the Nevada city where Papa settled us when he got rich. "Our Piper's Opera House showed *Romeo and Juliette* and *Hamlet* with a leading tragedian from the East...and...."

I also remembered a cowboy piece with horses and a St. Bernard named Jumbo that weighed two hundred pounds. Papa got us front row seats. I must have been about twelve years old.

Roddy pointed to a sodden, chewed corner of the *Times*. "'In rehearsal ...upcoming revival for the holiday season.'" Roddy winced. "*The Black Crook* for Thanksgiving? For Christmas? Bizarre."

He paused. "I wonder who's investing.... For the young ladies in tights, I'd guess a Vanderbilt. If a horse is involved, I'd say Oliver Belmont. But if buying up the Knickerbocker Theatre property is a plan, I'd bet money on Eli Fryer. That man is a real estate vulture. He's gobbling up land on the west side of the park where the apartment buildings are going up."

I rolled my shoulders, relieved that Roddy got the Templars' names and the woman whose body was found at the Pergola was not an Irish housemaid. "Enough of this, Roddy" I said. "Enough."

"...for the moment," my husband said, "but why was Clayton Philbrick's cigarette case found near her body?"

Chapter Ten

RODDY WOULD VISIT THE Philbricks to learn whether a "John" or "William" struck a chord as Clayton's friend. If yes, he would go to the Templars Club and, as one city club man to another, make acquaintance and inquire about the missing man's whereabouts.

"Club members gather at the close of day. You needn't wait dinner."

But I would. For now, I changed into a comfortable shirtwaist and skirt. I was also hungry.

The afternoon took a turn. Roddy had gone, and I demolished a plate of two-day-old chicken fricassee and spoke further to the footman about our dog's health. After the inky newsprint, Velvet looked listless and shot a baleful glance when I said, "Good dog" and freshened her water.

I was about to take her upstairs when Sands approached, flicking impatient fingers against his thumb.

"Excuse me, Mrs. DeVere…. A woman has rung yet again at the front entrance. We informed her that employment in the household is arranged through an agency."

Did we need another housemaid or someone in the kitchen? If she could brew a decent cup of coffee or bake sourdough biscuits, I would be interested.

"The woman insists that her purpose is not employment and that you will receive her."

"Who is she?"

"Evidently…." He touched his throat, as if the words pained him. "Evidently, she is a person without calling cards."

Laughable, but a serious breech in Society. "Did she say her name?"

"A name that we find to be suspect, ma'am. A name that Mrs. Thwaite and I both regard as highly improbable and unlikely to be authentic." He stood at full height, his swallowtail coat and trousers perfection in service. He ignored the languid little dog at my feet.

"Her name, Sands. May I ask her name?"

As if tormented to utter the syllables. "Flowers," ma'am. She calls herself Miss Flowers."

I managed not to exclaim, "Oh, no, not her." My husband and my friend Cassie (and the etiquette manuals) all warned against confiding in servants. Sands, nonetheless, had not worked for DeVere family for eons without sensing every current in the household air.

"Sands," I said at last, "did Miss Flowers indicate the purpose of her intended visit?"

"She did not."

"A charity, perhaps? Is she seeking a charitable contribution?"

"I wouldn't know. She wishes to speak with you, ma'am, on the basis of an alleged acquaintance."

In terms of the western square dance, my "do-si-do" with the butler had ended. "Please show Miss Flowers to the *Fleur de Lis* drawing room." When Sands was out of sight, I murmured, "Come, Velvet. The lady of the house needs you."

Annie Flowers's brisk footsteps meant purpose. Slight of build, she pulled up a Rococo side chair and gazed at the gold silk wall panels. From a sea foam armchair with Velvet in my lap, I watched her narrow dark eyes squint in disapproval. Her toe tips barely touched the floor.

"Miss Flowers," I said, "we meet again."

"We do." Her black serge skirt, muslin shirtwaist and lightweight cape were too thin for autumn weather, and her short cape no match for the sharp winds to come.

"It's been...two months, I believe."

"Six weeks, Mrs. DeVere," she said, "since your visit to my jail cell."

"—at the Halls of Justice and House of Detention."

"The Tombs."

The slang term better fit the granite fortress in lower Manhattan where I had visited this woman and tried to help her. Last July I had met Annie Flowers in her Lower East Side tenement garret when she cared for a fatally ill cousin of my friend Cassie. Soon afterward, she was jailed for "creating a public nuisance" in support of women's suffrage. Our attorney arranged for her release and the payment of her fine. Roddy predicted that we had not seen the last of her.

If she came give thanks, I saw no sign. "I trust that you continue to support votes for women," I said.

"Absolutely I do. As Scripture says, 'God is in the midst of her, she shall not be moved.' Psalm Forty-six."

The same verse she recited when we had met. I also recalled the sole object on Annie Flowers's Lower East Side walls: a Christian cross.

"However long it takes, we will vote."

"I agree. And I am prepared to contribute to women's suffrage. In Nevada, we women can already vote, and I support a national law."

She waved her fingers. "I'm not here for suffrage today."

"No?" I stroked Velvet. The dog had looked toward the visitor and closed her eyes.

"I am learning typewriting."

"Very good."

"To prepare for a new job."

"Excellent," I said. "I wish you well."

She sat forward, as if fronting a typewriter keyboard. "I will be employed by the National Consumers League. Have you heard of the League?"

"Consumers' League...? Something new?" Perhaps Annie Flowers would accept a few of the greenbacks that were tucked in a hallway Ming vase for incidentals.

She crossed her ankles and pulled her skirt to the floor, though I had glimpsed her sad mended stockings and well-worn boots.

"Remember the handkerchief you brought to the Tombs, Mrs. DeVere? The cotton hankie to wipe my chin?"

I had brought the suffragist prisoner a luncheon basket with a ripe peach and a cambric handkerchief in case the juice dribbled. Annie Flowers had objected to a handkerchief that was washed and pressed by a laundress.

Indirectly, she blamed me for supporting child labor. At least, that's what I felt.

In this moment I wished that Sands had sent the woman away, though I pictured her entrenched on our front steps.

"What might I do for you, Miss Flowers?"

For the first time, she acknowledged my dog. "Your dog..." she said.

"Her name is Velvet," I replied. "She may not feel well. It seems she chewed the morning newspapers."

"They all love to chew," Annie Flowers said, "but don't worry, the pulp paper won't do real harm." She reached forward and gently touched Velvet's head. "A purebred dog... am I right?"

"She is a French bulldog. A rescue."

"How enviable... a luxury dog."

She spoke softly, but I felt guarded, doubting that Annie Flowers would be moved if she knew that I once awoke in a bedroll when a dog barked a warning that a wolf had come near our camp in Colorado.

"A pet without a care in this world." She sounded wistful. "Your dog gets good veterinary care, I imagine."

I nodded. Velvet had awakened, her ears back, her little black nose twitching. I stroked her back, thankful that Roddy's mother was nowhere nearby. She had recently suggested that I train Velvet for the next Westminster dog show. ("Now that the French bulldogs are a certified breed, Valentine, the opportunity is yours.")

"Nourishing meals and a warm bed..." Annie Flowers continued. "If only the children and families in his city could have as much as this nice dog." She sat farther forward and seemed about to kneel in front of Velvet.

"So many children toiling in factories, Mrs. DeVere, and so many workers who cannot support a family on starvation wages...really, 'starvation.' Young women work out their lives in laundries...mangles and vats of boiling starch."

She paused to meet my gaze. "And those murdered girls, getting by the best they know how...killed."

"Which murdered girls...?"

"Working girls. Your park is no playground for them, Mrs. DeVere." She wet her lips. We were eye to eye. "A girl has got to eat, pay rent, dress halfway decent. You think she makes out trimming hats, starching petticoats? No, she works a second shift." Annie Flowers spoke slowly, intensely.

"Night work in the park. The men know where to find a girl. It's dangerous. The girls shouldn't be risking their lives."

"But the park police...."

She laughed. "It's a big park, Mrs. DeVere. Too many secret places. The men that dreamed up the park made a nightmare from the start...peoples' lives ruined...ruined."

"Whose lives?"

"...before it was a park, others had homes...don't you know?"

"...Olmsted," I said. "Frederick Olmsted and Calvert Vaux designed the park. Everyone knows."

"...knows what they want to know, Mrs. DeVere."

The moment hung. Velvet licked my wrist. "Miss Flowers," I said, "have you ever—?"

"—shown off my leg with a lacy garter in Central Park in the depth of night?" She shook her head no. "But I know those who need to."

"I didn't mean—"

"—maybe you meant, have I toiled from dawn to dawn on machines that will break a girl's back? No, but I have seen it, Mrs. DeVere, and it must be brought to an end. You will receive a letter from the Consumers League."

I struggled from the chair, Velvet wriggling in my arms. Our butler was nowhere in sight, so my next questions would be private. "Miss Flowers...about the men that go into the park at night...."

"What about them?"

How to ask the question? Nevada's Virginia City had celebrated its Queen of "D" Street, "Madam" Julia Bulette, who wore an opera cloak of white silk and purple velvet. Her "D" Street patrons climbed up the social scale from the lowliest miners to the exclusive Washoe Club. Her generosity made her a beloved legend. The drifter who strangled her for her diamonds and furs was hanged in the public square, and every saloon served whiskey on the house.

"What about the men?" she repeated. "You mean, who are they? They are all kinds."

"Gentlemen...?"

Her cynical smile. "If you say so."

The dog licked my thumb as I rose and started toward the front hall. Annie Flowers followed. At the door, she turned to me. "The National Consumers League will change things for the better, Mrs. DeVere. Improved working conditions and decent wages...and the park for safe, daytime pleasure. Daytime only. You understand?"

"I'm not sure I do," I said. "Is this your purpose in coming, Miss Flowers, to alert me to expect a letter?"

"Many ladies in your circle will join the board, Mrs. DeVere. Reform is underway. You will hear from the League. You will be invited. I will graduate from typewriting school in a few days. I will typewrite your letter. Good afternoon."

She was gone, her call for support a split-open Pandora's box. Sex for money under the bridges, in the shrubs. And ruined lives...and murder.

Chapter Eleven

WE DID NOT ENJOY our usual cocktails this evening but sat over lamb chops, green beans, and roasted potatoes. Roddy had arrived as the hallway clock struck seven p.m. and thundered from the foyer, "The morning newspapers, I must have them."

The butler's voice, in counterpoint, "Trash, sir. All disposed of...your little dog chewed—"

"—retrieve them, the whole lot...the *World* and *Times*, the *Journal* too... every single one. We must have them... immediately. No, I will not dress for dinner this evening. And where is Mrs. DeVere? I must speak with her at once."

Bursting to ask about street walkers in Central Park at night and the lives somehow "ruined" so long ago, I also puzzled over my husband's turmoil. "Why order the chewed newspapers again, Roddy? We found Roxie LaRue. Is it something about that play, *The Black Crook*?"

"Maybe...indirectly." He paused as a footman poured us red wine.

I sipped slowly but stewed in thoughts of my own. Roddy had not told me the park became a trysting place at night, nor said a word about other "ruined" lives. He cocooned me in the "tender mercies" that spared ladies the hard facts. Where was the honesty we had promised one another across the male-female divide? How different from the West.

"Good burgundy," I said through clenched teeth.

"Pinot noir, I believe."

"So many different grapes," I continued, "clever, the French...."

Roddy shot me a look, put down his knife and faced me. "Val, are you dodging something?"

"Aren't we both?"

We glared, and my husband's chest expanded against his shirt studs as he declared the lamb to be just short of mutton and called for serrated knives for us both. "Shall we flip for who goes first, my dear Val?"

"...shall," I said, and Roddy plucked a nickel from a pocket for a heads-or-tails quick fix, a move that sometimes spared us a tiff. The face-up Liberty head gave my husband his moment.

"Let me start with the Philbricks," he said. "They were in a state of shock, barely speaking to one another. The police returned to interview them this morning, the same detective and two officers in uniform. They asked to search

Clayton's apartment. Victor refused, but Gladys thought a search might help them locate Clayton. Victor pounded his cane and swore. Gladys tried to calm him down, but he fumed all the while."

"What 'while?'"

"During the search. Gladys led the detective and one policeman into her grandson's apartment. The other officer stayed with Victor in the reception room, which inflamed him."

"And?"

"And something of 'material interest' was found."

"What was it?"

"That's the question. The detective fingered a few things and rifled some papers. Gladys couldn't see what was taken... seized."

"Evidence?"

Roddy lifted his knife. "Let's not get ahead of ourselves. Whatever they found might help the police find Clayton, as Gladys hopes. I arrived just before two o'clock, and the couple were still distraught. Telling their story reignited strong feelings. Victor needed a brandy, and I joined Gladys for a pot of mint tea."

"And the Templars Club names?"

Roddy sawed at his lamb chop. "It took a while. Victor recognized three of the names you memorized from the jeweler. Gladys thought she might have been introduced to a fourth name, a John Grandison, but she had no information about him."

"...meaning that his family is probably not in Society." Roddy had no rebuttal. The Four Hundred knows its own. I moved on, ready to bring up the nighttime park rendezvous. "So, you went to the Templars clubhouse," I said. "And—?"

"And let us not have lamb until next spring, Val. The French call this *agneau de présale*, but it might as well be mutton from an old ram. Maybe Velvet will like it."

"For certain."

My husband called for fruit and cheese, and a footman apologized for the delay recovering the newspapers. ("We should have them presently, sir, and do you wish them to be placed on the same table as earlier today? Or would you prefer them to be brought to you here?")

We would inspect them immediately after dinner, Roddy said, adding that if the staff could not find the papers, he would lend a hand.

Another hour within those dreary ochre walls and yet another delay before I could bring up the "ruined" lives and the possibility that the women strangled in Central Park were "working girls" desperate for an extra dollar to pay the rent, girls trapped by a killer—as our friend Theo said, by Central Park's own Jack-the-Ripper.

Camembert and Roquefort wedges were before us. Roddy waved off the footman and sliced a pear.

My patience ebbed, but I waited.

"...about the Templars clubhouse on East Fourteenth Street," Roddy said, "I arrived at five o'clock and took a chance on Gladys's John Grandison. Luck was with me.

The man left the bridge table to spend a few moments with a Philbrick family friend. I suspect he was losing and welcomed an excuse."

"I thought gambling was forbidden at the gentlemen's clubs."

"A friendly game of whist or bridge doesn't count as gaming."

Roddy quartered an apple. "Anyway, Grandison is a pleasant fellow, and we spoke in roundabout terms, easy to do over scotch in a club lounge—a very handsomely furnished lounge indeed. Theo is right about the extravagance. If the Templars go bankrupt, someone will snap up everything from floor to ceiling."

"But you asked about Clayton Philbrick—?"

"—after small talk about next month's Horse Show. Would Dickman Brown's "Meadow Brook" win again this year? Or Colonel Astor's "Typhoon" carry the day? We got nowhere until a fellow Templar stopped to have a few words, and a very good thing that he did."

Roddy cut cheese for each of us. The meal felt endless. "The second Templar," he said, "his slogan might be *in whisky veritas*. At least I hope so."

"He was drunk?"

"Let's say he had enjoyed more scotch than was prudent. He's a young bond salesman named Brainard... Andrew Brainard. A Wall Street windfall let him celebrate with an early visit to his club."

Roddy reached for another pear.

"Was the man sober enough to make sense?"

"Barely. He hadn't seen Philbrick lately but hinted his fellow Templar would probably be found at a Broadway stage backdoor on any night of the week. 'Look for the man with a blooming blond moustache that's turned up and waxed. He'll hold a bouquet of roses and a matching boutonniere in his lapel. Look for the yellow moustache and a bouquet of orange and yellow roses, that's Philbrick.'" Roddy paused. "Andrew Brainard started to say more, but Grandison stopped him."

"What do you suppose it was?"

"Something about a number of Templars eager to set eyes on Philbrick. It seems that nobody has seen him for the last ten days."

"Before the third woman...before Roxie LaRue was found."

Roddy nodded. "Brainard gave me his card. 'If you see brother Philbrick, tell him that certain Templars are eager to meet with him—and he'll know exactly which members.'"

"Why don't the Templars go to the stage doors themselves?"

Roddy leaned close. "Val, guess how many theatres are operating in the city?"

"About a dozen?"

"Closer to thirty," he said. "And shows can change every two weeks, which makes it nearly impossible to find one silk top hat with a yellow rose boutonniere. Picture it, one young man with a stylish moustache crowded with others at the stage doors."

I plucked a small cluster of grapes. "It sounds like those backdoors attract quite a few theatre door Casanovas." I ate a grape. "Who are they?"

Roddy laughed. "Stage door Johnnys…young gentlemen, Val. Fellows on the town."

"—meaning that Clayton Philbrick could hide somewhere in the city and appear at a different stage door every night?"

"Unless one particular show girl has captivated him." Roddy pushed his plate to the side. "If so, he would follow her from one show to the next, and one theatre to the next." My husband added, "He would give her flowers and chocolates and jewelry."

"But the jewel she yearns for is a diamond engagement ring…."

"Of course. She hopes he'll marry her, make her a wealthy woman. Occasionally it works. Think of Edith Gould. Before she became Mrs. George J. Gould, she was on the stage."

I was stunned. We socialized with the Goulds in Newport and the city. George resembled his railroad baron father, the same heavy beard and suspicious eyes. But the statuesque Edith was a great beauty, and so gracious.

"A fairy tale that came true," I murmured.

Roddy's gaze suddenly went faraway, even dreamy. He held the pear in his palm, as if to warm it. "A chorus girl," he said, "is an actress of sorts, and her fellow is waiting after the show. He whisks her into a hansom cab for a starry ride through the park."

My husband seemed to cuddle the pear. "The twosome enjoy one another's company, and then he takes her to a lobster palace for a champagne supper... a lobster, and then... the evening is young...."

"What palace restaurant?" My voice tightened. Delmonico's was palatial. So was Sherry's. Both of their menus featured seafood, but neither had been called a "lobster palace" in my hearing. Was this a secret code?

"Rector's is a lobster palace," Roddy said. "So is Murray's Roman Gardens." He sounded nostalgic. "Everything glitters, champagne flows, and the orchestra plays an overture from the young lady's show...that is, if her escort has made arrangements with the Maestro."

"Roddy, are you speaking from experience?"

My husband flushed.

"Chorus girls? How many chorus girls?"

"A few times, Val. Every bachelor in the city...at least once." He dropped the pear, which missed his plate and thudded on the tablecloth. We both stared at it, me frowning, Roddy embarrassed.

Or so I thought.

He took my hand. "You must understand," he said, "the college years are a season of bachelor freedom." He looked into my eyes. "A very short season, and it came to a halt when I met you, Miss Valentine Mackle."

He laced his fingers in mine and put the wayward pear in the fruit bowl.

"And let me add, my dear, that a stage door Johnny's life quickly becomes a stale routine, at least for most young gents. The newness fades fast."

"But a few persist?"

"Always a few," he said, "the exception to prove the rule."

"Roddy, I have a question—" The grapes squeezed in my free hand, and I burst out, "Did you ever go into the park at night?"

"I just told you...a hansom cab ride...."

"I mean, by yourself?"

"By myself? What in the—?" Suddenly staring as though I spoke Urdu, he blinked twice, cleared his throat, and bent forward until our foreheads touched.

The grapes crushed in my fingers.

"Whoever put such a thought into your head?"

Grape juice trickled down my wrist.

"Annie Flowers called this afternoon."

"That suffrage woman."

"We had a talk. She hinted that lives were 'ruined' when Central Park was created. Do you know what she meant?"

"No idea."

"She also told me that working girls rendezvous with men in the park at night. For extra money. Do you know about this?"

He paused. "Somewhat."

"How much?"

"Val—" It took a moment. My husband looked half insulted, half amused. "There's a magazine for men, *The*

Police Gazette. Every barbershop and barroom has a few issues. They run sensational pieces like... 'How an Innocent Lass Was Done for by a Gothamite after Midnight.'"

"Why didn't you tell me you were a stage door Johnny?"

"You would have been offended."

He was not wrong.

"So, you never...."

"I never...No, I never...." The cheese knife clanked against the plate.

I had stopped. He looked offended. "But suppose Clayton Philbrick..." I said.

Roddy dabbed at my wrist with his napkin, wiping grape seeds and skins from my fingers. "Val, I am doubtful. The young gentlemen in Society are warned against catching the 'French disease' in casual romances."

"Syphilis," I said.

"They are warned that it can be deadly."

"And just as deadly for a woman."

Exasperation hovered around Roddy's eyes. "Right now, we are talking about Clayton Philbrick. We can discuss public health another time." Would you like to hear my thoughts?"

"I would."

"It's hypothetical, a possibility...."

"I'm all ears."

Roddy sat back. "There's a reason to review this morning's newspapers. We know that Clayton Philbrick has become a stage door Johnny. At times, a 'Johnny' becomes smitten with his show girl *cherie* and sometimes announces the intention to lead the young lady to the altar."

"Like George Gould."

"Edith Gould is one in a million, Val. Believe me. The usual chorus girl imagines that she will be the next Cinderella if she plays her cards right. She dances for the prince in the fairy tale. On the other hand," Roddy continued, "the young gentleman's family fears a gold digging harlot will infest their home."

"Or a silver mine 'harlot' from the Wild West?"

He stopped, smiled, and we both enjoyed a little tense laugh.

"In such cases," Roddy continued, "the family takes measures to put a stop to the nuptials."

"But what if the young man is legally of adult age?"

"The threat of disinheritance usually does the trick. The specter of life without funds is bleak enough to stop the romance."

"But Gladys and Victor told us that Clayton had come into his 'all.'"

"They did but the terms of his inheritance were not specified."

"Terms? Could Victor Philbrick retain some legal rights to his grandson's inheritance?"

"Legally, it's possible," Roddy said.

"And it's also possible," I said, "that Clayton has been involved with the dead woman...Roxie LaRue." Roddy nodded. "Suppose that he read about her death in the earliest edition of the newspapers and went into hiding, grief-stricken. Or...."

The *or* hovered, just like the *if*s.

Pausing, we both heard "ahem" at the doorway, a footman inquiring about dessert. Would we wish a sweet? Coffee? Tea?

"Nothing for me," I said. That weak coffee, so dispiriting.

"Perhaps later, Chalmers," Roddy said to the footman. "And what about the newspapers I requested?"

"Sir, they have been retrieved from an ash barrel and put out for you as you wish. They have been spread as best Bronson and I could manage."

Roddy stood and held my chair. "Shall we—?"

"We shall."

The shredded newspapers looked terrible, dusty and crinkled. We squinted, hesitant to touch them.

"In the ash barrel with coal ash and clinkers," Roddy said. "Ridiculous. I'll speak to Sands."

The chandelier cast jaundiced light against the ochre panels of the reception room, and our shadows dimmed the print.

"What exactly are we looking for?" I asked. "We know about *The Black Crook* and Roxie. What else—I"

"—the friend," he said. "The 'crazed' friend. What's her name?"

I bent close to a torn sheet dimpled with our dog's bite marks. "...friend...Miss...Taylor, here it is, Roddy... Miss Lola Taylor."

Roddy bent with me, our temples touching. He made out two more words, "ballet" and "*Crook.*"

"We could have looked for the friend's name this morning and saved ourselves the trouble," I said.

My husband touched the paper and freed a plume of ash. "Lola Taylor," he said, "is the murdered woman's friend and a member of the Black Crook cast. That's what we need to know. It's time to talk to this 'crazed friend.'"

Chapter Twelve

WE BOTH FELT GRATEFUL that my friend, Cassie, agreed on shortest notice to go along with me to the theatre at Thirty-eighth Street and Broadway to inquire about a cast member in the upcoming revival of *The Black Crook*: Miss Lola Taylor.

Roddy begged off because Eli Fryer suddenly complained that the cocktail my husband created for the gentlemen at the Bicycle Tea needed strengthening, and he needed a new blend right away to have it readied for the Tea.

"No point riling the Cycling Club president," Roddy said. "The recipe calls for plenty of rye, but I'll tinker with the bitters." The zinc-topped table in Roddy's study was arrayed with bottles of whiskey and various bitters, a siphon, glasses, oranges, and a jar of maraschino cherries.

"Tea for the ladies, and cocktails for the men," I said, my sarcasm flaring. "The cycling Tea," I asked, "...next week?"

"Monday...the third Monday in October. And we will be on time, Val. You remember last year...."

I remembered. The Tea was delayed because one couple was late. Eli took offence and sneered at the husband's cycling skills. "The Martendales, wasn't it?" I asked.

Roddy nodded. "Eli and Arthur Martendale haven't spoken for months."

My husband uncorked a bottle. "I don't understand," I said, "why Eli Fryer has such power. He's a boor and a nuisance. Why put up with him?"

"Business, Val," Roddy said. "And don't discount ancestry, because Eli is Old New York on his mother's side. And the man has an eagle eye for investment. By now, he owns whole city blocks. He's connected to Tammany and City Hall and Mulberry Street too...too important to ignore."

Roddy smiled. "The Tea is the last outdoor event of autumn, so let's enjoy it." He added, "...and a perfect opportunity for your new 'wheel.'"

"Wheel." I grinned at the deliberately old-fashioned name for the bicycle replacing the one that was wrecked this past summer in Newport. I had not yet tried out the new "bike," though cyclists were everywhere these days, and some park policemen patrolled on bicycles.

"Weather permitting," I said.

Our thoughts merged in the next moment, and silence hung like a cloud. Central Park "weather" now meant murder.

"Eli will plan on Riverside Drive this year," Roddy said, "He'll avoid the park.. So, Riverside Drive next Monday for sure." Roddy added, "Give my best to Cassandra, and thank her for saying 'yes' on short notice." My husband added, "And watch over Cassandra."

"I will."

"You understand what I mean."

"I do. I promise."

Our qualms about the morning with Cassie had been silently telegraphed between us. Roddy and I had promised strict secrecy to the Philbricks but decided to break the promise by involving a good friend.

Not without risk. Cassandra Forster was the soul of discretion, but a loose word or two could make the Philbricks a "juicy" item in the scandal sheet devoured by all Society, E. D. Mann's notorious *Town Topics*. The elder Philbricks would never forgive us.

Equally important—our sensitive friend's wellbeing. "*To the manor born*," as the saying goes, Cassandra Van Schylar Fox Forster patiently tutored me in the niceties of New York etiquette, so different from Virginia City, Nevada, where I went about on foot or saddle, strolled the wooden plank sidewalks lining "C" Street, and chatted with miners and bankers, dressmakers and farriers. Skipping by, I saluted bartenders through the saloons' plate glass windows and dined with papa in the Silver Queen Hotel & Saloon dining room with its whisky bar in plain sight.

Cassie, however, had patiently warned against freewheeling in New York, lest I appear in the gossipy "Saunterings" section of *Town Topics* and jeopardize the senior DeVeres' social standing. Gracious to one and all, my close friend, Cassie could sometimes nudge the far West to the back of my mind.

Among her friends and acquaintances, however, Cassie Forster also experienced atmospheric currents that were nowhere in others' thoughts. She sometimes "saw" colorful auras surrounding people. She saw spaces tinted in hues that were invisible to companions. Not quite superstitious, our friend, but she was close to it, as friends recalled from childhood dancing school.

I blamed her manicurist who doubled as a spiritualist medium, a Madam Riva who used manicures to promote her profitable sideline of evening séances. Cassie, however, told me of her beloved childhood nanny, Saffira, who gave her the love that was denied by her cold and angry mother. A warm, caring woman of the "Islands," Saffira schooled Cassie in the lore of spirits that surrounded her, and Cassie learned to sense them too, to see sights invisible to others, to feel what escaped others' attention. Alarmed, her parents sent the nanny away, but Saffira's gifts endured. When her husband Dudley was home from his fossil hunts, I relied on his scientific mind to keep Forster family séances off limits.

Still, Cassie's premonitions could prove uncannily accurate, and I trusted her second "lens" for whatever we might learn from Miss Lola Taylor. Roddy and I agreed that for gathering information, a pair of women had the advantage.

Promptly at 9:30, Sands announced that Mrs. Forster had arrived. I went downstairs. "Cassie, good morning."

"Good morning to you, dear Val.... Shall we...?"

On the sidewalk, our ears tuned to carts and horses, and eyes darted from the sunlight splashed on the colorful fall trees to the tall buildings on Fifty-ninth Street.

"I hear the Plaza Hotel will soon be torn down," I said.

"They're building a new one, even taller," said Cassie. "They say that widows will live there, with diamonds and dogs."

We set a brisk pace. The petite Cassie Forster glowed with her soft brown eyes and auburn hair, her perfect posture in every inch of her five feet in height. An azure blue cloak draped Cassie's hourglass figure, and her heart-shaped face was framed by a teal bonnet with birds' wings at the crown. I wore a russet walking suit and matching cape and the obligatory hat, a cocoa brown tam o'shanter with one cockade feather. The colors, my dressmaker had assured me, harmonized with my dark "dishwater" blond hair and olive complexion.

Cassie and I wore gloves and short boots with low heels. Walking, we always said, would do us good.

"Do you have your nickel?" Cassie asked.

"I do."

"Today, Val, we are ladies with coins."

My friend obeyed the rule against ladies carrying cash, though nickels for the "El" were an exception. (I secretly tucked a silver dollar into a pocket handkerchief. Some western customs were unshakable.)

We would ride the Sixth Avenue "El" to the theatre district because private carriages parked outside theatres at odd hours could attract attention. The public horsecars were pokey, so we chose the elevated train, which squealed and rattled and puffed black smoke and cinders—but sped at fifteen miles per hour.

"Remind me which theater we're visiting, Val?" We had climbed the "El" station stairs to the platform, felt the oncoming train rumble under our boot soles, boarded a car, and found seats. "Which theatre? The Princess?"

"The Knickerbocker," I said, "at Thirty-eighth and Broadway."

"The Knick...." She suddenly looked crestfallen. "Oh, no, not that one...." She wrung her gloved hands. The train groaned.

"What is it? What's wrong?"

Cassie's words were nearly drowned by the squealing wheels. "It wasn't the Knickerbocker years ago," she said. "It was Abbey's Theatre before the terrible fire. I saw *The Red Lamp*...my parents took me....Lily Hanbury in the lead. She was my father's favorite actress...and my parents were happy then."

My friend seemed to gaze into a distance beyond this time and place as the train ground on, halting conversation about Cassie's parents' bitter divorce, now in final stages. She had recently inherited a great deal of money from a deceased relative, much to the fury of her mother, who raged at being bypassed in the family inheritance.

Everyone hoped that Cassie's husband Dudley would delay his next scientific adventure to faraway shores rich with fossils. He was needed here with Cassie and little Charlie and Beatrice, their children.

"Next stop, Cassie."

We went on foot, toward Broadway and Thirty-eighth Street, and south of Times Square near Bryant Park.

"Could we sit in the park for a moment, Val?"

"Of course."

"To settle down," she said.

"Good idea."

Side by side on a shaded green bench, we felt an autumn chill. Cassie drew her cloak tighter.

A word about the two children and Dudley would surely lift her spirits. "Cassie," I asked, "what are Bea and Charlie doing this morning? An adventure with their daddy?"

She briefly brightened at their names. "Dudley insisted on the park," she said. "He got a permit for leaf collection, and they're off to the park with a lunch. I'll meet them near the Dairy when we return…. Dudley promised ice cream treats."

She bit one gloved finger.

"Perhaps I'm too cautious, Val, but I hoped Dudley would take them to F.A.O. Schwarz for toys, far from the park, not even the zoo…." She shuddered. "Those three young women that were found dead…the park feels haunted."

Haunted? I shuddered too, in fear for my friend. I touched her arm. "Notice the sunshine, Cassie. It's a gorgeous day. The park will be safe and festive."

"You sound like my husband."

Cassie gazed into the distance and seemed to muse to herself. "My Bea will choose the brightest colors, and Charlie will recite botanical Latin names. He'll want an album for specimens, and my little girl will ask for a vase to hold the leaf bouquet."

Cassie turned to me. "Do I sound jaded, Val? No such thing. The children are sheltered in innocence, and I envy them...and try to give them a childhood free of cares. As my own childhood was not."

"...your parents' difficulties...?"

She shook her head. "Because of the auras...because I see things...things others do not see. And feel certain things too." She pressed closer. "Val, you praise me for my manners...."

"Impeccable manners," I said.

Her smile turned morose. "Manners can conceal auras... cover up premonitions. There's a famous doctor, Dr. Beard... my father took me to him when I began to see things. I was very young, and the doctor was very old. He said I suffered from strained nerves." Cassie paused. "It seemed best to go along, and I did...and I have...all these years."

Almost morbid, she fingered a fan-shaped leaf that had dropped to our bench at that moment. "The Chinese ginkgo," she said. "Dudley says it's a tree from ancient times. Sometimes I feel ancient...."

"Nothing of the kind. Cassie, I have 'stolen' you away this morning. I plead guilty."

I watched my friend collect herself. With effort she sat up very straight and joined me in this present moment.

"Val," she said, "If you bring Velvet for a visit with my children, all will be forgiven." She dropped the leaf. "Now then, who is it we want to see at the theatre? And why, exactly, are we here?"

Chapter Thirteen

KNICKERBOCKER THEATRE WAS CARVED in stone above the darkened entrance, but the six-story structure could be mistaken for a modern office building. It looked deserted.

We had tried the doors and peered at the glass. "Locked tight," I said.

"Do you see anything?" Cassie asked.

"Our reflections."

I knew nothing about theatrical rehearsal schedules, but by late morning—it was almost lunchtime—surely some actors or dancers or musicians would be here. Or stagehands. Roddy had said *The Black Crook* involved "specialty performers," from jugglers to sword dancers to the celebrated flock of chorus girls.

"You're certain that Miss Taylor is a dancer?" Cassie asked. "Or perhaps an acrobat? You're sure—?"

I wasn't sure. "Let's go around to the back."

Down the alley, past the trash barrels and horse droppings, the stage door was a flat black steel plate. Like a tomb. A gray and white cat meowed and dashed off.

"There's nobody," Cassie said.

"I'll knock." I slipped off a boot and banged the heel against the door. Cassie looked amused.

The pounding brought a scuffling, the rasp of keys, and the door slowly opened. "What is it?"

We faced a paunchy man in a sleeveless undershirt with suspenders buttoned to his denim work pants. He wore rubber boots and held a mop.

"You two with the ventriloquist?" he asked.

"I don't think so."

"The ventriloquist is due this morning."

"We are looking for a member of *The Black Crook* cast," I said.

He shifted a bulge from one cheek to the other. Snuff? Chewing tobacco? "Cast?" He said. "There's a hundred or more in it."

We said we understood.

"Nobody's here," he said.

"No one?" asked Cassie? "Surely someone is expecting the ventriloquist." She looked winsome, just short of a smile. "Perhaps we might have a word with whoever is inside…just for a moment?" Her voice sounded like meringue.

He shifted the mop handle and eyed our hats. "There's no show going on now."

Shutting the door, he paused when Cassie said, "Only a very few minutes...if you please...."

Just then a deep voice bellowed from the dark depths. "Bring in the ventriloquist!"

The "doorman" ushered us into a cave-like interior as dark as a Hallowe'en haunted house.

We followed the squishing rubber boots in single file. Eyesight was useless, and the air smelled like old clothes. Did we walk one hundred twisting steps? Two hundred? My shin banged against something bulky that did not give way, but the labyrinth at last opened onto the stage, a vast wooden plane dimly lighted by electricity that flickered in an orange glow. I saw no one, but the bellowing voice commanded, "Not another step... watch the chalk. Watch it...."

From nowhere behind the stage a slim figure bounded forward wearing a striped jersey and white duck trousers. His hair was a mass of dark curls, and he was shoeless, somehow boyish and wizened.

"Where's the ventriloquist?" He glared at Cassie and me, frowned in disgust, and accused us of trespassing.

"I let them in," said the mop man.

"Never mind, Freddie, I'll show them out."

"Wait—" I said. "Just one minute...."

"You're stepping on the chalk, lady."

I looked down. My left boot smudged a white chalked line. Many such lines criss-crossed the stage and intersected with outlines of circles, squares, rectangles.

"Don't dare move."

"I won't."

"Neither of you."

Cassie and I stood like children in a game of Freeze.

He came forward to grab our arms, then stopped. Actresses might be man-handled, but ladies were untouchable. What's more, ladies might had connections to powerful men, including Broadway investors. He beckoned us into a clear spot. "You don't know what you're seeing, do you? You don't...."

"Won't you please tell us?" Cassie asked.

"Blocking," he said. "Architects make blueprints. Scene designers chalk the set." He glowered at me. "You stepped on the bell ringers' pedestal." He pointed to Cassie's feet. "The ventriloquist's throne and his dummy doll—right there, unless I change my mind." He gnawed his lower lip and pointed over my shoulder. "The stampede will start from back there."

"Stampede?" I asked.

"Snagged from the Buffalo Bill show. Everybody wants the Wild West."

Cassie winked at me. "Wild West? What would that be?"

"Gunfights," he said. "Annie Oakley stuff."

Annie Oakley's fame now rivaled "Buffalo Bill" Cody's stardom. His show featured sharpshooter Annie and a cavalry fight against real Indians. Last year, Eli Fryer tried to get up an outdoor party. We would have taken the ferry to the stadium on Staten Island, but the plan died with rumors about "splintery" benches.

"That girl shoots at glass balls tossed in the air," the man said, "and she never misses. *The Black Crook* would double its run if we could afford her." He shook his head. "This show is already over budget, and she'd cost a bundle. The investors would raise holy heck. Anyway, we'll cast an 'Annie' that's not afraid of heights. Both of you, look up."

We craned our necks to see a maze of ropes, pulleys, and cloth bags that looked stuffed and tied up—all in gloom.

"She'll fly down, guns blazing. She'll fire away, smoke and fury." He seemed lost in the imagined scene. "And a tribe of war-painted Indians will drop dead. Audiences will love it."

We stared as if bodies lay dying on the hardwood stage. The moment was deadly quiet.

"But not actual guns, surely...." Cassie ventured. She began to look troubled, as if the sketch of gunfire and death prompted new thoughts...or feelings. Her eyes widened, and she gripped my arm for support. Was she dizzy? "Guns...," she murmured. "Not real guns...?"

"The magic of the theatre," he said, ignoring my friend's distress and dusting his palms together. "Tryouts have begun," he said, "and with fifty dancers on the payroll, the director will get his 'Annie Oakley.'"

Cassie released her hold on my arm. Her eyes seemed filmed. Our opportunity could vanish in seconds. Trying for an admiring tone, I said, "The director? Aren't you the director?"

"Not this time. David Drake will do the honors. *The Black Crook* is a monster... half vaudeville, half three-ring circus and showboat too."

"But so many dancers—?" I said. "Fifty? Trained in ballet?"

He snorted. "Ballet? Try the Moulin Rouge can-can."

Our minutes with this man could expire in a heartbeat. The ventriloquist could arrive and ruin our chance. I smiled indulgently. "It's a dancer that has brought us here…a young woman we believe to be in the cast. We would like to speak with her."

"What for?"

"It is a family matter," I said. "I'm sure you understand."

He sucked the side of his cheek. "They come from all over. The names… they change their names."

"We have a name," I said. "Lola Taylor… Miss Lola Taylor."

He showed no sign of recognition. "Rehearsal starts at three," he said, then frowned. "You will not be admitted under any circumstance. Rehearsals are closed."

Cassie said, "But perhaps you have an address? A directory?"

Head to toe, he appraised us. "It's not the *Social Register*."

"But a listing," I said, "so we might find Miss Taylor without troubling anyone at the Knickerbocker Theatre." I deliberately put iron in my voice. "And without troubling anyone whom we might know personally to be an investor in this costly new production."

One hand pinched at his trouser leg as he heard my message. A money threat often worked.

"Wait here."

He left us standing in the weird orange electrical light, daring us to step even once on his chalk lines.

Cassie suddenly fanned her face. Inches from me, her eyes widened in fear. "Do you feel it, Val? Do you—?"

"Feel what?"

"The fire...the Abbey's Theatre fire...the flames...from backstage...." She pointed into the orange gloom. "It started there. Don't you feel it?"

No, I did not...no such thing. What to say? Cassie turned her face aside as if she felt scorching heat.

"Here we go, ladies. Here...." A scuffed leather binder cradled in one arm, the man stood between us. He glanced at Cassie. "You all right?"

She managed to nod.

"Let's stand over here...watch the white lines, ladies."

He led us to a nearby electrical bulb. We stood on each side of him as he thumbed through loose pages.

"I'm not supposed to do this...."

"We so appreciate it," I said. He smelled like chalk and licorice.

"Here.... Here they are. You said Taylor?"

I repeated the name, and he pointed to the entry. "See... Taylor, Lola... 641 West Thirty-fifth Street. Probably a rooming house. That's the address, but they move...one week to the next."

"Thank you."

"I'll call Freddie. He'll lead you out."

"One more thing...." I said. I had noticed the list marked DANCER, was alphabetical. "In the listing for the letter 'L,'" I said, "...might we see another name?"

"What name?"

"LaRue? Is a LaRue listed?"

Showing no sign that the murdered woman's name was familiar, he flipped back to the L's, eager to be rid of us. "Laffer... Lappé is that it?"

"Not sure," I said.

"That's all the L's...goes to Morris."

"But I see one name crossed out. Who would that be?" I pointed midway on the page. "Can you make out the letters?"

He lifted the binder. "Anybody that's x'd out has left *The Black Crook*. One reason or another, there's a few of them."

We waited. It felt like forever.

At last he said, "Looks like LaRue... LaRue, Roxie. She's not in the cast any more. For sure, she's inked out. Anybody inked out is a goner."

Chapter Fourteen

WE CROSSED STREETS CHOKED with delivery wagons, cabs, horses, and men. The sun arced to high noon when Cassie and I reached a row of sad brick houses with high front steps on West Thirty-fifth Street. We stopped to catch a breath.

"Those teamsters...." Cassie said. "Why do they all curse?""

"Or whip the poor horses?" I added. "Here it is," I said. "Number 641. Cassie, do you feel well enough?"

My friend pinned up a loose strand of her beautiful hair. "Better, Val...now that we're away from the theatre."

"And that awful 'chalk' man,' I said, not pressing about my friend's "visions." We faced a front window sign that read: FURNISHED ROOMS. "Careful," I said, "these steps are cracked." We climbed. The bell was dead.

"Let's try the door knocker."

A hard rap, and a face appeared through the door glass panel. A stout woman in a head wrap opened the door while fastening the top button of a sweater over a faded, flowered housedress. Odors of baking bread and cabbage rose as she eyed us eagerly—then, inspecting our clothing—fixed us with a cold stare.

"You're not here for a room, are you?"

One simple *no*, and the door would shut. "May we have a word?" I asked.

"What word?"

"We would like to visit a resident," I said. "Are you the landlady, Mrs.—?"

"Mrs. Demple. This is a private house."

"Of course...."

"A clean house. Respectable."

We both nodded. I slipped the toe of my boot under the door frame—a wedge, just in case. I said, "We are looking for Miss Lola Taylor."

"The police already came. Woke up the boarders, poked into things." She anchored her hands on her hips. "I take no responsibility for what goes on outside my premises. Terrible things happen in the city, but not in this house. I won't stand for it."

"We sympathize." Cassie's voice matched her words.

"We wish to see Miss Taylor," I said, "but may I also ask, did a Miss Roxie LaRue previously lived here?"

She ignored the question. "I told the police I won't stand for it. My boarders come and go, but inside the Demple boardinghouse, everyone is accounted for. Twenty-four rooms, twenty-four accounted for. They sign in and sign out, so I know." She pointed to a book and inkstand on a foyer table. My eyesight isn't what it was, but I know."

She wiped her face on her sleeve. "I favor a curfew, but the young women...they keep all hours day and night." She seemed winded. "I gave the police lunch. The police...you give your bit."

Cassie said, "We have cards to present."

For once, I had remembered my calling cards, but the two Bristol board cards printed with *Mrs. Roderick Windham DeVere* and *Mrs. Dudley D. Forster* and our addresses disappeared into a pocket of the housedress without comment.

"Is Miss Taylor at home?" I asked.

"Unless you're invited, this house is private."

A stalemate, and my toe in the door. And yet—a silver dollar in my pocket. "Mrs. Demple," I said, "If Lola Taylor is at home to receive us, we can make it worth your trouble."

Cassie looked puzzled.

I took the dollar from the handkerchief in my skirt pocket and flashed the face of Lady Liberty on the front and the Eagle on the back. *E pluribus unum.*

Greed did its work. I palmed the dollar into Mrs. Demple's soft wet hand, and the front door opened wide.

"You could use the front room parlor. There's a piano. There's sliding doors. I could bring you tea."

"We will visit Lola Taylor in her private room," I said.

"Rooms. She's got a sitting room for two more days… third floor on the left. Number Five. Watch you don't trip."

Glancing back, I saw her rub the coin and clamp it between her teeth. 'It's a Morgan silver dollar,' I wanted to say, 'minted in 1890, my papa's big year.'

The stairs squeaked, and the handrail wobbled. The narrow hallway led past numbered doors, all shut tight. We turned the corner to a door painted blue with FIVE in dull brass.

Deep breaths, and we knocked softly, waited, and knocked again. A female voice finally called, "Two more days, so leave me in peace."

"Miss Taylor—?"

"I said 'two more days.' I'm paid up."

"Please, Miss Taylor," said Cassie, "won't you open the door?" Once again, my friend's sweet-as-nougat voice, and the door opened.

"Who are you?"

Backlighted by early afternoon sun through a dirty window, the woman was outlined in a corona of light. Her slight, fragile figure was somehow forceful. She wore a kimono printed with bamboo leaves, and behind her, a half-dozen suitcases and a trunk ranged at odd angles on the floor.

"May we come in for a few minutes?"

Cassie turned to me. "Our cards."

Two calling cards were offered and our names read aloud in a voice newly trained, I felt sure, in elocution. Or perhaps music.

"We would prefer not to talk in the hall," I said. "Please...."

Holding our cards, she led us inside, around the suitcases and the upright steamer trunk topped with a huge shiny hand mirror, bottles and jars. We entered a "sitting room" furnished with a small table and a dusty chandelier with bronze gas jets. A green velvet rocking chair faced a matching loveseat that was draped with a lace doily that barely concealed a mustard colored stain. A wall calendar from an insurance company hung from a nail, the illustration for the month a harvest scene with pumpkins.

Lola Taylor took the rocker, and Cassie and I the loveseat. Odors of stale cigarettes and a heavy scent traced to an open perfume bottle and a full ashtray on the table.

"On your cards," she said, "there's only your names and addresses." We nodded. "You're not from *The Dramatic News*?"

"No."

Disappointment and confusion mixed in the large blue eyes that dominated Lola Taylor's narrow face and pointed chin. We found ourselves scrutinized by this pale woman with orange-gold hair colored with a henna rinse, her crinkled ends crisped with a hot curling iron. Facial makeup almost concealed the dark circles under her eyes.

"Are you from Koehler'?"

"I don't understand," said Cassie.

"Koehler's Costume Shop," she said.

"I'm afraid not."

"A booking agency? Nicely's?" She looked from Cassie to me. We shook our heads.

"This is something like a social call," I said.

Disappointed, she pouted.

"Miss Taylor," I said, "an unfortunate event has brought us here. Your name has appeared in connection with the death of an actress who is said to be your friend…. I speak of Miss Roxie LaRue."

Her shoulders hunched, she reached into the wide kimono sleeves for a handkerchief, patted her eyes, and sniffled. "At least you're not reporters."

"We are not," Cassie said. "Nothing of the kind."

"Newspaper blood suckers…worse than police, and they're bad enough."

"We cannot imagine," Cassie said, "how difficult at this time…."

"My best friend…and all her things…."

She straightened her shoulders and slowly swept one arm as if sculpting the air. Her bright red nails pointed to a shelf, where a burned-down candle had dripped wax over a gleaming, ornate brass candlestick. Beside it lay three china kittens tied with black grosgrain bows. They looked like carnival prizes.

"Those were Myra's." She closed her eyes.

"Myra?" said Cassie. "Who was Myra?"

"Roxie," she fairly burst out. "Roxie was Myra…." She looked at us as if we came from the moon. "Roxie was her stage name, her theatre name. She was Myra Keckenmeyer from Chagrin Falls, Ohio."

"But not 'Roxie?'" I asked. "The newspapers all reported—"

"—reported what I told them, what the *Black Crook* management spouted." She stared as if facing two zoo creatures on the loveseat. "You think my birth certificate says Lola Taylor? How about Dolores Fleck?" Her voice mocked an announcement. "'Now appearing at the Lyceum Theatre: Miss Dolores Fleck from Youngstown, Ohio!'"

She crossed her legs. "What would you think? Eager to see Miss Fleck from Youngstown?"

The woman suddenly crumpled into tears, sobbing, her body wracked. Cassie and I sat with hands folded, eyes averted.

"Crying my eyes out," she said at last.

"Oh, do not apologize," Cassie said. "Such a dreadful loss...."

She honked into the handkerchief, stared at the floor, and spoke in a flat voice. "We practiced our new names. I called her Roxie, she called me Lola. We met up in Cleveland, both runaways."

"You ran away from home?" Incredulous Cassie.

Lola seemed to smirk and agonize too. "What home? Roxie hated slopping pigs and milking cows in the barn, and I hated Youngstown, which is one big steel mill. Hang out washing on a clothesline, and it dries all soot black, so what's the use? Drudges... if we stayed, drudges for sure. The nearest big city was Cleveland. We went for it."

"You became friends?"

"In Cleveland. We were 'tavern wenches'.... You never heard of tavern wenches?"

We had not.

She looked back at the floorboards. "A German tavern... our first theatre roles, you might say, slinging beer and sausages and sauerkraut, which sickens me to this day.... We wore dirndl dresses, laced tight and cut low in the front. The men dropped dimes down our bosoms and laughed like no tomorrow... sometimes a quarter if we gave a big smile."

She touched her crisped curls. "Roxie's hair got her plenty of quarters...thick and wavy, and they'd touch her hair when she got near enough."

She sniffled. "Made us mad, but those tips added up. I took dance lessons. We both did. Singing too. We had our eye on New York...Roxie and me and every other runaway. The city's thick with us, every single one dreaming big."

She turned and pointed. "See that luggage? See this trunk? They're full of costumes we had to buy, mine and Roxie's. I'm still in hock...."

"You purchase your own stage wear?" I asked.

"Every stitch. Roxie played a maid in *Apples of Eden*, delivered one line in Act Two: 'Sir, if you please.' That was it, one line. The show closed in a week, and the maid's outfit cost triple what she made.

"Me, I was Jessica in *The Liars* at the Empire Theatre, a walk-on in a satin gown with pearls to the navel, hoping a scout might see me, but all I got was a bill for the gown and fake pearls." She patted at her eyes. "You take your chances, and maybe it pays off. The pay stinks, the hours are godawful, you never relax, and they treat you like scum. You heard of survival of the fittest?"

The motto of every Wall Street mogul.

"Some make it big, some hightail it back to the sticks they came from." Lola wet another cotton puff. "Some get tired of the game and blow out their brains, boys and girls both."

We cringed.

She fixed us with a hard stare and looked from one to the other. Somehow, I was mindful of our foolish hats. "Roxie," she said, "was brisk and bright and bright, up to the mark. She was on her way."

She bit a thumbnail. "One less in the rat race now. She's back in Chagrin Falls."

"For burial?" I asked.

"Her brother took her back. Big Bozo farmer in overalls and clodhopper boots. He got himself from Ohio to the city morgue. Then he came here for money."

"Money?" I asked. "For train fare?"

"You'd think so, wouldn't you?" Lola ran a hand through her frizzled hair. "Turns out, it'll cost you for the body. Eight dollars and fifty cents, the Coroner's own sweet deal. Some gobbledygook about medical inquiry… like the cause of death wasn't plain to everybody. Everybody in this whole city."

"Yes…all the newspapers," I said. Cassie and I nodded. My friend swallowed hard and blinked, her eyes appearing to film once again, and that faraway gaze as if seeing and not seeing.

"Live and learn," Lola said. "Not one body can leave the morgue till the bill is paid up. Good thing there's pawn shops." She pointed to the ceramic kittens. "See the kitties with the ribbons? I tied the bows black for mourning. Roxie draped them with jewels…diamonds from particular gentlemen." She gave a short laugh. "They're in the Liberty Loan pawn shop now. You might say the diamonds bought Roxie her liberty. The city would've put her in a common grave."

The very thought prompted a silent moment among the three of us. Cassie's eyes looked strangely glazed.

Lola pointed to the several suitcases. "Her things… the brother wouldn't take one thing, like the theatre was the pox. The dress she was killed…she died in, all torn and ripped. So I gave him the plainest dress she had…nice pink organza. She had a parasol to match. Looked so pretty…."

Lola's chin trembled as she fought back new tears. "The pawn shop money, I gave the brother all of it for the funeral back in Ohio. She'll get a headstone. He promised a headstone with carving."

"Your friend is laid to rest in her hometown," Cassie said softly. "Resting in peace…." The words were appropriate, typical for sympathy—but somehow Cassie's tone was remote, otherworldly. Despite myself, I shivered.

Lola threw her head back. "Let's say Myra Keckenmeyer is back in Chagrin Falls." She faced us. "So, what do you want to know about?"

"A possible friendship," I said, "between Roxie and a certain gentleman... perhaps a gentleman who gave her the diamonds."

Wariness crept into her eyes. "What gentleman?"

"His name is Clayton."

She shrugged. "Clayton what? Maybe Clayton's his real name, maybe not. Sometimes the men change their names too."

Should I say "Philbrick?" Gladys and Victor would be mortified. "A young man with a very blond moustache," I began.

She shrugged.

"He probably took her to a lobster palace for late night suppers at Murray's Roman Gardens. Does that sound familiar?"

"Murray's or Rector's," she said. "One or the other."

"And he liked to give roses."

"Lady, every florist in the city peddles roses to gents. What color?"

Cassie tapped my wrist before I could speak. "What color did Roxie like best?" she asked. Her voice sounded far away. "Was it lilac for caution? Perhaps pink for happiness? Or red....?"

Lola mulled this over, as if she understood Cassie as I did not. My floral "language" consisted of apologetic bouquets when I botched social occasions, not to mention Roddy's annual gifts of American Beauty roses—my namesake flowers—on Valentine's Day, my birthday. Vases upon vases, every room in the house.

"Orange and yellow," Lola suddenly burst out. "Orange and yellow...always mixed...that one particular gent... only him...."

"Ah," said Cassie, "orange for passion, and yellow for jealousy."

Lola sobbed, and Cassie's touch signaled me to silence.

"She called him Phil," Lola moaned. "And it got her killed...killed."

"Phil" blared like a klaxon. Phil for Phillip? Or Phil for a family name? The orange and yellow mix narrowed on Clayton.

"Miss Taylor—" I began in a voice as sympathetic as the circumstances allowed. "Lola...do you know why Roxie would have been in Central Park late at night? Do you?"

A moment passed. "Life happens off the paths," she said.

"I don't understand."

She eyed my wedding ring. "You don't have to."

She said nothing more. We waited while she twisted the sodden handkerchief. "What else? I've got rehearsal. I've got to get ready."

Putty-colored makeup had smeared her handkerchief, and bruise-black half-moons undershot both eyes. She sat up straight.

"Witch Hazel," she said, leaning toward a bottle on the steamer trunk. "Witch Hazel for my eyes." She reached for the big hand mirror and wet a cotton ball. "I need my eyesight for the audition."

"For *The Black Crook*?" I asked.

Somehow, Lola Taylor's face did not evoke pity. She eyed me sharply and patted each eye. "The show must go on."

"But aren't you already a member of the cast? Why would you audition?"

"For a bigger part." A leering grin played at her mouth. She put aside the cotton and the bottle but flashed the mirror. "Here's our deal. We both tried out for Betty Bang-Bang and made the first cut. We were ready."

Cassie asked, "What Betty?"

"Bang-Bang. Like Annie Oakley, but another name so they're not sued. Think of it, the chorus is a lineup of spangled leggings...but Betty will fly down in crystal and fringe. She'll swing from a catwalk, her pistol firing. Bang, bang, the lights will shine on her."

Lola gazed upward, as if the lights shone at this instant.

"Don't go for heights if it scares you," she said. "And if they do, get over it. When we tried out, Roxie pretended there was a featherbed at the bottom. For me, it was a swimming hole in July. There's three of us in the running now that Roxie's gone, so odds are one in three."

Cassie suddenly gripped the arm of the loveseat as if she might fall. I clasped her shoulder.

"You all right?" Lola looked at Cassie, then at me. "Your lady friend feeling all right?"

"We're fine," I said. "My friend is a little bit woozy."

She stood to shoo us out, and I helped Cassie to her feet. "So, in two days I'm moving into a single on another floor," Lola said. "Small, but it'll do. Maybe it's better...without Roxie everywhere here in Number Five." She opened the door. "I don't know if you got what you wanted, but I'll tell you this: if Miss Lola Taylor gets to play Betty Bang-Bang in *The Black Crook* of 1898, she will dedicate every performance to her dearly departed friend, Roxie LaRue."

Chapter Fifteen

THE FLOWERS FAMILIAR TO me in Colorado mining camps were the sand lily and wild onion. Those to dodge were larkspur and locoweed.

None spoke a "language."

So, I kept quiet while Roddy listened to Cassie recount our venture in the boardinghouse with Lola Taylor, pleased to find my husband had finished work in his cocktail "laboratory." And relieved to see my friend regain her poise. She and I had clasped hands in the hansom cab all the way from the boardinghouse up Fifth Avenue. Cassie kept her eyes closed, seeming to recover herself. "All too, too much..." she had murmured. "All too much...." She said nothing more, but clenched my fingers in a grip so tight my hand cramped.

At my insistence, she stopped here for a quick bite, but eager—almost desperate—to join her husband and children in the park, pausing just for a snack and the polite conversation.

"...never dreamed that the language of flowers would be so useful," my friend concluded. "I memorized it as a little girl."

"And my mother knows it by heart," Roddy said.

My friend and my husband linked in a social compact. For proper etiquette, Roddy would now volunteer to escort Cassie into the park—and my friend insist that our butler or a footman provide that service since no lady walked solo.

Gloves on, Cassie stood to go, but suddenly cried out, "Just for an hour, would you both come...please...would you....?"

Her voice struck a plaintive, minor key, but an afternoon in Central Park could be bracing, especially after the weird theatre and anguishing interview with Lola Taylor. Roddy looked eager, and Cassie needed supportive friends.

"Would you both...? It would help me...help me so much...."

Let's do," Roddy said. "The sunshine will do us all good."

"You must bring Velvet too," Cassie said. "Bea and Charlie almost think she's their dog."

It was settled. Velvet was harnessed and leashed, and off we went toward the Central Park Dairy, all the while a scene took shape elsewhere that hovered in my thoughts: a grieving, ambitious young actress seeing herself spotlighted in crystal and fringe, plunging from a catwalk with pistols blazing.

∽◎∽

"Mommy! We got autumn leaves and ice cream cones. I got chocolate, two scoops. It comes from a bean, the *theobroma cocao.* Daddy says means food of the gods in...did you say Latin, Daddy?"

"Greek, son. Ancient Greek."

Six-year-old Charlie Forster stood on tiptoe and raised his cone like a trophy.

"Mine is vanilla...very stupen...really big."

"Stupendous, Beatrice," said Dudley to his daughter, who was four years of age. "Your large ice cream cone is *stupendous.*"

Dudley's hazel eyes sparkled at the sight of his children and his lovely wife, who took his arm, nudging aside the canvas bag that held the gathered leaves.

"And look who's here, children!" cried Cassie.

"Velvet!"

"It's Velvet!"

"It's Mr. and Mrs. DeVere...Auntie Val and Uncle Roderick. Let's not forget our manners. What do you say to our friends, children?"

Both Bea and Charlie had knelt to greet our dog whose zeal for ice cream amused the little girl in her kilt skirt and tartan jacket and the taller boy in a tan corduroy short pants suit. Both recited "How-do-you-do," devoured their ice cream, and frisked with Velvet, who rolled over in canine ecstasy.

"Splendid day in Central Park," said Dudley.

"Nothing out of the ordinary?" asked Cassie. Her voice strained, as if the park that usually welcomed the Forster family now loomed like woodlands in a dark folk tale. "Nothing?"

"All's well enough," Dudley replied. "Count on sunshine and a breeze to bring out a few kites…an artist…bicycles… and amateur botanists." He gestured to three women closely matching leaves with their guidebook. "I'll wager those ladies are using the old *Trees and Shrubs of Central Park*," Dudley said. "It's out of date, but the basics hold true."

Dudley's short, dark goatee and moustache gave his angular features a marked severity, but the warmth of his voice and sparkle in his eyes softened this man who had won my friend's heart.

A trim figure just under six feet tall, Dudley Forster often flouted Society's gentlemanly dress code. His thick flannel shirt, leather vest, and trousers tucked into lumber-jack's boots announced a scientist devoted to field work and indifferent to men's fashion. Cassie had made peace with her scientist husband's vocation and appearance. ("Impeccable manners in a woodman's husk," sniped *Town Topics*.)

He smiled at Cassie and me and turned to Roddy. "Good to see the ladies return to our neighborhood, DeVere. Traipsing into the theatre district in the daytime, our two charming belles might have been cast in a stage play."

"And us, buying tickets," said Roddy.

The slight banter ceased at the sight of three dandies in checkered coats quaffing mugs of ale just purchased at the Dairy.

Roddy's annoyance spoke for us all. "To think," he said, "that this Dairy with Holstein cows once dispensed fresh, free milk for city children, but now sells ice cream and ale."

"And further back," said Dudley, "this whole area was a marshland covered with poison ivy." He jacked one knee on a rock outcropping and looked ready to examine whatever specimen might come into sight, preferably prehistoric fossils. "Twenty thousand years ago," he said, "this park was covered with ice. Today's park is actually a glacial record of geology's ancient upheaval, for instance, the Promontory and the Umpire Rock."

Everyone who enjoyed the park knew these massive rock formations on sight. Boys challenged one another to climb the Umpire, which produced an amazing number of broken arms. Young Charlie had been forbidden to venture near it. ("Not until you're out of short pants, young man!") Usually thick with young "mountaineers," the Umpire looked strangely bare this afternoon. Dead leaves swirled at the base, but the rock looked deserted.

"Shall we take a short walk?" Cassie nervously toed the gravel. "Hold Velvet's leash, children...yes, both of you."

"Don't let her pull you," I said. "You are in charge."

They squabbled over the leash as we moved along the path toward the carousel that was blanketed in a winter tarpaulin.

"Like a shroud," Cassie murmured.

"Nonsense, my dear," Dudley rejoined. "Think of the plants...dormant until spring,"

The children jogged in the lead, tugged by our dog, who showed impressive strength. A Frenchie, after all, is a bulldog.

Two by two, Cassie and I strolled in front of our husbands. Dudley had shouldered the bag of prize leaves. "Black cherry and horse chestnuts for Beatrice," he said, "and silver maples for Charles...and a few sycamores." His hearty voice rose. "The autumn presents New York's best show, Central Park in the month of October."

"Agreed, said Roddy, "but why so few New Yorkers this afternoon? We almost have the paths to ourselves."

True, the crowd was much smaller than usual for the season...no youngsters on the Umpire rock, and a scattering of grownups on the paths. Instead of celebrating, we felt subdued.

Roddy recharged the moment. "How many acres altogether, Dudley?" he asked. "Do you remember?"

"Around eight hundred-fifty, I think...from Fifty-ninth Street to 106th Street. America's own Bois de Boulogne."

"And Hyde Park too," said Roddy, "because our grandfathers decided Paris and London must not upstage the U.S.A. And the grandfathers triumphed, thanks to their Midas touch for real estate and the fur trade. Hats off to John Jacob Astor."

Our husbands seemed at ease behind us, though Cassie and I kept a watch on nearby figures in the deepening shade—the brawny man in a denim coat who stood strangely motionless by an oak tree, and another who spread out on a bench playing solitaire. His bushy beard hid everything but the eyes.

Each seemed alone, as if waiting.

For whom?

For what?

Each one eyed us as we passed.

It's their park, as well as ours, but what drew them here? I shrugged, as if to shake off thoughts of the park as a killer's hunting ground.

A park policeman hastened past, excusing himself as he broke into a run and disappeared into a thicket of shrubs and trees. Two city policemen followed at full speed, panting, nightsticks raised.

Whatever was the matter, Roddy and Dudley merely paused, exchanged private words, and then nudged forward on the path, but slowly. Their exaggerated gait reminded me of our carriage horses. Both husbands made a show of ease in the presence of us ladies.

"Charlie...Beatrice...not so fast." Cassie kept a close eye as they skipped to keep up with our dog.

The sun, I noticed, was beginning its slow decent, and the shadows lengthening.

Chatting behind us, Roddy and Dudley found a familiar topic: their "Pro-Park" grandparents. Their voices rose just enough to be intentionally heard, as if to demonstrate a confidence they might not feel. The names Astor and Vanderbilt and Livingston mixed with Forster and DeVere, but the stagey tone was unnerving.

"New York's Founding Families, those grandparents," Roddy said in a too-bright quip.

"My father talks about boulders blasted to make way for the park," Dudley replied, "and the work gangs that sledgehammered rocks and yanked out foliage. Half the workforce was on the city payroll."

"Before the Olmsted and Vaux plan was approved," Roddy continued, "the place was a squalid eyesore unfit for human habitation."

We paused to gaze at the colorful trees, the curving walkways, rolling hillocks and deep dells. For the first time, I felt struck by the park's deliberate enclosure. On all sides, we were wrapped in nature, nearly cocooned.

Somehow, it felt claustrophobic. Cozy in the bright morning, but another story in late afternoon...and then, after sundown....

"The scene looks natural and permanent," Roddy said, "as if for centuries."

"Deceptively so," said Dudley. His voice turned solemn. "The park is a human design, and our cosmos is constantly in flux. Darwin and Lyell teach the lesson—but will we learn it?"

"Please, no lessons on this beautiful afternoon, my dear," said Cassie. Both children gripped Velvet's taut leash as the dog pulled them toward a curve that was yards ahead in the pathway.

With one eye on her children, Cassie also spoke of the park's origin, a safe topic for all Society. "Truly," Cassie said, "people find it impossible to believe that in the old days before the war, a few people really lived here."

"—or existed," said Dudley. "My Forster grandparents remembered the squatters' filthy lean-tos and shanties on this very site. They farmed pigs and scavenged garbage."

"Who were these squatters?" I asked.

"Dangerous foreigners," said Roddy. "According to my family, they spoke little English and had no respect for the law. They had to be removed."

"Where did they go?" I asked.

None of our group knew.

"Who 'removed' them?" I asked.

"Probably the police," Roddy said. "And the Fire Patrol...."

"They burned their dwellings?"

"Foul shacks," said Dudley, "nothing like the grass houses in the South Pacific."

"But what about the people?" I asked. "The freezing winters?"

No one was interested in my question. My own great grandparents, I did not mention, were surviving in huts near peat bogs in County Donegal, Ireland.

"My Forster grandfather compared the park to a years-long military campaign," Dudley continued. "Cranes and carts, crews of blacksmiths and carpenters. Stone carvers and masons too. Until the Olmsted-and-Vaux plan was approved," he said, "the place was an eyesore unfit for human habitation."

A quiet moment passed, as if to let us meditate on the transformed earth we trod.

"Too bad Olmsted can't be around to see today's trees all grown up," said Roddy. "They say his health is piteous. He's seldom lucid. And Vaux's drowning was a shock."

Those names again—Frederick Olmsted and Calvert Vaux—the deities of Central Park. Distracted in that instant, I thought of the monumental Griffith Park in our farthest West Coast City of Los Angeles, and its famous ostrich farm.

Suddenly Cassie burst out, "Drowned...but not by accident."

"I beg your pardon..." Confused, I looked from Cassie to Dudley.

"Secrets of the park," she went on, "Calvert Vaux feared for his life, and Gravesend Bay is his tomb. There are secrets here. Madam Riva discussed it with me."

"Madam Riva...." Dudley and I both bleated the name.

"My dearest...." Dudley began, "you mustn't...."

Cassie clutched her cloak and fell silent, as if she had unwittingly blurted the forbidden name.

"Can we go see the sheep?"

"Can we?"

Little Bea and Charlie tugged Velvet, both eager for another romp. The Sheep Meadow was not far, but the late afternoon sun was fading, the shadows long and deep, and the curving pathway would take more time. Cassie and Dudley exchanged glances, as did Roddy and I. The golden light flared, but twilight would come, and then the darkness. We all looked skyward. The children ran ahead, as if to scout the sheep around the curve. We looked west toward the sinking sun. Dudley murmured to Roddy about how much shorter the days, and Roddy replied that we soon would exchange our carriages for sleighs.

Cassie's sudden cry jolted us all. "The children...where are the children?"

"They were...right here...they were...." My throat closed.

They were nowhere in sight.

Suddenly, nowhere. No dog, no children.

Cassie wailed. "Charlie...Bea...Beatrice...?"

Dudley cupped his palms at his mouth and shouted, "Charles...?"

Roddy sprang ahead to the curve and gazed around it, the sun glaring at his face. Then he waved, and he beckoned. "They're right there...children, Velvet, come back...come now." He stood at the curve, a sentinel until the little parade appeared—the dog, the little girl, the boy.

"We wanted to see the sheep," said Beatrice with a pout.

"The Southdown ewes," said Charlie.

"You need to stay with us," said Cassie.

"No wandering off," said Dudley.

I gripped Velvet's leash, expecting the children to be scolded.

They were not. Cassie knelt to hug them, and Dudley circled his family in widespread arms, a Forster tableau.

We all glanced about in the next moment, as if sharing the same thought, the lovely afternoon felt under eclipse, and the park was ours only until sundown, no matter how many others continued to stroll the paths, the Mall, the Belvedere Terrace....

The scene changed before our eyes. Departing couples quickened their pace, and kites were pulled from the sky.

The sketchbook artist had vanished, and the botanist ladies were nowhere to be seen.

"I'm afraid we won't be visiting the sheep today," Cassie said.

"Not today," echoed Dudley.

"And Velvet must soon have her supper," I said.

"She must," said Roddy.

Pitiful, I thought, that a little black French bulldog became the excuse for adults who could not bear to speak their truth: that sundown in Central Park could feel like the deadly woods in a tale by the Brothers Grimm.

Chapter Sixteen

MIDWAY DOWN THE STAIRCASE, dressed for the theatre, I was stopped by the drama in our front hall. We were to attend a comic opera, *His Excellency*, and dine afterward at Sherry's. The evening ought to be the perfect antidote to this strange afternoon with the Forsters in Central Park. Roddy loved grand opera but agreed that *Götterdämmerung* at the Metropolitan would be too much tonight. Cassie and Dudley had other plans and could not join us this evening. From the front hall, I heard—

"*Not* now, *not* this evening...*not*...."

Our butler sounded like a waif in a Dickens novel. "Just a very few minutes, sir, if you will...."

The voices dropped low, then Roddy cracked. "—ten minutes at the very most, only if Mrs. DeVere—"

"—right here, Roderick." Full names in servants' presence. "Coming down."

The stone spiral stairs defied my every step in a long silk gown and a sable evening cloak. On the marble tiles at last, I found two men at a standstill under the gleaming chandelier, Roddy cemented to the tiles and Sands frozen fast.

"All ready," I said in forced bright tones. "Shall we go? Is something the matter?"

"Your police detective is here," Roddy said, tight-lipped. "Fillmore, is it?"

"Mr. Finlay? Here?"

"Sands admitted him. He's in a drawing room."

Before me, a sheepish butler in his formal coat and the irked husband in evening dress with his top hat, gloves and ebony walking stick.

Sands murmured, "In the French Second Empire room, ma'am."

My most-avoided drawing room, furnished by my mother-in-law, with dark varnished mahogany, wallpaper like a fever dream, and one hideous table with carvings like warts.

"I felt obliged, ma'am. He wishes a word with you and Mr. DeVere. He expressed some urgency…."

Roddy cut him off. "Ten minutes, no more. Time it, Sands, and prepare to show him out."

"Yes, sir."

With that, we marched to the mahogany cavern where the detective inspected a painting of a DeVere ancestor counting his gold coins, supposedly the "school" of Rembrandt, according to my mother-in-law.

Mr. Finlay turned, his bowler ("plug") hat in hand—and the corn-colored hair streaked white, the long arms, the same mail-order black suit, somewhat shinier.

"Mr. Finlay, good evening." I introduced him to Roddy, who did not offer a handshake. The last time I saw two men size up one another like this was a prize fighting ring in Reno, Nevada, just before the match.

"Let us sit down," I said. The bulging upholstery embroidered with lizards mocked all efforts at comfort. Roddy and I sat side-by-side on the sofa, the detective on a side chair. "Mr. Finlay, our time is short this evening," I said. "How may we help you?"

I feared a firearm when he reached for an inside pocket. Instead, the familiar envelope from three days ago. He waved his credentials like a matador with a cape.

I said, "Your badge and certificate...I remember them both, Mr. Finlay, and also your promotion from the uniformed service. Unless Mr. DeVere wishes to see them, we might proceed."

Roddy scowled, and Finlay pocketed the envelope and cupped palms over his knees as if ready for a contact sport. My husband slipped out his watch and glanced at the time.

"A detective works by himself, you see..." Finlay began, "but a man had best not lose touch with officers in uniform... his old shipmates."

"Shipmates—?"

"It's lingo from sailing days, ma'am. Clings like a barnacle. A seaman stands watch, and a patrolman reports for duty…pretty much the same hours, four on and four off. Point is, if he stays in touch, a detective might learn of incidents."

"What 'incidents?'" Impatient, Roddy pretended boredom.

"In specific," Finlay said, "a man assigned to a certain crime scene in Central Park might recall that a couple on horseback…a lady and gentleman…arrived in the early morning of October twelfth and appeared to be very interested in a certain spot…to search for a lost gemstone."

The Pergola. Roddy shot me a look, and my hands dampened inside my kid gloves. Roddy tapped his walking stick. "What's this about, detective?"

Finlay moved on. "And suppose a case led to a jewelry establishment…with diamonds and silver that sparkle like the open seas on a sunny day, and learned that a certain lady had visited the jeweler to inquire about a young man customer who belongs to a private club."

His gray eyes fixed on the bridge of my nose. I refused to say Black, Starr, and Frost aloud. I would not.

"I believe my reference is clear," he said.

"It is," I admitted.

"And within hours," Finlay went on, "a certain gentleman paid a visit to that same private club and made inquiries."

A grandfather clock chimed the half-hour. Where was Sands?

"Detective Finlay," Roddy said, "Mrs. DeVere and I must excuse you."

"We have evening commitments, Mr. Finlay, as you see."

The detective did not budge. "Another few minutes if you will...because the fact is, we are jointly in private discussions with a particular couple."

"You needn't be coy, Mr. Finlay." Roddy set his hat down and squeezed his hands into fists. "The Philbrick family has been friendly with the DeVeres for many years," he said. "Their grandson has disappeared, and the Philbricks have called upon us."

With eyes raised to the coffered ceiling, the detective said, "This situation binds the civilian and the police...like knots."

Roddy blinked. I stared.

"Take the half-hitch," he said, "...maybe the clove hitch." His fingers flexed as if tying ropes. "Finally, I think the bowline is best," he said. "No matter how tight, it's easy to untie."

Was he deranged?

Roddy said, "Mr. Philbrick, you must—"

"—Sir, it is you who must release yourself from the New York Police Department's search to locate...." He leaned forward, hands on knees, and slowly intoned, "Mr. Clayton Rogers Philbrick."

Roddy crossed his legs, and the tip of his boot pointed at Finlay's shin. "Is that your message, sir?"

The "sir" dripped acid.

The door opened and Sands appeared. My crushed gloves told how unsettling these last minutes, as did the rippled brim of Roddy's top hat. The evening's silly stage drama suddenly felt like a chore, and the late-night supper a nuisance.

Before Sands could speak, Finlay reached for his own hat. "Mr. and Mrs. DeVere," he said, "I have kept you long enough. On behalf of the New York Police Department, I thank you for your time. I had hoped to discuss my work in relation to recent events in Central Park, but the hour draws late." He moved as if to stand up yet kept his seat.

I never knew whether Colin Finlay silently wagered that we would forfeit the theatre to take his "bait." Strategic or lucky, the detective reeled us in with mention of Central Park.

Sands was dismissed, and Roddy loosened his topcoat. I slipped off my cloak. Two tickets to *His Excellency* at the Broadway Theatre would go unused this October 14, 1898.

"We are most interested in the park," I said, "and prepared for whatever will help."

Finlay tugged at his celluloid collar, a device sure to chafe his neck raw. "My orders," he said, "come from headquarters."

"—Mulberry Street," said Roddy.

"Indeed." He rested his hands. "We call it 'The Castle of Joy and Sorrow.' It's 'Sorrow' for officers that face a hearing that seldom goes a man's way. A disciplinary hearing will send a man to the worst patrol...the manure pits by the East River...perdition."

"And 'joy?'" My turn to cue.

"Joy," he said, "for those of us getting promotion orders, such as patrolman to precinct captain...or detective."

Did he expect congratulations?

"A detective's work," he said, "is like a sailor's. At sea, a man learns currents, tides, depths...and squalls." He looked from Roddy to me. "On the lookout, that's the detective's job...to learn the currents running in the neighborhoods... and the storms. To keep watch, that's the nub of it."

Did he intend to tell us about early life as a mariner? Were the sea and the land fused in his mind?

What about the park?

"I got my land legs patrolling the Bowery and the Lower East Side," he continued. "From helmet to badge to boots, fully uniformed."

Or was this nostalgia?

"A man pays it off," he said, "every last cent...to begin with, paying for the job itself." He looked from Roddy to me.

"You paid a bribe to become a police officer, is that it?" Roddy confirmed what he knew for a fact and I'd heard rumored.

Finlay nodded. "First to get the job, and then the overcoat and trousers, winter and summer, the whistle and the revolver and holster and cartridges. And gloves and the locust wood nightstick. No end to it, nearly a man's year of salary."

I clucked in sympathy.

"Myself," he said, "I got a break. A widow sold me the whole lot on the cheap, and just three holes in the overcoat." He eyed my cloak. "A lady would think of moths."

"Or bullet holes?" I replied.

He flashed a touché. "Patrolman Michael O'Doul," he said, "was shot dead in a robbery. The widow O'Doul sold me the coat that I buttoned up every day or night for seven years. The coat was mine and O'Doul's every time I shut down gambling dens or arrested hooligans or racetrack touts or con men. And when I held back panicked crowds." He hesitated and looked at Roddy. "And when I worked vice."

As if the lady was unaware that "vice" meant prostitution.

He flexed his arms and adjusted the stiff shirt cuffs, also celluloid. "I made friends," he said at length, as if deciding what to say next.

"And I made enemies too."

"Very sobering, Mr. Finlay," said Roddy, "but I don't see—"

"—the point? The point, Mr. DeVere, is that 'joy' can disappear in the blink of an eye. A patrolman, you see, has his brotherhood, but the detective can be the odd man out."

He stopped again, as if we needed lessons.

"Some detectives," he continued, "are born to the job. They get favors and have 'pull.' This one, however, does not. My promotion, I warrant you, is meant for failure."

An extreme statement. Could it be true?

He bit a thumbnail and went on, "This detective risks a forced resignation or removal quick as a wink. So much for the 'joy' of it. Right now, I operate out of three precincts—the Central Park Arsenal and the precincts on East 88th and East 104th Streets. They all cover the park. You understand?"

"It's huge acreage," said Roddy.

"And God's gift to every soul in the city—up to now." He faced me. "The murders...that's what you wanted me

to talk about last Tuesday when we met, Mrs. DeVere...
everybody's topmost fear, the murders."

"Of course."

"The pressure on us...the force can be a political game.
There's nowhere to hide. Inside every precinct, it's a boiler ready
to blow. Five thousand police in Manhattan and the Bronx, the
precinct officers, the park police...everybody's after the strangler."

He broke off, and Roddy and I exchanged a glance, ready
for Finlay to prod us about Clayton Philbrick.

He did not.

"The murders get all the attention, but other vicious
crimes are happening in the park, and nobody knows why."
He studied our faces. "You might think thieves, or ruffians
hurling rocks off bridges when folks pass underneath...
crime that fills newspapers."

"We read about it every morning, Detective."

"No, you do not, sir. This is under wraps, so far. You
can read about park rules broken, the shrubs trampled and
flowers stolen. Or games of three-card monte. But this is
different." He cracked his knuckles.

Roddy asked, "How different?"

"Different as slitting the throats of sheep."

"In the Meadow?"

"In the sheepfold. Three Southdown ewes. We sent them
to an orphanage for food."

"Horrid," I said.

"And dynamite."

"An explosive word," Mr. Finlay," I said.

"An explosive. Period." He leaned close to us, his coat straining at the elbows. "I mean a cardboard cylinder filled with nitroglycerin, all good for mining and quarrying—and also for bombs. Do you know the Glen Span Arch in the park woodlands?"

Roddy nodded. "Built from boulders, wasn't it? For a rustic effect?"

Finlay nodded. "Somebody blasted it a week ago, set off dynamite. So far, it's been kept quiet. Officially, the department will say that Mr. Frederick Olmsted hired stone masons that made mistakes. It's under repair."

"A crime scene," I said.

"A crime scene. And there are others. Someone set fire to the Shadow Bridge. And the West Drive arbor...it's wood too. East or West side, seems all the same. There's somebody out there with combustion fuel, and somebody with powder to blow up bridges."

His voice rang with irony. "The chief has done me a 'favor.' I am to ignore panhandlers or pick pockets or visitors snatching leaves without a park permit. My assignment," Finlay said, "covers the violent destruction of property—and murder."

The grandfather clock chimed the hour, eight bells that tolled slowly. We sat with downcast eyes until it passed.

"And you suspect," Roddy asked, "that the two might be connected....?"

"We don't know. I don't know."

"But somehow," I said, "you suspect that Clayton Philbrick might be involved?"

"It's a lead, Mr. DeVere. I follow leads. Detective work is no deep mystery. It's following human nature in all its phases. I'm here," he said, "to warn you to stop the amateur snooping. You must untie yourselves, release the knot."

Roddy bristled.

"Because friendship can lead to mistakes, Mr. DeVere. Goodwill can be dangerous. Mrs. Philbrick praised you to the heavens, both of you. Whatever you did on your summer vacation, she sang your praises."

I bit my tongue. "Mr. Finlay, I'll have you know that our efforts were crucial in a trial for attempted murder that is scheduled this fall in Rhode Island, and—"

"—and this is New York City, Mrs. DeVere. It's a different country. Your summertime effort was well meant, I am sure. But—"

"—but you suggest that Mr. DeVere and I simply inform Mr. and Mrs. Philbrick that we will no longer help to locate their grandson…and that Detective Sergeant Colin Finlay will take complete charge?"

Once again, Finlay surprised us.

"In fact," he said, "I have come to ask for your help."

From insult to plea, what was he thinking? Bizarre, this man. We simply waited on the terrible furniture while he readied his request.

"The upper East side…your neighborhood," he said, "is worlds away from the Bowery and the Lower East Side…so different, but the same problem for police."

He cracked a knuckle. "I patrolled the Lower East Side, all immigrants… Jews, Italians, a few Germans. They sell everything in the street… beer, cheese, eggs. Their vegetables get washed in the public hydrant. The carrots are 'improved' by the public bath.

"But tragedy strikes too," he continued. Tempers flare, and the gun or knife does its work, or a razor or a rock. You try to help, but they turn scared as rabbits. No matter if they're robbed or swindled or worse, they shut like clams if you say 'police' or 'law.'"

I would not give him the satisfaction of knowing I had shuttled among the pushcarts on Orchard and Hester Streets. Roddy and I sat perfectly still. It was Finlay's turn to blush.

"…so different, but the same problem, the silence. Don't get me wrong. When our nightsticks hold back the crowds at your fancy balls and big funerals, Fifth Avenue is very happy. And police officers gladly escort your parties that go 'slumming' for an evening in the Lower East Side. Or when a Victoria or a brougham carriage gets stuck or topples over, we help."

True enough. Carriages got wrecked.

"But otherwise, in a manner of speaking, we hit a wall. Especially in plainclothes. We ask questions and get no answers. If it's a mansion or a gentleman's club, everybody is polite, but a detective gets a little scrap or else big fat zero."

Roddy nudged my arm. So, this was Finlay's offer—that we spy for him, solely under his supervision.

I said, "Mr. Finlay, you propose that Mr. DeVere and I work undercover for you? Is that correct?"

He swallowed hard.

"Perhaps," I said, "you recall that I grew up in mining country in the West? Just for the record, we had a word for this sort of thing: 'snitch.' And a 'snitch' was detested."

His cheeks flushed a deep rouge, and he pushed to the edge of his seat. "Consider this, Mrs. DeVere...the greater good and the safety of Central Park. Do you know it's called the city's 'lungs?' The city must breathe, Mrs. DeVere. Right now, people are afraid. Attendance is way down."

He turned to Roddy. "You, sir, are a man of affairs in this city. You called at Mulberry Street, I believe, to demand that the Chief order day-and-night police patrols throughout the park."

Roddy scowled but nodded. One more trace of our whereabouts over the last four days.

Finlay continued to wind up his planned speech. "This year's new organization of the force is a chance for a fresh start. If it sticks, the longtime rot will be gone. The gangs might be broken up, and the gambling dens shut down. I don't suppose you heard of the Batavia Street Gang? Or the Hudson Dusters?"

We had not.

"Never mind. As of tonight, you have the choice—sit by and see what happens or cooperate and help us." He added, "I remind you both, the calendar is not with us."

Black or white, light or dark, we needed no reminder. The days shortened by the minute.

"A stirring plea, Mr. Finlay," Roddy said at last, "but Mrs. DeVere and I have agreed only to help the Philbricks' search for their grandson. Our efforts are confined to the search. Good evening, sir."

We rose to end the interview. In that moment, none of us needed to say the "search" also meant the saboteur who had slaughtered sheep and blown up a bridge—and the Central Park strangler who might, in weeks, seize another young woman by the neck and choke her to death.

Chapter Seventeen

THE MORNING OF OCTOBER seventeenth—the day of the Bicycle tea—dawned bright and crisp, with the deep blue sky a broad canvas that was lavishly painted with puffy white clouds-upon-clouds.

Would today be the recess we needed? The past few days had been tense and frustrating. We had learned nothing further from the Philbricks nor from the detective. Roddy had learned nothing new about the investigation, not from members of the Union or Union League Clubs or from downtown sources at Tammany Hall or Mulberry Street or the city courthouse. He heard no "scuttlebutt" at taverns or saloons.

The Finlay challenge hovered. To help the detective or keep our distance?

Newspapers, meanwhile, spewed the same purple prose about fraud, graft, and politics. We breakfasted with Velvet and with Pulitzer's and Hearst's warring views on "despot" Boss Platt, and on Roosevelt's "Rough Rider" campaign for governor. The new crimes reported in Central Park included panhandling, tulip bulb theft, and a runaway carriage smashed to smithereens near the Mall.

The mail brought invitations to musicales, luncheons, and a ball. We endured a dinner in honor of a German prince from Hedwig Holstein (Karl Friederich von Holstein-Gottorp) who was soon to marry a copper heiress from Montana. He would fill his family's depleted coffers in exchange for making his bride a certified princess.

No dinner guest mentioned the murders in Central Park.

A brochure had arrived confirming our box at the Horse Show, gratis Rufus and Eleanor DeVere, heralding several November days when we would admire prize horseflesh at Madison Square Garden in the company of my in-laws.

But not today.

"Great day for cycling," Roddy announced, "exercise in fresh air with our friends on Riverside Drive."

"Along the river," I said, "and nowhere near the park."

"Nowhere near." My husband nodded, the picture of health in the fishnet undershirt he wore to lift barbells. "No cobwebs this morning." Roddy had finished and set two barbells on a rack in the little gymnasium that he had built off his bedroom. I perched on a wood bench in the "gym" to enjoy the sight of his fitness routine.

I had "substituted" as his valet since last night, lingering as Roddy undressed. In my silk nightgown and peignoir, I had "visited" his suite and "assisted" as he doffed his coat and tie, his shirt, trousers, underthings. My peignoir slipped off, and my gown, leaving all our clothing in a pool at our feet. We took it from there for the nighttime hours.

"Last night," I said softly, "was a Val and Roddy jubilee."

"Playing at St. George for a change," my husband said.

"And the 'agony of bliss' was ours to share."

"A night to remember, Valentine." He leaned close and kissed me. I kissed him back.

Our spirits stayed high through the morning and lunchtime, even as the azure sky turned overcast and the clouds turned a drab gray. From the front windows, we saw leaves scatter from branches in the park. "Breezy out there," I said.

"Bit of a wind," Roddy looked at the clock. "We're to meet at Columbus Circle by one-thirty for the ride."

"Weather permitting—?"

"It's Eli's call. He would have sent word of a cancellation. His butler has two gallons of the Bicycle Tea Cocktail … premixed with rye whisky and extra bitters, ready to serve at the finish line."

Eli Fryer was the president of the club he had founded, named after a French blacksmith who invented the modern two-wheeler. The route was always Eli's surprise, supposedly fun for all.

"So it's a *go*."

Our footman, Bronson, was sent to inflate our bicycle tires, while Roddy dressed and I sought Calista's help because of the complex costume. *Bicycling for Ladies*, a gift book from my mother-in-law, demanded "knickerbockers, shirtwaist, stockings, shoes, gaiters, sweater, coat, hat, and gloves." Cycling ought to be casual, I thought, but no, the whole rigamarole.

Fastening the leather gaiters was a chore, but crucial to keep the spokes and chain clear. The gaiters looked a bit like cowboys' chaps, which made me homesick.

'Never mind, Val,' I said to myself. 'Cycling will be fun, a New York treat.' We had no bicycles in the mining camps, nor on the steep mountainside of Virginia City. My patented bicycle shoes guaranteed comfort ("soft as a glove"), but my left heel protested as Roddy and I walked our "bikes" along Fifty-ninth Street toward Columbus Circle, where a statue of Christopher Columbus stood on a column discovering America and hosting scads of pigeons.

و6ك

"Brave ladies and gentlemen of the Cycling Club, I bid you welcome to the final Bicycling Tea of 1898! Prepare to pedal!"

Severe in a slate gray cycling suit with a big gold watch chain across his ample front, Eli Fryer had to feel disappointed by the meagre turnout. His pomaded gunmetal gray hair flattened against his head, and dark whiskers shadowed his cheeks. He fingered his watch chain ornament like a worry bead.

The weather could be blamed for the turnout—or was it the "fear" factor?

The dozen of us stole skyward glances during greetings. The Vanderbilt girls had come, and Mrs. Ogden Mills with one of her daughters. I waved to Carrie Astor Wilson and to Theo, whose bicycle looked as new as mine. We greeted the Pembroke Joneses, James Van Alen, the Grahams, the Bains, and Colonel William Jay (previously introduced to me as a Van Cortlandt of Old Knickerbocker ancestry). The Martendales were nowhere in sight, doubtless to avoid a repeat of Eli's scorn for Arthur Martendale's skill on two wheels.

Would Clayton Philbrick magically appear among us, as Roddy had suggested to his grandparents?

Wishful thinking.

The Forsters came from the "Inventors Gate" entrance. My friend disliked cycling. Her light touch on the reins of Bella was the envy of every equestrienne, but she struggled with a two-wheeled "mechanical horse," though our friendship would not have blossomed without it, for we first met one summer afternoon two years ago in Newport when Cassie took a spill, and I helped with a tire pump.

Well past 1:30 p.m. and time to get going, Eli requested a short delay, flashing his oversize gold watch, maybe hoping latecomers would make a stronger showing. He bellowed his usual checklist.

"Chain and gear?"

"Sprocket-wheels?"

"Nuts and washers all in place and screwed home?"

We nodded and saluted, though Theo's "Aye aye, sir," sounded dutiful. Our park police detail stood by impassively, eager for the tips they would earn by escorting us to the destination where ladies got hot tea and iced cakes and Roddy's drinks awaited the men. The police were advised about the route in advance. The air felt bone damp.

"Very good to have the police escort this year," Carrie Wilson remarked.

"Especially considering dreadful recent events," replied Rupert Bain in his deep bass voice. Several of us nodded. The unsaid would go unsaid.

"Definitely Riverside Drive this year—and I believe the temperature is dropping." The soft southern tones of Pem Jones voiced complaint. He chafed gloved hands and tightened his neck-muffler, doubtless yearning to be at home in South Carolina, where he served guests mint julips. He repeated, "…Riverside Drive."

Murmurs of "no doubt about it" and "a sure bet" mixed with remarks on Eli Fryer's habit of testing friends' hardiness in foul weather. Theo, a Bostonian to the marrow, rolled his eyes, pulled up his collar, and whispered about glowing fires and cognac.

"Let's get on with it, Eli," Colonel Jay called out. "What's the route?"

"Before today's ride, my friends, a special announcement—" Eli spoke over our heads, as if to a large crowd. "The Cycling Club membership will soon receive invitations to an evening event. Messengers will be dispatched to each and every residence. As host, I will welcome you, one and all to a splendid evening…a surprise."

"But Eli, what about today's route? Riverside Drive, yes? Shall we go?"

Eli cupped his palms at his mouth. "Hallowe'en is nigh," he called out, "and the headless horseman...poltergeist...."

Just then, two wagonloads of coal rumbled by on the Avenue, and the iron shoes of eight Clydesdales drowned Eli's voice a second time.

"What did he say?" asked Carrie Astor. "What 'horseman?'"

"Headless?" One of the Vanderbilt girls laughed nervously. "Mr. Fryer, you did not say 'headless.'"

But he had. "A toast to Halloween." Eli unfolded a cardboard megaphone and clapped it to his mouth. "A tribute to Old New Amsterdam, my friends, and the haunting legends of Diedrich Knickerbocker."

"Who is that Diedrich?" Isabel Bain asked. "Do we know him?"

"A stage play," replied James Van Alen. "*Rip Van Winkle* at the Harlem Theatre...last April, I think."

Mrs. Bain looked relieved. The Bains had come recently from Indiana, having amassed a fortune from gas wells.

"Legends of the haunted..." Eli continued, "the 'Spuyten Duyvil' the 'spouting devil' creek by the Hudson River. And the horseman slain in our Revolutionary War...slain the Battle of White Plains... headless and 'ever in quest of his head, with rushing speed, like a midnight blast.'"

"Nonsense," Dudley muttered. His red-and-black checkered mackinaw jacket had seen years of service. "Headless horseman, my eye...."

Megaphone at his lips, Eli slowly and very loudly announced in sepulchral tones that we would proceed to ride to sites of 'haunting' in Central Park.

The wind whined in the bare branches, and James Van Alen protested in a reedy tenor, "Central Park is not haunted. And never has been haunted. No such thing." A loud silence followed.

Unfazed, Eli clapped one hand over his heart. "'In the gloom of night, as if on the wings of the wind....'"

Someone murmured, "Property investor thinks he's playing *Hamlet*."

Theo leaned close and shivered. "This sounds familiar... the headless horseman, I knew it...'The Legend of Sleepy Hollow.' It's Washington Irving's horrible story." He turtled into his collar. "It scared the daylights out of me as a boy."

"All of us," Roddy said, "and that's the solemn truth."

"I was terrified the headless horseman would ride into my nursery," Theo continued. "Nightmares...couldn't sleep a wink." He shuddered. "Brings it all back." Theo shrugged as if to slough off old fears. "Eli is scraping bottom, deviling us. Nobody wants to bicycle in the park, nobody. What's the man up to?"

All around us, gloved hands tightened on handlebars.

Theo said, "I'll spread the word that it's Sleepy Hollow."

Our friend threaded his way among the bicycles as Eli gazed skyward into the gray gloom. "'His haunts are not confined to the valley,'" he intoned, "'but extend to the adjacent roads.' My friends, we will ride those roads this afternoon in the park...into the haunted Central Park."

"Oh, no, no...please, no....!" Cassie's wail was unmistakable.

Good manners fought with disappointment, anger, and anxiety all around. We all came to be good sports, to rally. I had lent Cassie *Bicycling for Ladies* and had read her lines on "the sociability about cycling." None of us, however, expected this creepy plan of the club president.

"No such thing as 'haunted!'" Colonel Jay shouted.

"Dudley," I heard Cassie say, "won't you please take me home?"

Dudley Forster encouraged Cassie for health's sake. Cycling was promoted as an elixir, and every maker of bicycles won support from scientists.

"Haunting? We'll find out," Eli continued. "The Headless Horseman of Halloween is our quest this afternoon, and our gray skies set the mood—so, my friends, prepare to mount, and we'll start through Merchants Gate. And here we go! In the spirit of the Cycling Club, what could be better?"

Better would be the capture of the Central Park strangler, as everyone knew. Roddy and I would also add an end to the vicious crimes. The zoo was under heavy police patrols, probably because of the Southdown ewes. Mid-November loomed, another date with death somewhere in the park.

By the Reservoir?

Near Harlem?

Or perhaps close by the crushed gravel roadways where we drove carriages and rode horseback?

Or pedaled bicycles. I hung back, sending the Forsters ahead of us, and Roddy stayed at my side, though I was a "natural" on two wheels. It would have been easier to pedal faster, but the group straggled, and the wind made for heavy going.

Why Eli led us onto the bridle paths from the wide drives, we could only guess. The cycling became rougher, and we needed to rest at the Pine Bank Arch. Alfred Graham suggested that we keep an eye out for the headless horseman galloping along the bridle path. The polite titters sounded thin and strained, but heads turned to see the path, just in case.

Eli raised the megaphone to announce the site as "'the region of shadows in the bosoms of spacious coves....'"

"What 'bosoms?'" Carrie Wilson asked, warning that she hadn't strength to complete the ride in the wind.

The Vanderbilt girls sulked. Our ten-minute "rest" became a trial. Cassie put on a stoic face, as did Isabel Bain whose hat "ripened" with clusters of cherries despite advice that headgear decor be "abbreviated."

"On to Drip Rock," Eli called, and we pushed off, single file, wheeling over and around horse droppings on the path. I caught up with Cassie by the time we reached Drip Rock, where Eli called another halt.

With the megaphone covering half of his face, he went on. "...bewitched from the early days of the settlement." With the voice of a dramatic actor, he proclaimed, "'…Haunted spots…and twilight superstitions…poltergeists.'"

Theo shuddered.

So did I. Eli Fryer reminded me of a mine foreman my papa had fired, a man who scared us when he laughed and left his men in total darkness when their candle burned down. He made them work when the air got bad. Two men did not survive. Papa said the foreman "danced with the devil" and got what was coming to him. His body was found on a heap of mine tailings.

"Drip Rock," Cassie whispered to me, "is a likely hiding place for Calvert Vaux's secret papers…papers that involve his death. This might be one of the 'haunted spots.' Madame Riva urged me to look."

Dudley held her bicycle while Cassie felt the rock for chinks and crevasses, her gloved hands trembling as they moved. Her husband barely hid his dismay. Lapels and scarves were tugged tight, and top buttons fastened. Pem Jones reached for a second pair of gloves, and I overheard a man's low voice "…damnably stubborn…damnably cold… demented…whatever he's cooked up for a 'surprise' evening, count me out."

Before pedaling on, Colonel Jay insisted that Eli disclose our final destination.

"Belvedere *Castle*," Eli fairly roared. He held up his gold watch to signal that we had time enough. "The *Castle*," he bellowed, "…'castles in the clouds that pass, trances and visions…voices in the air.'"

Cassie murmured something about the castle's "cockatrice," a mythical, monstrous beast. She began to weep.

I fumbled for a handkerchief, but Dudley dabbed her face with a chamois cloth. My friend weeping, the air colder, and the gray light dimming by the minute. Hands and feet and ears ached with cold, and the park police escorts stared into the distance as though the Upper East Side cyclists were an alien species.

Chapter Eighteen

THE BICYCLE TEA—AND THE arc of our lives—bent double in the next moments. Eli Fryer ceased the Hallowe'en "hauntings," and led us off the bridle paths toward the broad drives, where we pedaled with grim zeal with the wind at our backs. Oncoming carriages pulled aside—mainly grooms exercising purebred horses and terrified of collision.

Winded, we stopped at Cherry Hill to catch our collective breath. Even the policemen panted.

My left heel had blistered, and I bent to loosen laces when Roddy tapped my shoulder, face to the wind, and asked, "Do you smell it, Val? Something acrid?"

"A little bit."

He pointed. "Look there...beyond the lake?"

"What is it?"

A thin brown wisp rose in the distance. "Looks like smoke," I said.

"It does."

"I smell it now. Maybe the gardeners are burning leaves."

"Not this late in the day."

Our fellow cyclists had not noticed in the darkening afternoon. They huddled—and fussed—about the fastest routes out of the park, excusing themselves from the tea, the cakes, and cocktails. Dudley and Cassie said goodbye to Roddy and me and fled. James Van Alen, the Pembroke Joneses, Theo and Carrie Wilson thought it best to proceed to Fifty-ninth Street. "To the Scholars Gate, you DeVeres... practically your front entrance. Let's all have tea at the Plaza. Better yet, champagne and cocktails."

Roddy thanked them, wished them godspeed, and peered again across the lake.

"Buttered rum, DeVere...don't miss out. And Valentine, the Plaza awaits, lest you think about your blustery old Wyoming."

"Nevada," I said, but the word got lost. In seconds, Roddy and I were left by ourselves to gauge the thickening shaft of smoke across the Lake.

"Let's go"

We cycled toward the smoke, a gray-brown column that wafted slowly toward the clouds but hung in a haze around us. Nostrils and throats stung, and wood smoke filled our mouths—and a nasty chemical.

I sneezed, and Roddy clapped his muffler scarf over nose and mouth, one-handed on the handlebar grips.

"The boathouse," Roddy called. I nodded, eyes watering.

A short-cut took us onto a walking path where I skidded to a stop on rotting leaves, slid off the seat, and stood before a scene that Roddy and I faced together in the next thirty seconds.

"The boats," Roddy said, his scarf muffling his voice, "The rental rowboats."

"On fire...."

Fire patrolmen stood braced before a row of boats upturned for the season, blazing and hissing as hoses turned on the flames. Before us, one boat had blackened to ash, a second reduced to steaming ribs, and a third was licked with flames as jets of water thrust and splashed at the scorched hull. The patrolmen gripped their nozzles, aimed, and blasted like gunmen firing at fire.

"Stand back!"

I jumped, and Roddy retreated a few steps, his muffler over nose and mouth. Uniformed policemen skirted the scene. We pushed the bicycles to the side. The chemical smell shot to my head. "Dizzy..." I murmured.

"Back! Stand back!"

Lightheaded, blinking, I did not know the voice, but the scar was unmistakable. The patrolmen wore identical rubber coats and helmets with brass "Fire Patrol" badges on the front. Several sprouted whiskers, but one man alone stood out for the crescent scar carved into his sooty cheek—the sergeant who had barged into our house, inhaled my workroom glue and notified the police of an arsonist inside.

"Val…." Roddy sat me down on the cold ground, his scarf something like a mask. "Val," he said, "look who is here…."

"Who?" I felt faint. "Who is it?"

On the ground, at eye level, the black trousers came into view, and the long arms as I gazed upward, then the celluloid shirt cuffs, the suitcoat. "Detective Finlay," I said.

Roddy had knelt on one knee beside me, and Finlay hunkered down. Both men begged to summon a doctor, but I refused. "I'll be fine…a few minutes."

Finlay spoke to us both, his pale hair and gray eyes too close. "You need to know," he said, "this fire is no accident. The captain suspects gasoline. We could have lost every boat. The fire patrolmen could have been burned or blinded."

He looked from one of us to the other. "One more vicious crime in the park," he said, then drilled us with a stare. "Murders and damage," he began, leaning yet closer. "Mr. DeVere…this park got its start from families like yours. Your grandfathers built it, and now somebody…or somebodies…they're after ruin…a bridge in rubble, wood structures burned, the boats in ashes…and those pitiful young women."

His eyes searched ours. "People are afraid, Mr. Devere, so tell me this—how much more death and damage before you and Mrs. DeVere cooperate to save the park that your forefathers built?"

Chapter Nineteen

THE NEXT MORNING, RODDY tucked a canteen of water under one arm, looped Velvet's leash around one hand, and chose a rattan walking stick. I slipped two Spratts dog biscuits into my jacket pocket and took an umbrella just in case.

"Here, Velvet."

"Come, girl...we're going for a walk."

With all four paws planted on the Persian rug, our dog did not move a muscle until a biscuit enticed her into the harness and leash. From all appearances, we merely sought fresh air to exercise our little dog on the path by the Pond at the southernmost entrance to Central Park on this Tuesday morning, the eighteenth of October. Thin clouds signaled changing weather on this cool autumn day. We did not speak until reaching the Pond, where we paused near the water's edge.

Velvet sniffed a fern. Our dog was a pleasure and a pretext. We needed to talk far out of servants' earshot.

"A cheap trick by Finlay..." Roddy said.

"I don't agree," I replied.

Ahead of us, a nanny pushed a pram and disappeared around a curve. A pair of ducks paddled nearby, and Velvet's "bat" ears bent back in interest. No one else was in sight.

"He needn't have tied me to my grandfather... great-grandfather," Roddy said. "The Bicycle Tea was disastrous, and the boats on fire...destroyed.... Still, it was coercion."

"Of a sort," I replied. "But Finlay is desperate for help, Roddy. He made his case to us nights ago. Nobody will give him information, and Clayton Philbrick is...nowhere." I pointed to the nearest bench that faced the Pond. "Let's sit down. The heel blister stings...that cycling shoe...."

We sat. Velvet buried her nose in a shrub, and Roddy looked skyward where a flock flew south in a V-shaped wedge. "Amazing how birds know to do that," he said. "Every autumn, follow the leader and migrate."

My annoyance at his focus on birds melted when my husband turned and said, "No choice in the matter, Val. We must help."

On my tongue tip, the next question—how?

Roddy tapped the walking stick against his boot. "First, we ought to find out more about the boathouse fire."

"Finlay said 'gasoline,'" I said. "But who called the Fire Patrol? It was nearly dusk when the boats caught fire...."

"And was anybody seen dashing away with a large jug? Or a tin?"

I paused. "Possibly Clayton Philbrick? Is he out of the question?"

Roddy peered across the Pond where the ducks dived, resurfaced, swam out of sight. "We need to know more about Clayton Philbrick, Val. Victor and Gladys are doting grandparents, and so far, they paint a picture of a young blood feeling his oats, rather lazy but not much different from his friends. I have gone along with them, drinking mint tea and commiserating." He unscrewed the canteen. "No more."

Canteen water trickled into Roddy's palm, and Velvet lapped and licked. Softly he repeated, "No more."

"Would they hide him?" I asked. It seemed unlikely. "Could they be that desperate?"

"Desperate people, desperate measures." Roddy capped the canteen. "I want to know what Detective Finlay took away from Clayton's suite when he returned for a search. Gladys said she did not see the object of 'material interest.'"

"Finlay ought to tell us," I said. "If he wants our help, he ought to help us to help him."

"Too many 'oughts.'" Roddy looked skyward. "Cold rain by tomorrow," he said. "A good soaking ought to discourage arson. But first thing in the morning, I will track down a certain young broker...." He reached into his tweed jacket pocket and showed me a card:

Andrew D. Brainard
Broker in Stocks and Bonds
Thirty-Six Wall Street
New York City, NY

"He's the young man you spoke with at the Templars Club?"

"Yes. He was eager to say more about brother Clayton. I hope he's still eager and won't corner me into buying shares in a failing railroad." Roddy pocketed the card. "I'll also revisit the Templars clubhouse."

And I...." I hesitated. "I will ask Noland to drive me to a rooming house on West Thirty-fifth Street. This time I'll go alone. Miss Lola Taylor might be persuaded to say more about the stage door Johnny and her murdered friend."

Chapter Twenty

THE MORNING DAWNED WITH sprinkles turning into heavy, cold rain. Calista tiptoed into my dressing room with a rumpled envelope on a silver tray.

We often bypassed the servant-to-mistress scripts in the etiquette books. I reached for the tray, but she tugged it back. "Ma'am...if I might explain...?"

"Of course," I said, "but Noland expects to drive me downtown, and I need your help with my wardrobe. The tray," I said, "what's on the tray?"

Her apology began with our dog. "You see, ma'am, I played a little game with Velvet. 'Chew-and-chase,' I called it. Mr. Sands was not troubled, but Mrs. Thwaite was unhappy. She found this letter under one of Velvet's little beds...it arrived three days ago, but somehow Velvet got hold of it and...and...." My maid wrung her hands.

"Don't worry, Calista," I said. . It's sweet of you to play with Velvet. Give me a look at this…and do see about my daytime outfit, nothing fancy…."

I slit the flap with Papa's Barlow knife and smoothed a typewritten letter postmarked New York City and signed by a stranger named Lillian Wald. The next moment became a back-and-forth between me and my maid, who was in the dressing room while I read the letter. "Calista, have you ever heard of Lillian Wald?"

"No, ma'am."

"How about Florence Kelley?" I looked again at the letterhead. "Or the Henry Street Settlement?… How about the Consumers League of New York City?"

"I'm afraid not."

"You're sure? Consumers League sounds vaguely familiar…."

"I'm looking at your two-piece Mountain Dress, ma'am."

I agreed to the skirt-and-jacket outfit with no-nonsense lines and rows of little horn buttons on the jacket.

"—and a hat, Calista. No feathers…too much rain."

"Yes, ma'am."

Signed by a Lillian D. Wald, the letter invited me to a meeting—this very morning at eleven a.m.—of a newly-formed national organization: The Consumers League, to meet at the Henry Street Settlement, 265 Henry Street.

The "League" surfaced as a hazy memory until I saw the telltale clerical initials under the signature —af. Who else, but Annie Flowers? Each word in the letter was typed by the newly-hired secretary who had graduated from typewriting school and would probably take notes at this morning's meeting, a gathering that I could not possibly attend, fortunately.

Relieved to be free of Annie Flowers, I was jarred when Calista bent down to retrieve a slip of paper on the floor by my writing desk.

She handed me a half-sheet in crabbed handwriting with a message to "**Mrs. DeV.**" I took it to the window, saw the rain coming down in sheets, and read,

> —most important you attend Consumers League meeting because of what they did to the Uptown Land you call Central Park and ruined lives. Anger boils.
>
> Yours truly,
> Annie Flowers

Whose anger? And who were "they?" What "ruined lives" and what "Uptown Land?" I never heard the park called by such a name.

"May I help you any further, ma'am? Ma'am....?"

"Thank you, Calista. That will be all for now. I need a few minutes to think...."

By ten a.m., wearing the Mountain Dress with a felt hat, a Macintosh and "rain" boots, I stood under the umbrella that Noland held to assist me into the phaeton hitched to

Apollo, one of our high-stepping black Hackneys. In cape and coverings, both Noland and the horse defied the foul weather.

"And we will be going to West Thirty-fifth Street as ordered, ma'am?"

"No, Noland. My plans have changed. We are going to 265 Henry Street to an address known as the Henry Street Settlement."

The three-story brick building on Henry Street was dead-center in the notorious Lower East Side. In a pounding rain, Noland had driven around pushcart venders standing knee deep in rain-filled gutters awash with trash and spillage. They vied for space under awnings, pulled rags over the pushcart displays, and touted their wares in guttural languages. From the closed carriage window, I glimpsed vegetables, fish, hernia trusses, hardware, and children's stockings ("*bambini piccolini..calzini per bambini piccolini….*").

Twirling his nightstick, a policeman in rubber raingear patrolled the street, aiming for a cobblestone "island" with each step. I imagined Colon Finlay on this "beat," scouting gambling dens and gangs.

Children's and venders' cries mixed in pounding rain, and I stared at the swarming children in tattered, sodden shifts and knickers who spilled into the street. Little girls swaddled babies in their arms, and both infants and girls got more soaked by the minute, while young boys gawked at our horse that was blanketed in his own Macintosh from mane to withers. The boys poked twigs in the spokes of the phaeton wheels.

Why weren't they in school? This was a Wednesday, mid-week in October, so why weren't these children in school?

I would ask this question of Miss Wald or whoever convened the gathering in this building that Noland had located amid foul tenements, fire escapes, and a saloon on every corner. Last summer, I had briefly viewed such a scene from a hansom cab with Cassie but was too preoccupied to absorb the enormity of it.

"This is the address, ma'am." Umbrella raised, Noland assisted me into the street and front entrance. Rainwater dripped from his hat brim, and the coachman's disapproval was written in his clenched jaw. "I'll have us somewhere on the block, ma'am, and be waiting for you."

My "Thank you, Noland" was drowned in the street-side splashing, but when the door to number 265 opened, I entered a paneled reception room scented with herbs and antiseptics. An earnest young woman arranged tight rows of Thonet chairs, the clever bentwood utility chairs that could be stacked and stowed. A small table at the front was piled with books in paper wrappers and surrounded by three chairs. A coal fire had been lighted in a nearby grate, a notion of warmth.

I sat at the back, unfastened the Macintosh, and looked around at space that my mother-in-law would cherish for its history and pity for its cramped size. The room reeked of history in the carved moldings that banded the high ceilings, though the space was too small for today's New York extravaganzas. Nonetheless, our 1890s was probably set into motion by the Old New York men who reaped fortunes in this room with the stroke of a goose quill pen on parchment.

Were Roddy's ancestors among them?

Whatever "settlement" meant here, it was not like the settlements I knew from the Nevada alkali creeks where squatters scratched a living and fought off Paiute Indians.

The space filled quickly with two dozen ladies who sat hip-to-hip in narrow aisles. The rainwear and umbrellas left little puddles on the waxed hardwood.

I did not see Annie Flowers. Her handwritten note might have been a ploy to bring me here. "Uptown Land"...what did that mean? What "ruined" lives?

Where was the woman?

And who was Lillian D. Wald? Several young women in practical clothing and sensible shoes stood near the walls, welcoming arriving ladies who were dressed for a low-key social function.

Had others received letters identical to mine? Did curiosity bring them to the Lower East Side on this raw, rainy day? Did Annie Flowers slip handwritten notes to them?

This much I could say: my feet were wet, my toes clammy inside the stockings, and the heel blister sent messages in its own Morse code.

And Annie Flowers was nowhere in sight.

So far, a waste of time.

Then, suddenly, "Valentine DeVere, what a lovely surprise!" A familiar figure made her way to the chair beside me.

"Good morning to you, Daisy Harriman," I replied. "Have a seat."

Daisy (Mrs. J. Borden Harriman) was a social friend and occasional doubles partner on the ladies court at the Newport Casino in July. She sailed a catboat in the bay, and she "sat" her horse as elegantly as Cassie. Though firmly embedded in Society's Four Hundred, Daisy Harriman was rumored these days to be trumpeting peculiar ideas about laborers' wages and workplace safety.

"Drenched," she said, doffing gloves and rainwear to reveal a ribbed woolen skirt and long jacket in coppery shades. "Raining cats and dogs," she said. "Of course, when Lillian Wald and Florence Kelley call, one simply must heed that call."

Daisy gave me her lovely warm smile. "Lillian Wald and Florence Kelley—and The Consumers League," she continued, "what could be more exciting?"

My papa had advised that ignorance could always be fixed ("but stupidity, my dear—never!"). I told Daisy (Florence Jaffrey Hurst Harriman) that neither woman's name was known to me.

A blank second passed, as though I had been asleep for a century, and then—"Oh, I forgot, Valentine...you come from...South Dakota? The Badlands?"

"Nevada and Colorado, Daisy. But in the West, a settlement is a frontier colony... not quite a town, but on the way." I gestured at the artful molding and the wall paneling. "Nothing like this," I said.

She laughed. "Classic Federal period house," she said, "these days, a health clinic for nurses, and a rooftop playground too. Lillian Wald started it all, Lillian and her friend Mary Brewster, two trained nurses who saw the crying need in this part of the city. Do you know they invented the visiting nurse program...*voila*, house calls in the tenements."

She snapped her fingers and looked up. "This old Federal building might have been torn down, but the Settlement got it three years ago. Thanks to Eli Fryer."

"Oh?"

"Bordie says he owns buildings all over the city. He buys distressed property, vacant lots, whole blocks...even gentlemen's clubs."

"Clubs?"

"The Arcadian is no more, and the Standard is gone. They say the Templars is on borrowed time, but no loss on that score. The settlement house here on Henry Street is his first charitable contribution. May others follow...so many in our city need help."

Daisy pointed to the young women standing against the walls. "They're recruits, young nurses that live here, thanks to Lillian and Mary. They treat children in the schools too. You saw the children outside in the pouring rain? Wondered why they weren't in school?"

"I certainly did."

"Not enough seats…sixty children to a schoolroom, and three to a desk. It's criminal. The first public school in New York City—School Number 1—is here on Henry Street, but children are turned away. And so many poor families keep their boys and girls at home to work because they need the pennies. But change is on the way. A committee is at work to expand the schools and educate these parents."

"…huge effort," I murmured.

Daisy smoothed her skirt and spoke quietly as the room hummed with soft conversation. "A city settlement, Valentine," she said, "reaches out to the new populations to help them get settled…the many immigrants flowing into our cities …Chicago, Pittsburgh…Cleveland…."

Cleveland—where Lola Taylor and Roxie LaRue had become friends in the German tavern. Distracted, I lost track of Daisy's words, looked for Annie Flowers, and strained to listen once again to the voice at my ear.

"…and Ellis Island busier than ever, so think of it, tenements, no fresh air…children and parents at death's door… germs and rotten food…."

Daisy gestured toward a window glazed with rainwater. "They're bursting with energy, and they need help. Murderous living conditions…downright murderous."

That startling word drove Central Park roaring into my brain. Righteous anger had sparked Daisy's gaze, not the fear of unsolved homicides in the park. In truth, no one in Society was speaking directly about the murders, not at the dinner for the German prince, not at the dreadful Bicycle Tea.

Daisy and "Bordie" Harriman, I recalled, spent the autumn outside the city in their Hudson Valley home in Mount Kisco. If the killer wasn't caught, would Society abandon Fifth Avenue and flee into the Hudson Valley?

Would we?

Where was Annie Flowers? I could be at the boarding-house questioning Lola Taylor.

"...and so you'll specially want to join the Consumers League, Valentine. The workplace, as you'll soon understand, is at the root of social progress, and Florence Kelley will inspire you. It's full speed ahead...and look, here she comes now...."

Applause rose as three women approached the table. Daisy whispered, "Lillian Wald is on the right, and that's Florence Kelley beside her. How strong they both look— so splendid. But the young woman on the left, I don't know her...."

"Daisy," I said, "the young woman on the left is a secretary, and her name is Annie Flowers."

Chapter Twenty-one

BOLTED TO THE CHAIR, I glowered at Annie Flowers as if willpower might telegraph my presence and prompt a wink or a wave. Seated, she opened a notebook and began penciling. Her pale blue shirtwaist and navy skirt looked new, and her hair was neatly pinned. Not once did she glance toward the Thonet chairs.

No choice for me, but to settle for the duration. The room hushed, and I braced for two hours of sentimental prayers, soulful speeches, pious tributes—and a plea for funds.

No such thing. A fire-and-brimstone tirade began when Lillian Wald welcomed us and gave the floor to "our Mrs. Florence Kelley, direct from Chicago to New York."

A large-featured woman came forward, pushed her jacket sleeves to the elbows, and thundered, *"Philanthropy!"* as if the word tasted rancid. *"Philanthropy,"* as if Satan's own scourge.

"Satisfied to patch and cobble," she growled, "so philanthropy mends and cobbles... and sweeps tragedy under the rug ...tens of thousands sacrificed...an industrial system that destroys its own workers, men, woman, and children, our very future ...ruinous...salt in open wounds...."

Who was this woman with the gusting voice and a gaze that pierced the room? She could be a ranch woman facing down cattle rustlers in the West.

"...lives crushed by toil...children in mills and factories... pasty-faced ...doomed...."

Beside me, Daisy Harriman nodded prayerfully, as if in church. What would her financier husband, J. Borden Harriman, think of his wife in rapture at this buxom, middle-aged woman dressed in mismatched clothing, no jewelry, and a coil of dark braided hair wound from ear to ear?

Florence Kelley declared herself the General Secretary of the new Consumers League, laced sturdy fingers, and paraded her interlocked hands up and down the center aisle. "On the one hand, the League will be devoted to the education of consumers...and who are they? You who shop at Macy's here in New York, or your cousins in Filene's in Boston, or Chicago's Marshall Field...or...."

I glanced at my lavalier watch. The department store roster went on. At the front, Annie Flowers penciled, not once glancing up.

"From sea to shining sea... cotton fibers in workers' lungs.... children tending looms...slaves in our modern age...."

Kelley's utopian scheme promised school-age children would be in classrooms, none in the streets, the one idea I applauded as practical.

At last, the woman finished and turned to Lillian Wald, who stood like Auntie Benevolence in a stage set. "Lillian, if you will…?"

The founder of the Henry Street Settlement lifted a poster from the tabletop, held it high to show us a black-and-white drawing, and beamed. The poster showed a white bow-tie etched with phrases on "clean and healthful conditions."

She pointed to the table where Annie Flowers took notes. "This poster was prepared by the very first League employee. If we might give our thanks to Miss Annie Flowers—?"

The room applauded. Annie Flowers's demure nod did not interrupt her penciling.

"I bid you join the Consumers League. And we have a gift for each of you, a book you must read and take to heart before you waste precious hours on another foolish novel." Arms on her hips, Florence Kelley looked ready to dance the tarantella.

Applause, and then a swirl of raincoats and umbrellas, and conversations by ladies who shuffled past one another along the pinched aisles but stopped to sign the clipboards that were suddenly circulated by the young nurses.

"Please, ladies, your good penmanship for your home addresses so we can get in touch, because we will do so. I promise you we will do so!"

"Valentine, I'll see you at the Horse Show next month." Daisy reached for her umbrella. "And we'll get together at the next League meeting too. I must be off...train to Mount Kisco." She fastened her Macintosh. "Let me tell you something, Valentine. When Bordie and I married, I spent my days collecting American Revolutionary documents. Important as they are, our industrial system will have my energies from now on. Our system is a wonder of the civilized world, but it takes a tragic toll on people's lives. I'm on board to help fix it. You'll be needed too. It's the new pioneering. You'll be a pioneer. 'Bye for now."

She was at the door, where a young nurse distributed the paper-wrapped books. The room emptied. Lillian Wald took Florence Kelley's arm and departed through an inner door, trailed by the young nurses.

I glimpsed carriages as the front door opened and closed. Nearby, my coachman waited in the pouring rain. Our horse would need body brushing to clear mud from his legs and belly, and his hooves carefully dried to prevent cracking. A groom could do that work, but Noland deserved tureens of hot soup.

It was after one p.m., but I would not cross the Henry Street Settlement threshold without a word from the first employee hired by the Consumers League. She was near the wall as I approached. "Miss Flowers."

"Mrs. DeVere."

Inches taller than Annie Flowers, I wanted to tower over her. Silly me.

"Shall we sit down, Mrs. DeVere?"

We sat. Annie Flowers pulled a Thonet chair across from me, and our knees nearly touched. She held one of the paper-wrapped books. "I have a few minutes for you, Mrs. DeVere. I must help Mrs. Kelley unpack."

"Oh?"

"She will have a room upstairs."

"To live here?" She nodded. "Is the Consumers League is upstairs too?"

The young woman laughed softly. "The League's office is located in the United Charities Building on Twenty-second Street and Fourth Avenue," she said. "Our workday begins at eight a.m. and I must be 'thoroughly presentable' to receive visitors from far and wide." She added, "We have two adjoining rooms."

The smug "we" sounded both amusing and irritating, like the jail cell meeting that put me at a loss. I said, "Miss Flowers, you put a handwritten note inside the letter inviting me to this meeting."

"I did."

"The note began, 'Dear Mrs. DeV.'"

"Yes."

"Referring to 'Uptown Land' and boiling anger and 'ruined' lives." She nodded. "I have no idea what that means, or why it matters."

She winced. "People forget so soon," she said. "Lives get brushed aside, and no one cares. Lives are disposable."

"Miss Flowers," I asked, "has someone close to you passed away? A family member?"

She looked over my shoulder, her eyes moistening. "Power does what power does," she said. "In a valley north of here, good farms with crops and cows, but that city wanted water, and they dammed the whole valley, filled it up, drowned the farms. The people scattered. Power and money...."

"I'm not sure I understand."

"...so, understand Central Park in New York City." Her eyes beamed at me, her knees pushing mine. "It used to be the 'Uptown Land.'"

"I believe with squatters and trash," I said. "Shacks... shanties...."

"With *people*," she burst out. "With carpenters and tailors, and gardeners and laborers too. Some of them owned property on the 'Uptown Land.' But power wanted its park, Mrs. DeVere. The land was condemned, the homes were burned to the ground."

She paused while I fumbled with my Macintosh collar.

"Lives were condemned and burned too," she went on, "whole families.... So, the question is not, '*What* was on that land?' The real question is, '*Who*?'"

"Who is angry, Miss Flowers? You wrote that 'anger boils.' People from that land...that was years ago. How many are living? Who is angry?"

She sneered. "Think about it, Mrs. DeVere. How would you feel? Would you like to know who is angry? If you would, let me know, Mrs. DeVere, because I can have you meet them."

I swallowed hard as she thrust a wrapped package into my hand. "A book for you, Mrs. DeVere. People can forget, but a curse is timeless."

Chapter Twenty-two

HOME FROM HENRY STREET, I was told Mr. DeVere could be found in the billiard room. Shedding rainwear, I stowed the wrapped book on a shelf in my boudoir and dashed upstairs.

The "click" of billiard balls meant that Roddy was brooding. When troubled, he often retreated to our billiard room where the emerald green table, a cue stick, and a rack of colored balls helped him sort out stormy thoughts.

I kept still until the cue ball struck its target and sent it rolling to a thump in a pocket. Roddy's skill on the green felt table was formidable, though my agitation whirled like a Nevada sandstorm.

"Roddy—" I began.

"Val…." He turned and smiled politely, though his furrowed brow signaled trouble. "So glad to see you home… wretched weather." A peck on the cheek, and he laid the cue stick down. "Have you eaten? Shall we—? Perhaps a cocktail?"

"Roddy, let's take a moment right here...lots to talk about...but please turn that tiger rug around." The glassy-eyed tiger, its jaws wide open, teeth flashing, was kicked to a corner, and we sat together on a leather bench under a painting of polo ponies.

"How was Lola Taylor?" Roddy asked. "Did you bribe her landlady again?"

"Roddy," I began, "I did not see Miss Taylor today. I went to the Lower East Side...a meeting. It's a long story, and I have serious questions." I gestured at the billiard table. "But something is on your mind, or you wouldn't be here alone."

"Probably not."

From the look on his face, I knew my issues better be on hold or Roddy would rely on born-and-bred politeness. Patience was never my strength.

"Is it Wall Street?" I asked.

"Depressing place, Val. The exalted 'Street' is a warren of cramped offices, rickety staircases...dingy basements."

"You saw the broker?"

"Andrew Brainard, the Templar. Yes, I met with him. Likeable chap. His office is small, but the firm's ticker-tape stutters on. I took him for an early lunch at Del's...the old favorite at Beaver and William Streets. Over broiled trout and oyster pie, he tried to sell me stock in a budding manufacturer of faucets.

"And?"

"And I promised to consider it. I also asked about Clayton Philbrick, and Brainard seemed relieved to talk." Roddy's mouth tightened. "It's worrisome. Clayton has lost at bridge and poker, and he is deeply in debt to his Templar brothers. It seems that Philbrick lured the Templars with sleight-of-hand card tricks. He showed off, and the fellows played a few hands. Brainard said that Philbrick handled cards like a dealer at a casino...as if the cards were second nature."

My husband rubbed his cheek. "A clubman's gambling debt, Val, is called the 'old fatality' because it threatens to fracture the membership and put a club at risk of insolvency. The Templars are courting disaster. Their card table has become a casino."

I gazed across the room at a small bronze hunter shooting a bear. "So, Clayton Philbrick is hiding from men he owes...how much?"

"Brainard didn't say...or wouldn't say. He admitted the sums are 'substantial.'"

"Sums, plural?"

Roddy nodded. "Several Templars hold notes. Several have become his creditors."

"In other words, they've loaned him money, and they have his IOUs. And they still have no idea where he is...?"

"Not only that," Roddy said. "The members don't know exactly which Templars have loaned him money.... Some suspect that Philbrick repaid others, but not themselves...all before he disappeared. So, there's ill-will, and they've begun to taunt one another, mimicking Philbrick's high voice."

"—the tenor that his grandparents adored...."

Roddy nodded. "And they joke about his laziness... always claimed the most comfortable chair...ordered stewards to fetch anything beyond arm's reach."

"—which fits what Gladys Philbrick told us," I said. "Why walk, when a carriage is nearby?"

"Most times, yes. But every now and then, Clayton 'erupted' when something displeased him...something trifling. The fellows joked about 'Hot Lava Philbrick' but wouldn't go near him until he cooled off."

"No such word from the doting grandparents," I said, "though they must know about his tantrums." Roddy nodded. "And what about Brainard?" I asked. "Is he mixed up in the Philbrick affair?"

"I doubt it. Andrew Brainard heads the Templars social committee, and he's trying to keep peace in the ranks. I think he's afraid the club will go bust. Bankers have called about a new mortgage, and a Real Estate man had drinks in the card room to talk about buying the building to take it off the Templars' hands. Brainard remembers Clayton Philbrick ordering rounds at the table."

"For the banker?"

"The Real Estate man. Brainard doesn't remember his name, but his hair was slicked with perfumed pomade, and his watch chain clanked on the card table. I wouldn't be surprised if it was Eli Fryer. Brainard remembers Clayton riding off in the Real Estate man's carriage. It was shortly before he went missing. Of course, Brainard offered to sponsor me for membership."

"Roddy, tell me you wouldn't…not even for inside information about Clayton Philbrick," I said. "You don't owe Gladys and Victor that much, not for old times' sake." I pressed a finger at his chest. "Not for our sake."

A faraway look crossed Roddy's face. "I'm thinking of a man I knew at law school," he said, "a poker player. He'd play in Boston on weekends. Heading south for the holidays, he'd find a game on the New York Central. He'd stop overnight in every city to find a poker game until he got home to Baltimore. We joked that we ought to wager on whether he'd make it home by New Year's Day."

"And—?"

"I never knew what happened to him. We heard he'd lost everything. He dropped out of law school and disappeared."

"So, you think Clayton Philbrick might be on the run…a gambling vagabond?"

"Two points to consider, Val. For some men, gambling is like opium. They can't stop themselves."

"Clayton…."

He nodded. "Not having met the man, I'm only guessing. But a card table could be his addiction. We don't know whether his grandparents are aware of his gambling."

"What would they do if they knew?"

"I believe Victor and Gladys would quietly settle their grandson's accounts." Roddy brushed back a wave of hair.

"If Clayton had confessed to his grandparents, it's doubtful that they would have appealed to us."

I paused. Our own lives felt taken over by the Philbrick "case," as if we were in eclipse. Whether these recent days would have been richer without the Philbricks.... Calmer? More festive? Both notions were beyond me at this moment. "Roddy," I said, "you had two points in mind. Did I miss the second one?"

"It's simply this: a gambler in deep debt is vulnerable. His debt weighs heavily, and he is liable to go to extremes."

"What kind of extremes? Like the speculators I heard about in Virginia City?" My papa had said men failed when their mining stocks went down the drain and they 'lost their shirts.' I had pictured shirtless men roaming Market Street in foggy San Francisco. "Do you think Clayton Philbrick might borrow money to gamble on Wall Street stocks?"

"That's a possibility," Roddy said, "but I'm thinking Clayton might allow himself to be used...by someone, for some purpose. And that's more worrisome."

My husband looked past my shoulder toward a framed print, which showed a billiard table with a caption:

> "Let's to billiards"—Shakespeare,
> Antony and Cleopatra, 1606-1607.

I said, "The billiard table beckons when you're sorting out scrambled thoughts. Your morning meeting with the Templar...what else came up?"

"Nothing to do with Brainard, Val. But the park... I'm thinking about Central Park, the fires, the damaged bridges...." He looked at me and swallowed. "And I needn't add...."

"No, you needn't...because November is coming...."

Roddy said, "Consider this autumn, the splendid trees, but no boys climbing the Umpire rock when we strolled with the Forsters and their children...and the few visitors as we walked. How few when we bicycled. We all remarked on it."

"And nobody was around when we walked Velvet by the Pond," I said. "A nanny pushing a pram. No one else."

"And Finlay said that park attendance has dropped off," said Roddy, "not to mention the newspapers hammering the police for failing the investigation." He paused. "And the boathouse fire, supposedly an 'accident.'"

Roddy bit his lip. "But how much longer before a sharp reporter on the *World* or *Journal* takes a photographer into the park, talks to a stone mason, learns about arson fires burning wood bridges, and gets a Page-One exclusive on 'Central Park Sabotage?'"

"With photographs," I said.

Roddy nodded. "So, to think about the park...what it takes to shun Central Park...."

"Fear," I said, "and dread." I recalled Cassie's wish that Dudley would take their children to the toy store instead of the park. I said, "A deliberate scheme to arouse fear of the park? Is that what you're thinking?"

Roddy nodded. "Suppose that someone—or someones—have an interest in a dangerous Central Park...a park to avoid."

My smile was rueful. "Roddy, this very morning I saw Daisy Harriman at a meeting I attended. When she left for the train to Mount Kisco, I envied her. I envied the Harrimans living outside the city. The Hudson Valley was never more appealing."

"Exactly."

"So, you suspect that crimes in Central Park are a deliberate scheme for...for frightening us all into the Hudson Valley? Absurd.... Surely that's absurd."

Roddy was quiet. "Let's think about Clayton Philbrick," he said. "The stage door Johnny has distracted us. The engraved cigarette case found by the Pergola has seemed accidental."

I swallowed hard. "You don't think Philbrick might be... could be...involved?"

"I do not suppose anything, but we must open the possibility." Roddy gripped my hand. "Val, it is time to consider the possibility that Clayton Philbrick has committed serious crimes.... I will visit the Philbricks, and you must have your talk with Lola Taylor. This time, Val—" He looked into my eyes with reproof. "This time, try not to be diverted to a gathering of ladies on the Lower East Side."

Chapter Twenty-three

THE RAIN HAD STOPPED, but this morning I would skirt puddles, for I planned to visit the Demple boardinghouse.

Roddy, however, warned me at breakfast of a sudden "dark cloud" looming over my sojourn. "This from the *Herald*, Val," he said. "'*The Black Crook* to open Thanksgiving week and run through Christmas, declares director David Drake.'" He spoke slowly. "'...featured role of Betty Bang-Bang... intense competition ...awarded to Irina James.'"

"Irina James?"

He repeated the name. Roddy did not need to add that I would face a sullen, angry, disappointed young actress at her boardinghouse this morning. Nor that his visit with the elder Philbricks would test his skills as a family friend and inquisitor.

Our little dog snoozed at Roddy's slippered feet. "Nice life," he said.

"Without doubt." The German Junghans clock gonged, my signal to dress for the boardinghouse.

Our coachman was nursing a fierce head cold, so the new groom took the reins on the brougham box seat, and I endured a jolting carriage ride all the way to West Thirty-fifth Street.

Ready or not, I climbed the cracked steps, knocked, and faced Mrs. Demple in her housedress and sweater at eleven forty-five a.m. The landlady did not recognize the woman in the business-like double-breasted suit at her front door. My hair was pinned in a tight bun and the "military" blouse buttoned to the neck. Apart from a thin platinum wedding band, my sole ornament was a sterling lapel pin shaped like an oak leaf. I held a leather portfolio of Roddy's.

The landlady was cowed by the "professional" woman at her doorstep and relieved that the boardinghouse was not to be served legal papers. When asked about Miss Lola Taylor, she opened the book on the foyer table, ran a thick finger down a column of sign-out signatures under today's date, and saw none for Lola Taylor, proving that Miss Taylor must be at home on a floor above.

"They sign out and sign in, or they do not reside at this address. My eyes aren't what they were, but I see to the Demple rule."

Once again, I heard about the very "respectable" Demple boardinghouse until, at last, she sent me to room number six on the third floor.

Again, the same uneven stairs and the wobbly handrail and the yeasty odor of baking bread and boiling cabbage. Again, a dull brass number on a blue door—6.

I knocked softly. "Miss Taylor?"

A muffled voice. "—time is it?"

"A few minutes, if you please."

"—girl needs her sleep."

"Miss Taylor, if you would...?"

Back and forth we went, until my line. "...to make it worth your time, Miss Taylor." A suede purse stuffed with silver dollars was tucked inside Roddy's portfolio. "I can make it worth your time...."

"Wait a minute." Rustling, and then, "Come in...I guess...."

In the narrow door frame, she was an outsized figure against a tiny space crammed with the suitcases and steamer trunk that I recalled from the first visit. Beyond a cot with rumpled sheets and a blanket stood a single upholstered chair with burst seams and one splintered leg. The calendar with pumpkins was propped against a wall, and the china kittens on the floor beside the towering brass candlestick with the same melted wax like a frozen waterfall. A stain darkened the ceiling, and gowns hung like curtains from wall pegs, as if Lola Taylor's clothes were décor. Tobacco odors filled the air, and a glass ashtray with crushed cigarettes lay on the floor by the cot.

Lola's hair had yet to meet a brush, and the kimono once again wrapped her petite frame. She squeezed an atomizer bulb to spray a heavy scent into this small, dark, stuffy room. Droplets hung in the air. "You like gardenia? I like it," she said. "Gardenia or mildew, take your pick."

I fought the sneeze that rose in the thick mist. Lola looked fully awake. "I remember you," she said. "One of the ladies... the one in the dull red suit."

"Russet," I said, a pointless detail.

She eyed my clothing. "What character are you playing today? The lady doctor? The headmistress? Where's your hat?"

I flushed. Calista had offered a deep-crowned hat, but I went bareheaded. "Miss Taylor, may I sit down?" I claimed the chair without waiting. "I hope we might continue the conversation of last Friday—?"

"Without your friend."

I nodded, resolved to keep Cassie out of this. In a voice that tried for sympathy, I said, "I understand that another performer has been chosen for the role you hoped to play in *The Black Crook*."

She looked hard at me. "You heard about the casting couch? Irina James is a star of the casting couch."

"I am sorry."

"Not as sorry as me...." She perched on the cot. "I'm better on the stage. Roxie was too. Our Betty Bang-Bang had Irina beat by a mile. But Roxie remembered her from *Apples from Eden*. She got lines that belonged to Roxie. Same thing this time."

"I am sorry."

"I'm sorrier. Here's my *Black Crook* costume." She reached to lift a suitcase lid and pulled out a spangled, skin-colored garment, then opened the kimono and held it against her. "Neck to ankle," she said, "it's a body suit. There's fifty of us, all alike. The new girls are thrilled. Just out of the sticks, they got a part in a New York City theatre. Biggest deal of their lives, sprung from the farm or a mill. Could've been me a couple of years ago…and poor Roxie…."

She wiped her eyes on the kimono sleeve, careful not to dampen the costume. "You know what this cost? Take a guess?"

I shrugged.

"Nine dollars and sixty-eight cents," she said. "If you don't have it, management lends it to you…half your pay sucked out till they get their money. And Drake makes us practice in it. One tear, and I'll be on the hook for another one."

She laughed without humor. "They think we live on air and water, like plants. They call us 'butterflies' because our lives are short, because nobody thinks we're real human beings."

She folded the costume. "I'd like to wad it up and throw it out the window…if I had a window."

With the costume laid back in the suitcase, she peered at my left hand. "Where's your big diamonds today?"

Again, the actress caught me off guard. "Miss Taylor, please—" I opened the portfolio, reached for the suede purse, and jingled the silver dollars. "I would like to continue our talk about Roxie's gentleman…the man who gave her the orange-and-yellow bouquets. The man she called 'Phil.' Or maybe 'Clayton?'" I held the portfolio open so she would see the coins.

She said, "How much?"

"I beg your pardon?"

"Never mind the pardon, I got bills to pay." She looked hard at me. "And I don't go to the park at night, not anymore. Life happens off the paths, I told you." She wet her lips. "Death too."

She looked away. Somewhere water dripped. I had not decided whether to offer a lump sum or pay the dollars one-by-one, but I would not haggle with this woman. The suede purse held eleven silver dollars.

"Miss Taylor," I said, "I grew up in the West. In mining country, the greenhorns—newcomers—get excited by shiny rocks, which are phony silver. The real silver ore is dull as dirt. We know the difference." I met her gaze. "I am here for a fair trade. What can you tell me about 'Clayton' or 'Phil?' Aren't those two names for the same man?"

She wrapped the kimono tighter, crossed her legs, and spoke in low, matter-of-fact tones. "That yellow moustache," she said. She called him Phil, and he went for her. She was crazy about him, and he fell for her too. She was Cleopatra's maid in *The Wizard of the Nile.* No lines, she just reached into the basket and handed over the snake."

Lola ran a hand through her tangled hair. "He went to every performance, and then he'd wait at the stage door to take her on the town. He followed her to *Apples from Eden*. Same deal."

"Was her only beau this Clayton? Or Phil? The only one?"

She shook her head. "Stage door Johnnys," she said, "thick as flies because Roxie had sparkle. Even in Cleveland, she got better tips than me. It was her hair. They wanted to get lost in her hair." She shrugged. "Roxie caught the fellows' eye, and they wrote her mash notes."

"In Cleveland?"

"Here, in New York. The notes, the Johnnys, and Phil got jealous. I think she liked him jealous."

"How jealous?"

"Jealous enough to marry her, she hoped."

"That's what she wanted?"

"What we all want, lady." She pointed to my hand. "Third finger left hand, that's the diamond we want. All the others, karats galore...." She shrugged. "Only that one counts."

"And she expected a proposal of marriage?"

"She told me he had arrangements to work out. He asked for time."

"What kind of arrangements?"

"I don't know...business. That's what they all say. They show up with diamonds, but a rock won't pay the rent, a diamond bracelet won't buy you dinners. Sometimes you need cash...hard cash. A girl has to go out of her way...like I say, off the paths."

I paused. "And how much time did 'Phil' ask for?"

She bit her lip. "I think winter...maybe spring. They fought over it."

"What kind of fight? A quarrel?"

"She slapped him."

Did I hear this? "*She* slapped him?"

"I think he liked it. But sometimes, she came home bruised...said he got 'hot and bothered' for no reason. I think he scared her sometimes."

I shifted on the chair. "Miss Taylor, do you know Phil's full name?"

"I don't."

"Do you know where he is these days?"

"I wish I did."

"You're certain?" I jiggled the portfolio.

She narrowed her eyes. "Lady, if I knew, I'd go after him."

"For...romance?"

She laughed. "For the jewelry that'll soon be in the Liberty Pawn window," she said, "for the diamond necklace and bracelet and earrings...for the money it's all worth."

She stared hard. "The jewels were Roxie's...all from him. But who went to the pawn shop? Who got pawn shop money to get her out of the morgue? Who gave her brother money for her funeral and a stone with her name on it?"

She sprayed saliva. "Me, I went to the trouble." She clenched her fists. "Phil—? He never once showed his face."

A moment passed. She looked toward the calendar. "November fifth," she said. "A Saturday, I got it marked. The loan is up, the jewelry goes in the window, all for sale." She leaned forward. "Maybe you want more jewels," she said. "I could sell you the pawn ticket."

"I'm afraid not." My right hand closed around the suede purse. "But could we have a few words about other particular gentlemen who were interested in Roxie?"

She eyed the portfolio.

"The 'arrangements' that delayed the proposal of marriage," I said. "I believe your words were, 'That's what they all say.' I'm interested in whoever 'they all' might be, Miss Taylor."

Her eyes flashed like flint. "What are you, some kind of lawyer?"

I jingled the coins. "'Phil' was a special stage door Johnny," I said. "Were others also special?"

Her finger traced a bamboo pattern on the kimono. "What's it worth?"

To bargain with this woman? A bottomless pit. I too could narrow my eyes and could return flint with steel. I pulled out the purse and jiggled it in her direction, all while holding my stare.

The purse won out.

"Maybe another one...." she said.

I waited.

"At the theatre...."

"The Knickerbocker?" I asked.

She nodded. "An old man...pretty old."

"A gentleman?"

Her lips curled. "Lady, a silk top hat and a walking stick, they all look like gents."

I did not veer. "He waited for Roxie after rehearsals, is that it? At the stage door?"

"No. He came in."

"Into the theatre during rehearsal?"

She nodded.

"Aren't rehearsals closed?"

"Supposed to be." She eyed the purse. "He got in, no problem. He stood in the wings, took her by the arm when Drake finally let us out for the night."

"David Drake, the director?"

"That's him. You want to know what we call him on the sly? Simon Legree. Because he drives us like you-know-what."

"This 'gentleman,'" I said, "did he only wait for Roxie?"

She nodded. "Only her."

"How often?"

She held up two fingers, then three. "Maybe three times."

"With permission from the director?"

"Had to be," she said. "The stage door locks on the inside. Somebody let him in." She pushed at her hair. "The rest of us go backstage to change after rehearsal, but Mister Whoever scooped her up, spangled suit and all. And off they went. She never said where."

Lola exhaled, her chest narrowing. "That's all I know. Roxie said she could make him jealous, drive him insane, and he'd give her jewels."

"Jealous of Phil?"

She shrugged. "Never said, and I never asked."

"You don't know his name—?"

"I told you before, they use all kinds of names. You never know."

"Can you describe him?"

She shook her head. "Old gent, gray hair...almost gray. Nothing special...maybe his hair, slicked back...pomade. Who knows, maybe he's an investor. Investors can get in if they feel like it."

She looked ready to claw the purse from my hand.

"Nothing else?"

Eyes closed, her lids fluttered as if to search memory. Was it an act?

"Okay, one thing..." she said at last. "A watch chain, bigger than usual...and a gewgaw on it..." She pointed at the kimono waistline. "Right here...."

"At the naval."

She nodded. "Bellybutton. I saw him twist at it, like a lucky charm. Maybe he needed luck. I caught a good look at his face once. Gave me goose bumps."

She faced me and stood. "I got to get myself ready. A working girl's got rehearsal. The show must go on. She reached for the huge shiny hand mirror and flashed it in front of me. "Now, how about the dollars?"

Her smile became a sneer when she counted the coins I put into her hand.

"Maybe a millionaire Johnny will pick me out of the *Black Crook* lineup next month. Maybe I'll have a ring by Christmas. Maybe you and me will be ladies together. Wouldn't that be swell?"

Chapter Twenty-four

ARM-IN-ARM, RODDY AND I walked up Fifth
Avenue and crossed into the park to make our way to the
Central Park Casino. At this late afternoon hour, the Casino
normally bustled with late-lunch and teatime visitors and
stayed busy until the last diner has finished the evening meal.

The Casino dining rooms, however, were empty at this
four o'clock teatime. We had come to "count the house,"
to learn the truth of rumors that this popular restaurant
might need to close its doors for lack of business. A sea of
empty tables shone with silver and napery, but the space felt
cavernous. "No need to ask the *maître d'hôtel* for a quiet
corner," Roddy said. "We have the whole place to ourselves...
worse than we imagined."

"Far worse...." I unclasped my cloak. "Then again," I
murmured, "the Casino is close to the Pergola, isn't it?"
We paused, each thinking of the space we had viewed

days ago, the spot where the third young woman's body was found.

Where Roxie LaRue's body had been discovered.

"Sir, Madam, good afternoon.... If you please...."

We were shown to a small table by a window in sight of a single carriage and a mounted policeman passing outside on the drive. Not another soul.

In the center of the dining room, a young couple in traveling suits were seated and held hands under the table.

"Newlyweds from out of town," I murmured, "splurging to visit the Empire City. If only they could relax."

"—if all New York could relax," Roddy said, "but not these days."

"No."

The waiter took our drinks order: for me, Appolinaris water and a glass of champagne. For Roddy, the Casino gin fizz.

"Did you make up the recipe?" I asked. "Has the Casino asked for your advice?" My husband's sly smile said he would not tell me. His cocktail consultations were held in confidence. The bartenders got all the credit, but my husband worked behind the scenes to perfect the recipes. Our drinks arrived, and Roddy passed his tall glass to me for a sip.

"Refreshing," I said, but Roddy would be the judge:

The Gin Fizz
Ingredients
- 1 ounce gin
- ½ ounce lemon juice

- ¾ ounce clear syrup
- 1 egg white
- Ice cubes

Directions:
1. Combine gin, lemon juice, syrup, and egg white in cocktail shaker.
2. Shake with vigor.
3. Add 3 or 4 ice cubes.
4. Shake vigorously.
5. Strain into glass, spritz with siphon, and serve.

The waiter approached, and Roddy suggested his cocktail needed a stricter measure of lemon juice. "Just see your head bartender's notebook," Roddy said, and he ordered us cold roast chicken and Saratoga potatoes. "And are you serving many cocktails these days?" he asked. "And your wines?"

The waiter lingered for a moment. Scanning the room, he said, "Not so much these past weeks, sir. Something of a drought in the Casino."

He gave a quick look from our window. "A pleasant day like this, the carriages ought to be going and coming. And the dining room...as you see, sir...madam." He bowed slightly, promised to have a word with the bartender and see about our food, then vanished."

"As I guessed," Roddy said, "the Casino patronage has dropped...another sign that the park is off limits. We had to be certain." He gestured toward the newlyweds. "They're from somewhere else…with the wedding on their minds, they haven't heard the latest."

He raised his glass. "Salud, Val."

I raised my champagne glass. "Tell me about the Philbricks."

Roddy leaned close. "I should have guessed there was much more to Clayton's story. Gladys and Victor have been too frightened and embarrassed to tell the whole Philbrick tale of woe."

I sipped.

"They know about his gambling. It began in prep school with boys' games…marbles, mumblety-peg."

"Harmless fun," I said.

"Pennies and nickels, winners and losers. The headmaster spoke to Victor, and Clayton was disciplined. Gladys thought boys-will-be-boys and persuaded Victor to go easy. And he did. The boys learned their lesson, so they thought.

"College became more serious. The young gentlemen had private suites and brought their valets. Clayton discovered dice—and cards."

"Bridge?" I asked.

"Bridge, whist, poker…take your pick. Clayton learned card tricks and practiced with full decks until he could shuffle and deal the playing cards like a casino operator. He was, at best, a gentlemanly 'C' student. He failed to graduate."

Roddy reached into an inside pocket and put a tiny photograph on the table—a young man on a tennis court wearing a striped tennis blazer. A pale moustache bloomed on his upper lip. "It's a photograph of Clayton as a collegian," Roddy said. "Gladys said she would try to find us a studio portrait. The snapshot is for the time being."

I lifted the tiny square. "This could be any young man with a moustache."

Roddy nodded.

"And if he shaves—?"

"Our hope is his vanity," Roddy said. "His grandmother says the blond upper lip is Clayton's pride and joy. He had it 'barbed' daily at a hair-dressing salon with a barber called André. Maybe I'll pay a call...have a shave."

"And inquire about a young man on the loose," I said.

"And in serious debt." I handed back the photo. Roddy sipped his water. "Victor settled several college debts but fears that others are owed. Clayton would not discuss them. His grandfather admitted that Clayton's inheritance comes semi-annually from a trust fund. He suspects the young man might try hiding somewhere until the fund pays out at the first of the year."

"Nearly three months from now."

Roddy nodded. "Meanwhile, *Town Topics* was ready to publish something like...'Lady Luck Abandons Young Gentleman of Gotham."

I shuddered. The weekly scandal sheet had ripped Cassie and me for an event off Bailey's Beach in Newport last summer. Nicknames and sly hints let the paper avoid lawsuits, but everyone knew that last summer's "Mermaid" was Valentine DeVere, just as Clayton Philbrick was sure to be exposed.

"The paper planned to feature the *City of Brussels* disaster," Roddy said. "Society would recognize Clayton's drowned parents."

"But nothing was published?"

"—because Victor wrote a check to Colonel Mann to keep the scandal out of *Town Topics*."

I took a sip of wine. It was understood that the publisher of the weekly scandal sheet was an extortionist. When Cassie's parents were embroiled in their divorce, her father, Robert Fox, paid a large sum to keep the scandal out of Mann's scathing pages.

"A grandson deep in dept debt goes missing. And the police show up...." I paused. "Of course, the Philbricks are frightened."

"...not only because Clayton is in debt and missing," Roddy said, "but they suspect he is involved with someone who is sinister. Gladys used that word: 'sinister.'"

A word from a cheap melodrama, but chilling.

Roddy bent so close that our heads nearly touched. "Do you remember the Philbricks' longtime business...? Do you? It's quarries," he said. "Rock quarries. The Philbricks blasted rock from the mountains, and the DeVeres hauled the rocks away in carts, wagons, and finally railroads. And there's more...."

"Yes?"

"Gladys admitted she knows what the detective seized from Clayton's apartment. She told me that Finlay took two booklets, 'Rudiments of Chemistry for the Young" and 'Pyrotechnical Celebrations.'"

"Fireworks," I said, "...and explosives."

"Think of the Glen Span Arch here in the park,' Roddy said. "Suppose Clayton Philbrick is the saboteur...and the arsonist...unless he acts for someone else...as a hired 'middleman.' He could be frantic for a way out of his debt. A cornered man is desperate, Val. He will do whatever it takes." Roddy tapped a thumb against his glass. "He will be the stooge of whoever he thinks might help him."

"But who? Who wants to damage Central Park? And why?" I paused. "Another thing, Roddy...one more thing...." I cleared my throat and tried not to sound like speech class at the Fourth Ward School in Nevada. "The three murdered young women," I began, "...they are altogether a different matter." I reached for Roddy's hand and held tightly. "Property," I said quite simply, "is not human life."

As if a bell had tolled, we fell silent, holding hands, our appetites gone as thoughts swirled. The smashed stone bridge, the wood structures, the rowboats...the three young women—none of it made sense.

The moment was too solemn for food, but here it came, the beautiful chicken and the potato slices crisped in hot oil. Our waiter offered to carve, but Roddy took the knife with skill that reminded me of Papa at mealtimes around campfires. ("Another slice for strength, little Valentine," he would say. "You're a growing girl, so eat up.")

"Your favorite wing, Val, and slices. And look, we have companions."

Three ladies in hats of autumn golds were being seated for tea by a far wall and chirping like birds. The newlyweds met their courteous smiles with nervous nods. The young couple looked miserable, their plates barely touched.

Roddy signaled to our waiter. "The young man and woman," he said, "appear to be disappointed in their selections."

"Sir, if I may… visitors from faraway are sometimes displeased by our most popular shellfish."

"Clams Casino?" The waiter nodded. "We would like to extend a New York welcome," my husband continued, "so please suggest that the Casino provide other selections from the menu." Roddy glanced quickly at the couple. "Do include the assorted cakes," he said, "and of course, whatever they choose is charged to this table."

"Thank you, sir."

A moment passed as the center table brightened with cheerful murmurs. "A lovely gesture, Roddy," I said.

He shook his head. "A very small thing, Val, in the midst of horrors…a road to nowhere." He ate a potato crisp. "What would they call it in the West?"

"My papa would say our 'diggings' have got us into a 'blind lode,'" I said.

"Colorful."

"—and another stage door Johnny is no help, but my visit with Lola Taylor added confusion. If I were a dentist, I'd compare the morning to pulling a tooth."

We went on as best we could. I finished my champagne. "No idea who the other man might be?" my husband asked.

"No name, Roddy, just a vague description. He's older, but not yet 'old,' somewhat heavy, the usual evening suit and top hat. Lola remembered that he toyed with a watch chain 'gewgaw,' as she put it. He apparently had easy entry into the theatre during rehearsals."

"No waiting outside with competing Johnnys?"

"No," I said. "She thinks he might be an investor in the show. He waited for her in the wings."

"With flowers?"

"No flowers, but he swept her up the minute the cast was dismissed. She didn't change clothing."

"No idea where they went?"

"None."

Roddy paused. "A public dining room would require a gown."

"What about your Roman lobster palaces?"

"Val, they are not 'my' palaces, and Murray's Roman Gardens expects a woman guest to wear a gown." He gave me a wry look. "I suggest that we soon dine at Murray's or Rector's so you can see for yourself."

"Let's do...as soon as our 'diggings' make sense."

Roddy did not smile. "The second Johnny...was he in the picture at the same time as Clayton?"

"Yes. Lola says Roxie played on the men's rivalry to get jewelry. The two women kept their own secrets. Lola knew about Clayton because of the flowers and the jewels, but Roxie did not discuss the other man. Apparently, she went with him willingly, but Lola said the sight of him gave her goose flesh."

"She hasn't seen him since Roxie's death?"

"I don't think so. I'm not sure." We fell silent, and I thought of the questions I had failed to ask. Did Lola see the second man after her friend's murder? Did she have information I had not tapped?

Roddy's frown meant that questions might gnaw at him too, whether the grandparents shaded the truth to protect the young man.

I said, "You don't suppose that Gladys and Victor know where Clayton is hiding?"

A long moment passed. "No," Roddy said, "I don't think they have any idea."

I looked outside at the drive, the trees, the expansive lawns. The evening advanced, and sundown approached. "Roddy, I said, "before we leave the Casino, there's something I must ask...."

He looked up with that certain tilt of head, open to my thoughts, so endearing.

"About the park," I said, "the beginnings."

He smiled. "More park history? You got a heavy dose when we walked with the Forsters. I thought we bored you silly."

"It's the land clearance…" I began, "the 'vagrants' who were 'removed.'"

"Squatters," Roddy said. "Scavengers…petty criminals."

"I heard a different account," I said.

"Oh? What did you hear?"

I put down my utensils and sipped the tea. "I was told that the park acreage was called 'Uptown Land.'"

"It was. The city hub was downtown."

"—but those who lived on it were not 'squatters' or 'scavengers.'" Roddy looked puzzled. "I was told the people worked in carpentry and domestic work… gardening, tailoring…the trades …."

My husband looked bewildered.

"They were employed, Roddy. They earned wages. Not only that, but some of them owned property…the property we're sitting on right now. That's what I heard."

Roddy's mouth opened slightly. "I never…" he began. "Who told you such a story?"

I could have predicted my husband's response when I said, "Annie Flowers."

"That woman…." Exasperation on the rise, Roddy snapped down his fork. "Val, that Flowers woman is no end of mischief. How we helped her…got her out of jail for—"

"—for promoting votes for woman. For suffragist action."

"For making a public nuisance of herself. You ladies will get the vote in due time, but splashing in a public fountain cannot aid the cause."

I lowered my voice and spoke slowly. "Roddy, Annie Flowers sounded sure of her facts. I am simply inquiring whether you ever heard about the people on the 'Uptown Land' ...before it became Central Park."

"Never."

"Would you ask your father?"

"My father," he said, "or the elders on the Dewey committee." He reached for my hand. "I want to quash the rumor before it hardens into a 'fact' in your thoughts. Our wonderful park...it's not Eden, but the 'lungs' of the city give breath to us all. To slander Central Park with a crackpot story...it ought to be legally actionable."

I did not respond. The tremulous moment continued as we departed the Casino and went on foot from the park down Fifth Avenue to our home. The daylight was fast fading, the air chilly, and we quickened our pace to count off the numbered streets from the Seventies into the Sixties, a countdown that pitted us against the setting sun.

Crossing into our block, Roddy tightened his grip on my arm. We had slowed at the sight of a man pacing back and forth in front of our house. Like an impatient sentry, he pivoted and marched back and forth on the sidewalk in the dusk. Swinging long arms, he looked vaguely familiar, and, seeing us approach, he stopped to recognize us, as we recognized him.

"Detective Finlay," Roddy said.

"Your butler would not admit me," he said, "but he said you might soon return. I am here about a new case." He stepped very close. "A young woman was attacked in the park last night. She fled the assailant who tried to strangle her, and she's lucky to be alive."

Chapter Twenty-five

"JUST AFTER NINE p.m.," Finlay said, "near the Promontory."

Roddy winced. "That close."

We three huddled in our nearest drawing room, and a footman lighted an electrical wall sconce, which cast a dim glow. "That will be all, Bronson," Roddy said. "And no, you needn't summon Mr. Sands."

Finlay sat across from us and unbuttoned his peacoat. "She was crossing the park alone and tackled from behind... like football. She went face down, and the attacker slammed and choked her..."

"—choked from behind?" Roddy asked. "The attack was not frontal?"

"We think, from behind."

"We?" asked Roddy.

"The officer that heard her scream...Brennan, a man I know well. The attacker ran off, and Brennan chased him."

"—leaving the young woman?" I asked.

"Brennan couldn't...the attacker got away. A park policeman heard Brennan's whistle and came to assist."

"Assist the woman?" I asked.

Finlay nodded.

"And then the two officers helped her...or tried to."

"Tried...?" Roddy asked.

"'Hysterical,'" that's what Brennan told me. She tried to fight them off...bit the park policeman, took a chunk out of his thumb, couldn't listen to reason...like a sailor that falls from a yardarm and slams to the deck."

Roddy and I exchanged puzzled glances.

"Confused and hurting," Finlay said. "Both men lifted her, but she kicked like the police were on the attack."

"Was she taken to a hospital?" I asked.

"That would be her employer's call."

"I don't understand," I said.

Finlay let out a big breath. "She wouldn't say her name or where she lived. Brennan found a laundry slip in her jacket with an address on Sixty-fifth Street. He and the park officer carried her there, kicking and yelling her head off, but she fainted before they got her to the door. Turns out, she's a housemaid at that residence."

"Fortunate," I said.

He nodded. "The housekeeper was waked up, and the lady of the house too. They helped bring her in, but she woke up crazy. The housekeeper settled her down with laudanum."

"Opium for women," Roddy said.

"Dead to the world after that, Brennan said. Both officers left, and Brennan told me all about it first thing this morning. So, I paid a call at the residence by midday, to find out more…if the woman was in her right mind."

"You spoke with her?" Roddy asked.

He slumped in his chair. "Tried my best. They fixed her up in a little sitting room off the kitchen."

"In the basement?" I asked.

"Basement," he said. "She was propped up on a sofa, but one look at me, and she fainted…swooned. Maybe it was real, maybe fake, but the maids and the cook stood around like mother hens, and I got nothing. Maybe she talked to the servants, but not to me. 'Poor Mattie,' they said, so that's her first name. I finally gave them my cards, and left." He raked his fingers through hair that looked whiter than ever.

"Roddy said, "You are certain that she was attacked in the park? No doubts?"

"None. Officer Brennan is a true blue shipmate. One thing he remembered, the sound of the attacker running off…clean running. Like he knew where he was going."

We stopped to take this in. A clock chimed on the half-hour.

"Mr. Finlay," I asked, "why are you reporting all this to us?"

He looked at the bridge of my nose. "The house where she works is three blocks from here, Mrs. DeVere. It's your neighborhood, and she could have been one of your maids. Could you ask those folks to persuade her to talk to me?"

He fingered a peacoat button and reached for his notebook. "Number Four, Sixty-fifth Street."

I searched my mental map, but Roddy was faster. "The Martendale house," he said. "Three blocks away."

Finlay nodded.

"We are barely acquainted with the Martendales," I said. "We are not close friends."

The detective held his gaze. "It's your neighborhood, Mrs. Devere." He buttoned his peacoat. "In the interest of the neighborhood, I call on you to assist law enforcement in our city. I call on you to help us with the utmost speed. We're tacking against strong winds, and our sails must be trimmed tight."

With that, he stood, and Roddy showed him to the door.

⌒⌒⌒

"That damnable nautical talk," Roddy said. "Excuse my language, but Finlay ought to speak like the cop that he is…'yardarm,' for godsake."

"It's his native tongue, Roddy. And we agreed we'd help him. Will you tell him what you learned about Clayton's gambling? And your other suspicions?"

"I'll start with Clayton's barber. The detective ought to have a haircut by André."

"Roddy, admit it, Finlay rubs you the wrong way."

My husband loosened his collar. "Maybe so, Val. I don't trust the man. And I resent him yanking us into his case…

the appeals to my great-grandfather, and now our neighborly conscience."

"We are his best bet, Roddy. He's afraid he'll be fired if he doesn't solve this case."

"Then he can go back to sea."

"Oh, Roddy...."

My husband suddenly looked sheepish. "Sorry, Val.... I don't mean to bicker. It's just...I like to think that we make our own moves, not bossed around by a detective."

"Then I have a proposal. Never mind clearing the way for Finlay to interview the Martendales' maid." I rose to my full five feet, seven inches. "I'll be the one to question 'Mattie.' I'll write to Priscilla Martendale immediately. The sooner that 'Mattie' talks, the fresher her memory."

I recalled meeting Mrs. Martendale, who poured my cup of Oolong at an afternoon tea hosted by Carrie Wilson a year ago. As I remembered, Priscilla was a stickler for etiquette. Cassie had compared her to Emily Post, who is writing a manual on manners.

Roddy said "Fair warning, Val...the Martendales were good friends of the DeVeres until my father bought a horse from Arthur. The roan filly was infested with worms."

I grimaced.

"And you remember Arthur Martendale at last year's Bicycle Tea?" Roddy said. "How Eli embarrassed him?"

"So vicious," I said.

"Payback from a real estate deal gone sour, most likely. Martendale holds a good deal of property in the city, and he competes with Fryer. And Eli Fryer holds grudges. He probably waited for Arthur's foot to slip off his bicycle pedal so he could fire away."

Roddy took my hand. "Arthur is a hale-and-hearty fellow, always up for a good time, but Mrs. Martindale is a New Englander going way back to the *Mayflower*...starchy." He held my fingertips. "About the note you'll write to her, my dear...would you like help? I'm sure my mother...."

"No worries, Roddy," I said. "I'll do it right away." I pounded upstairs to my writing desk, thrust a sheet of the monogrammed stationary in front me, took up a pen and ink, and—stopped. Thoughts of my mother-in-law inspecting handwriting and word choices raised hackles, but a faulty note could be a deadend.

How to request access to a maid recovering from a murderous attack in the park? I plucked *Manners, Culture, and Dress for the Best American Society* and found Chapter Thirteen: "Letters and Letter Writing." Pages of samples appeared...Letters to Parents, to Children...the Family Letter, the Friendly Letter...."not too formal...nor too great familiarity."

I snatched phrases and strung them like beads. "I take the liberty...not without purpose...I pray you to accept... earliest convenience...a kind inquiry...on behalf of...."

I rang for a footman to dispatch the note that was properly folded, sealed in a matching monogrammed envelope, and addressed to Mrs. Arthur Martendale in Palmer Method handwriting learned at the Fourth Ward School in Nevada.

Bronson ferried a reply to my note. In penmanship that danced a ballet, it welcomed a visit tomorrow morning at nine o'clock. I got ready for a restless night. My bedtime reading would be *Manners* on "Conversation." ("The finest compliment that can be paid to a woman of refinement is to lead the conversation into such a channel as may mark your appreciation of her superior attainments.")

Etiquette "cramming" and bumpy dreams took me to Sixty-fifth Street the dot of 9:05 a.m. the next morning, when I offered my hand to the ivory-complexioned Priscilla Martendale, whose sharp dark eyes and soft, delicate mouth seemed at odds in a narrow face with a pointed chin and eyebrows arching nearly to the hairline.

We quickly became Priscilla and Valentine in the Louis drawing room whose silk wall panels almost matched her mauve morning dress and slippers. Pleasantries were exchanged, tea offered and declined, and my hostess took the lead before I could ease into "Mattie."

"You have an interest in our injured housemaid, Valentine? I should think the matter would best be left to the police. A detective was here last night, and no one had a decent night's rest, except Mr. Martendale. I did not awaken him. He needs his sleep. But the park is a matter for the police."

"We all have an interest, don't we, Priscilla?" I said. "The park—"

"—forbidden to the servants in this household all this autumn." Her mouth suddenly hardened. "I issued strict instructions, and I feel quite cross with our housemaid. Not that she is blameworthy for her injuries, but she will set an example to others, including the footmen and gardeners."

She smoothed an invisible crease in her skirt. "This young woman's disobedience is especially troubling because she is an American. Our staff is principally Irish and Swedish, but Mr. Martendale encouraged me to try her....a favor to me, since she grew up in my ancestral Massachusetts."

She twisted her wedding diamonds, one eyebrow rising higher. "I am willing to let her recover, Valentine, but she will be summarily dismissed."

"Dismissed..."

"And without a favorable reference, which will send a clear message to our servants and to all households in this part of our city." She spaced her words. "The message will be clear: to trespass in the park will cost your position."

"That single mistake..." I began. "Possibly fatal, was it not?"

"—fatal to a housemaid's employment in the Martendale home, yes indeed, Valentine. But the dismissal will deter all servants in this neighborhood from meandering into the park. Until safety is assured, the Martendale household is performing a great service to friends and neighbors. My Puritan ancestors from New England had the right idea. Those who misbehaved were put into the stocks for all to see."

"Shamed," I said.

"...to keep order in the village." Her mouth softened, but Priscilla's eyes bored into mine. "We reside in a sort of village, do we not, Valentine?

With the *Manners* manual urging flattery, I murmured, "Village, yes, so important...and service...to one and all."

Priscilla Martendale smiled, her features wreathed in triumph. On the edge of her needlepoint chair cushion, she signaled the moment for my departure.

How possibly to get past this fortress of a woman to see the maid?

Quite simply, I concocted a fast lie.

"Priscilla," I said, leaning close in confidence, "Mr. DeVere and I suspect that your American maid has been keeping company with one of our grooms, and I have promised Mr. DeVere to find out."

I gripped my gloves. "You see, Priscilla, the groom was overheard to say the name, 'Mattie' quite recently."

She listened, unmoving.

"Is it possible, Priscilla, that the maid's name is, in fact, Mattie? If so, I would be very grateful for the opportunity to speak directly to her. As one lady to another, you understand that I dare not return to my home until I can satisfy Mr. DeVere on that point...for we both understand that pleasing our husbands is of utmost importance...." I smiled and fluttered my fingers at my gloves.

And that is how I gained access to the basement sitting room of the Martindale home.

Chapter Twenty-six

"I THINK HE BROKE my nose."

"I'm sorry," I said.

The broad-faced young woman had answered to "Mattie" and managed "How Do You Do" through swollen lips as she searched my face with bloodshot eyes. She lay covered in stiff blankets on an Empire sofa in a musty sitting room off the Martendales' basement kitchen, where pots already bubbled on the stove. Ointment glistened on a cut at her chin.

"Banged up, that girl," a brawny kitchen maid muttered when she pointed to a chair and closed the door. A vase of wilting yellow chrysanthemums lay on a table beside the sofa, and assorted chairs and one candelabra made this space the Martendale servants' sitting room. Daylight filtered through a dirty basement window. I pulled up the chair and sat close to the sofa.

"How do you know if your nose is broken?" Mattie asked in the slightly nasal voice that harkened to New England, though not Theo's Beacon Hill Boston.

"Broken? I'm not sure," I said.

She patted her nose. "—blessing my teeth weren't knocked out."

I nodded, equally blessed after cascading down hillsides in Colorado mining country.

This was no moment to relay my mishaps. "Mattie," I said, "bruises do heal, but can you move your arms and legs?"

Her limbs stirred under the blanket. "Everything hurts," she said. "...hurts like when Mrs. Martendale makes us scrub the marble stairs on our knees. The heavy scrub buckets... our aching backs."

"But your arms and legs...your ankles...neck...." I stopped. Grey's *Anatomy of the Human Body* was in Roddy's study, but I was in over my head. "Has Mrs. Martendale offered to call a doctor?"

"I said *no* to that. It would come out of my wages, so it's no...." She slowly raised an arm and touched her chin. "The housekeeper put salve on my cut...knees too."

I would not ask to look under the blanket.

"Could you tell me...tell what happened?"

"My dress pulled up when he pushed me...from behind. I crashed down on a rock...or maybe roots. It was dark."

"The man who pushed you...it was definitely a man?"

"He grunted," she said, "grunted and growled deep... like, 'got you' or 'get you'...like a bear on top of me. His beard was on my neck...I smelled his breath...."

"Did he have a moustache?" I asked. "A yellow moustache?"

"On my neck...his hot breath...I know that smell, rotten teeth. And he grabbed at my throat."

Tears welled in her bloodshot eyes. At the moment she could not hear my questions.

"If I hadn't screamed...."

"But you did scream, and the police came to help." I gently touched her hand. "Did you see a moustache?"

"—top of my lungs, I screamed bloody murder."

Eyes shut, her hand clawed at the blanket.

"Mattie," I finally said, "may I ask why you decided to go into Central Park? Didn't Mrs. Martendale warn you not to enter the park?"

She tried to sit up. "Over and over, she did. But it was my evening off...my own time."

She searched my face, jacket, and scarf, as if to gauge trust. "The Martendales don't fool us," she said. "They think the park is for them, not the servants. It's supposed to be their private garden."

"—a public park," I said, "open to all."

Her eyelids fluttered. "So they say, but servants know better. We're to walk by the river with the stinking shanties and the stables and manure pits. We know our place."

To argue would be futile. I softly said, "So your walk in the park last evening was...your choice, on your own time?"

"Not exactly. I had an appointment," she said at last. "A friend waited for me."

"In the park?"

"No…near the statue of Christopher Columbus up high on the pole."

"Columbus Circle," I said, "at the south edge of the park, on the west side."

She nodded, flinched in pain, and whispered, "Yes."

"You decided to cross the park?"

"A short cut…," she said.

"And your appointment…?"

"He drives a hack," she said. "He promised me a ride in his night-hawk."

I nodded. The Livery stables rented all sorts of carriages, but "night-hawks" were the worst, usually lurking under "El" stations for passengers. The carriages were dilapidated, the horses broken at the knees.

"He's from Worcester," she said, "that's Massachusetts, where I was from."

"*Was* from?"

"A tobacco farm, way west in the valley" she said. "Eight brothers and sisters, and we worked the fields." She studied the blanket. "Tobacco makes you sick to touch the leaves. So, I quit school and went to Lynn…Lynn, Massachusetts. I lied about my age, and they hired me in a shoe shop."

"Selling shoes?"

"A *factory*," she said, as if the word had no other meaning. "It was wintertime…cold as ice, but the shop was steaming hot. I turned the leather into little seams and mashed them with a hammer. Twelve hours a day, Sunday off, and I got paid by the pair...worked up to four dollars a week."

She sighed. "Worse than tobacco. I was slow with the hammer, and the foreman lady said I should do housework." She gave a crooked smile. "And so here I am."

"All the way to New York City," I said. A pointless phrase, though Mattie seemed to be steadied.

"The policemen last night," I said, "I believe you misunderstood them."

"I did not."

"They tried to help."

She raised her eyes to mine. "They've got me fired from my job, Mrs...Mrs....."

"DeVere," I said.

"DeVere," she repeated. "If the cops brought me here, they'd tell where they got me. 'Central Park,' they'd say, and Mrs. Martendale would know, and that's that. She gave fair warning. Anybody that works for the Martendales and gets caught in the park gets fired." She paused. "And that's me."

I had no answer. I reached for a calling card in my skirt pocket. "I live close by," I said. "If you...if you need help, the address is on this card. Show the card at the door. Do you have a pocket?"

"I have a stocking," she said, and closed the card in her hand and under the blanket.

"Before you go, Mrs. DeVere," she said, "Would you touch my nose and tell me what you think? My friend says it's my best feature, and I hope it's not broken."

Detective Finlay perched on a fawn tapestry loveseat with his peacoat folded beside him, an open notebook across one knee. Roddy had telephoned Mulberry Street headquarters to request the visit and Finlay arrived promptly, expecting to interview the maid herself and irritated that facts would come from me. His pencil had scratched hard this last hour. Roddy sat beside me on a small sofa.

"You have no idea who the 'friend' might be, Mrs. DeVere? The 'friend at Columbus Circle?'"

"—only that he drives a night hawk livery cab, Mr. Finlay." I repeated the point for the third or fourth time.

"Night hawk…" the detective echoed.

"So, the night hawk driver must be a man, mustn't it?" I said. "Only men are allowed to drive liveries in New York." My voice soured, and Roddy gave me his "warning" nudge. This interview dragged on. Never mind that I had learned to handle the reins of a Conestoga pair of draft horses to pull a wagonload of lumber in Nevada.

"And once again, you didn't learn her full name? Just 'Mattie'"?

"Just 'Mattie,' Maybe it's short for Matilda. I ought to have asked her full name."

The detective nodded.

Roddy bristled.

My cheeks got warm.

"I believe housemaids are usually called by their surnames," Finlay said. "'Mattie' is rather odd."

He made another note. Roddy was eager to see Finlay to the door, but the detective flipped pages to review his notes.

"Think back just one more time, Mrs. DeVere," he said, "if you will."

His eyes narrowed like gray agates. I glanced from the window at the skeletal treetops in the distance in the park. "I don't mean to squabble," I said, "but surely we don't imagine the housemaid staged her own attack."

Finlay did not answer. "I was thinking further," he said, "about the attacker's voice. She said it was deep…like a foghorn?"

"A deep growl, as I said, Mr. Finlay. And possibly 'got you' or 'get you.' I don't know about foghorns."

Which was not entirely true, for I heard them in San Francisco with my papa when the city was in "pea soup" fogs.

"But Clayton Philbrick has a tenor voice," Roddy said. "His grandparents heard him sing in the church choir… definitely tenor."

"And the attacker's breath—" I said, "Mattie remembers how foul. Her words were, 'rotten teeth.'"

"But no yellow moustache,"

"Only 'whiskers,' Mr. Finlay," I said.

"A description," he said, "to fit ninety-nine of a hundred men in the city." Notebook shut, he rose, took his coat, and thanked me for my time, and hoped I could soon be his envoy to the Martindale home. At the front door, Sands ushered him out.

"...far beyond thorough," said Roddy.

It was nearly lunch time. "I did not tell him that Mattie would soon be dismissed," I said.

"His 'grilling' would have gone on for another hour."

"Roddy," I said, "about the teeth...please ask Gladys and Victor about their grandson's dental health."

My husband sighed. "Bad teeth and a basso growl...but no yellow moustache. What's your papa's old saying about a failed mine...a blind lead?"

"Blind lode," I said, "but maybe Finlay can make it pay off."

"Maybe...but before we have lunch...something I saved for you." Roddy reached into his blazer pocket. "Interesting column in this morning's *Herald*." He plucked out a clipping and read aloud, "'**Black Crook** *Star Turn... Hallowe'en Haunts New Production...Actress Gravely Injured... Free Fall Plunge...Irisa James Out....*'"

"Irisa James...? Roddy, that name.... She's the Annie Oakley character...the Betty Bang-Bang. What happened?"

I snatched the clipping. "'catwalk rigging...'" I read, "'falling star... no high-flying for Broadway starlet this holiday... precipitous tumble...merciful catch...juggler juggles falling star...prayers for recovery...out for the stuff.'" Then the predictable puns on "featured cast in casts...arm and leg...."

I looked for a picture. No picture. "It sounds as though another performer caught her," I said.

"A juggler," said Roddy. "*The Black Crook* sounds like a three-ring circus. Crazy."

"Roddy, did you see this at the end? '...replaced by the daring and dazzling Miss Lola Taylor...visits Miss James... tears flow at hospital bedside...declares show must go on... Taylor insists heights thrill, no fear of falling.'"

The clipping crackled in my hand. "Roddy, what do you make of this...something about a frayed rope...denial that any rope frayed. Why issue a denial if the matter hasn't come up?"

He took my hand. "The trapeze accident isn't our concern, Val. Let's not get sidetracked. Promise?"

I promised, yet gazed once again at the distant treetops in the park. "Roddy," I said, "about your father...have you asked him about the park? When it was 'Uptown Land?'"

"I gave it a try, Val."

"But—?"

A certain expression reminded me of my husband as a guilty schoolboy. "It's not an easy topic," he said. "And consider the source...."

"Annie Flowers..." I said.

"We know nothing about her...."

"She has a job with a new organization that promotes safe workplaces," I said. "She has learned typewriting...a modern skill."

"To write malicious rumors?"

"She offered information," I said, "which might have merit."

"Merit?" Palms slapped on his desk. "Val, I'll settle this thing this afternoon."

"Your father?"

"No, the Dewey Committee. Two or three are old enough to remember chumming with Olmsted and Vaux...if they don't fall asleep at the table."

He straightened papers on the desktop. "Trust me, I will find out about the 'Uptown Land.' I hope to hear no more about it."

We left it at that. Roddy reviewed documents for his meeting, and I caught up on correspondence from the Mackle Trust in Virginia City. A few household duties loomed but stalled when Calista brought out a paper-wrapped parcel.

"Ma'am, this package has been on a back shelf for a few days. It feels like the paper got wet and dried. It feels like a book."

"Oh, yes," I said, "I forgot... a souvenir from Henry Street."

The twine and brown wrapping somehow brought Annie Flowers barging into my boudoir.

Tempted to send the package back to a far shelf, I said, "Yes, let's open it," then reached for my Barlow knife and slit the twine. Calista slipped off the paper. "What is it?" I asked.

"The title is," she said, "*How the Other Half Lives*. The author is Jacob...." She spelled the name, "R-i-i-s. And should I take a quick peek, ma'am?" I nodded.

"It seems to have...a good many pictures, ma'am. I suggest you not look at them now." Calista's eyes widened. "The photographs, ma'am...of poor people. Ragged children... here in New York City. Too sad, ma'am, and it's early in the day. You better not...."

Closing the book, she stopped at the flyleaf. "It seems to be dedicated to you, ma'am."

"Can you read what it says?"

She cleared her throat. "'To Valentine DeVere... Best wishes for reading the book with secrets from the Uptown Land... Most sincerely yours....'" Calista looked up. It's signed with initials, ma'am."

I would guess an A and an F," I said.

"Yes, ma'am. Shall I help with your hair? A.F. it is."

Chapter Twenty-seven

"VAL, PLEASE COME JOIN me. Come look at this map of Central Park... I'm in the *Fleur de Lis* room. Val...? Val...?"

Roddy's voice called from afar, as if we were in different lands instead of two nearby rooms on the first floor. I had spent hours on a sofa with *How the Other Half Lives*, immersed in devastating photographs of immigrant groups...Chinatown, Jewtown...Italians and Irish too...and back-alleys choked with waifs and paupers...terrible pictures of girls in tatters and ragged boys hunched in alleyways. They scowled at the camera, their lives haunted in ways new to me. The rough Colorado mining camps had been filled with men and women whose eyes sparkled with hope for a better day despite hard and narrow lives. They had no stockings, and their boots rotted off their feet. They burned pine knots to keep warm and chased off bears that went for the wild berries they hunted for themselves. All the while, they saw a better day ahead. The scenes of the Lower East Side in this city, however, looked like circles of Dante's Hell.

"Val…? Valentine…can you hear me?"

"Coming, Roddy…coming." I jammed the book behind a cushion and wrenched my mind from the tenements. My husband's voice called me from a place as dark as Papa's deepest mine…deeper.

I found Roddy leaning over a table in the *Fleur de Lis* drawing room. A document was anchored with stone chess pieces at the corners. Every light in the room blazed, and Velvet snoozed under the table.

This was not the moment to bring up the Lower East Side.

"Val, are you feeling well? You look distressed. I thought you spent the afternoon reading. I thought you relaxed with a book…."

"…with a book," I mumbled. My mouth felt dry, my shoulders stiff. The tenements ran through my mind, but I gestured at the table. "What is this?"

"…the Bogart and Sibeth map of Central Park," Roddy said, "the engineer and the draftsman. I dug it out of my study. Look with me…Val, can you listen? Perhaps you need a few minutes?"

I stepped close as Roddy's warm palm touched my cheek. "The map can wait," he said. My spirited husband caressed a downcast woman at his side. "Something has upset you," he said. "The servants…Mrs. Thwaite?"

The housekeeper's name jarred me into the moment, a touch of the absurd. "I'll be fine, Roddy. Show me the map."

His voice deepened as his finger traced each area. "You see the greenery and drives and the walkways…all to scale." Roddy pointed to different shades of green for the foliage, blue for the waters. "…and see the places where sabotage happened… the Boathouse, the Glen Span Arch…Shadow Bridge…the Sheep Meadow…and here's the West Drive Arbor…." Roddy's finger moved quickly. "Here's the Promontory where the Martendales' maid was attacked…so near the Pond."

"—where we walked Velvet days ago."

"And here…" Roddy paused, searched my face, and pointed again. "…where the two young women were found, the first two bodies…."

I shuddered. "…strangled…."

Roddy nodded. "Yes, those are the sites, and we know the Pergola…but I've been mapping ideas about the crimes, Val…and about Clayton Philbrick. Let me start with the young gambler's losses that put him in debt to somebody that his grandmother called 'sinister.' The Philbrick family fortune came from blasting rocks, and wouldn't Clayton be just the man to use for 'sinister' sabotage?"

Roddy stepped to the side of the table and pointed to the north end of the map. "Look here…these streets, 100th to 105th on the West side…. Manhattan marches north to an area called Bloomingdale and Manhattanville. Land values are rising."

Roddy pointed to a green and beige edge of the park boundary. "Look here…a neglected section where real estate 'interests' are nosing in."

"What 'interests?'"

He straightened his shoulders. "That's what I heard at the Dewey committee meeting today—a rumored appeal to the Board of Commissioners to consider rezoning the park at its northwest corner...for private possession."

"Private...? Roddy, you told me the park is officially set aside for 'the public and posterity.' Forever."

My husband was seldom cynical, but his lip curled at the corner. "This is New York, Val. 'Forever' does not apply. The Boss Tweed years are over, but greed never ends."

My voice rose. "Whose real estate 'interest,' Roddy?'"

"You can guess."

"Eli Fryer?"

Anger shadowed my husband's face. "No name was spoken, Val, but let's look at the map again. I've been thinking... here's the route of the Bicycle Tea. Eli could have planned it with his own copy of this same map."

A sour reminder of the Tea, but the route wormed through bridle paths and carriage drives as I followed Roddy's finger to the boathouse. "Those boats on fire..." I said. "I can still smell the smoke."

"And the Glen Span Arch, Val...the boulders now under repair for 'mistakes' by the stone masons...to hide the sabotage...."

I turned to my husband. "And you suspect Eli Fryer is behind these crimes...."

"To downgrade the park," he said, "to increase crime and scare people off."

"I looked back at the map. "So, the Bicycle Tea," I said, "...the miserable afternoon, those 'Headless Horseman' quotes.... Was it planned to scare everybody? Hard to believe, Roddy. Eli Fryer loves the Tea, thinks he owns it."

"He loves money and power more." Roddy fingered the route from Columbus Circle once again. "Consider the cyclists—the young Vanderbilt women, the Bains, Mrs. Ogden Mills, Carrie Wilson...."

"Carrie *Astor* Wilson, the daughter of *the* Mrs. Astor, the queen of New York Society."

"So, suppose," Roddy said, "that everybody reported how nasty the cycling afternoon. Every cyclist would spread a negative report on Central Park."

"And the sale of a few acres would not be out of the question."

"—might be welcomed," Roddy said. "That's Eli, no stone unturned. First, lessen the value of the park, and then let a private interest step in to develop parcels of property and reap a fortune. One more fortune." A moment passed. "Shall we have a drink?"

We went to our favorite sitting room. Roddy pulled up a small table and signaled Bronson for the wheeled bar cart. "Something light, Val?"

"Something robust," I said.

Roddy stood to look over the bottles, scratched his chin, and said, "I will make for us...a drink in tribute to Old New York, the Knickerbocker...in an Atlantic spiral glass."

The Knickerbocker

Ingredients

- 1 wineglass Jamaica rum
- 1 dash Curaçao
- 3 dashes raspberry syrup
- Juice of ½ lemon or lime
- Cracked ice

Directions:

1. Squeeze lemon or lime into mixing glass with small amount of ice.
2. Add all other ingredients.
3. Stir well, stain, and serve in fancy glass.

"What do you think?" Roddy asked.

"Sweet," I said, "and robust too. One day soon, you'll make one for Dudley and Cassie...when this nightmare ends."

"I'll drink to that."

Visions of the flaming boathouse lingered. "Roddy," I said, "Eli Fryer's scheme...sabotage.... He couldn't commit these crimes alone."

"No." My husband rubbed his chin. "Right now, I'm thinking of the stockbroker who remembered Clayton driving away from the Templars Club with a 'Real Estate' man with pomaded hair.

"Fryer."

"—and I'm thinking of the pamphlets that Finlay seized from Clayton's rooms...on explosives." Roddy paused. "So, suppose that Fryer got wind of young Philbrick's gambling debts and agreed to pay them if certain destructive acts took place in Central Park...."

Roddy sipped his drink. "A Real Estate man knows what goes on in every part of town, and a wealthy young man known to play cards frequently in the city's gambling dens would be noticed. For his part, the young man would recognize the 'buzzards' that roost by the doors and do dirty jobs for cash." My husband gazed at the fire. "For a sabotage agreement to pay off his gambling debts, Clayton would take a 'deposit' from Eli, which both men would call a 'business expense.' Clayton would get his marching orders—and cash."

"And then—?"

"Simply this... Clayton Philbrick could leave a betting parlor in the Lower East Side or the Bowery. He'd scout for a muscleman, take him to a saloon for whiskey and outline a deal. He'd mention a 'pal' that needs jobs to be done by a firebug and a man that's handy with a stick of dynamite and a knife."

"But the 'pal' is him?"

Roddy nodded. "And flammable fuel and explosives are easy to get hold of in the city."

"But the 'muscleman' would set the fires and blow up the bridges, and kill the sheep?" Employed by Clayton Philbrick...and Eli Fryer?"

"But never to know Philbrick's name, let alone Fryer's" Roddy said. "The jobs get done, the cash changes hands, and no one is the wiser."

"Sabotage for a price," I said. "But whoever attacked the Martendales' maid has rotten teeth and a deep voice." I paused. "The 'muscleman' Roddy...would he also attack a young woman near the Promontory if the price was right?

Roddy sipped his drink. "Why not?"

We sat with our drinks. "Roddy," I said, "what about the murders... Do you think it could be Clayton? All by himself?"

"You're asking, could the young man overpower young women fighting for their lives? My answer is.... if he fights in a rage...yes, he'd be a 'Hot Lava' killer."

A silent moment passed. I drained my glass. You saw the Philbricks today. "What did Gladys and Victor have to say?"

"Very little, Val." Roddy put his glass down. "They have aged ten years in the past few days. Victor wants to offer a reward...to advertise in the newspapers. Gladys is horrified at the thought of publicity. They asked me for advice."

"And—?"

"And I urged them to wait, give the police more time. I even put in a good word for Finlay...lying through my teeth to help them feel better."

"And Clayton's teeth?" I asked.

Roddy's expression turned wry. "The Philbricks affirm their grandson has taken very good care of his 'pearly whites.'"

The fireplace logs crackled and sparks skittered on the hearth. "Roddy," I said, "The Martendales' maid was on her way to meet a 'friend' when she was attacked. She's being fired for disobeying Priscilla's rule. She needs a job, a place to stay. I gave her my calling card. We could hire her for a time, help her get back on her feet."

"The milk of human kindness?"

"Not entirely. The 'friend' she planned to meet drives a night hawk, and maybe rumors get around in the livery stables. Maybe we can catch a break...for once. And Roddy," I said, "there might be another way to help answer some questions. Do you know the book, *How the Other Half Lives*?

"Riis," he answered. "By Jacob Riis."

"Then you know."

"'About' it, yes."

"You haven't read it? Or seen the pictures?"

My husband shook his head. "It's a book about immigrants, isn't it? Are you thinking about your folks...from Ireland? What's the book got to do with the Central Park crimes?"

"Possibly nothing," I said, "but I'm not sure. Here's how the I happened to get Riis's book...."

I tried to be patient, slowly recounting the meeting on Henry Street, the Consumers League, the wrapped-up book, and how Calista retrieved it from a closet shelf. I expected Roddy's exasperation at the sound of name, Annie Flowers.

Instead, my husband quietly picked up Velvet, settled her in his lap, and gazed at the table where the map was anchored by knights and bishops. "So, you'll seek out the Flowers woman? Is that it?"

"Roddy," I said, "I doubt that Annie Flowers has the faintest notion about Clayton Philbrick. But she offered to put me in touch with...with people."

"The Uptown Land again? The woman seems fixated...."

Just then, a blazing log rolled forward and threatened to fill the room with smoke and fire. We both dashed forward, lunging at pokers as if ready to cross swords.

"On guard, Mr. DeVere," I said.

"On guard yourself, Mrs. DeV." I did not tell Roddy that Annie Flowers's note was addressed in that very same shorthand.

Chapter Twenty-eight

FLURRIES WERE PREDICTED, and wind stripped the maples bare. Roddy and I watched the wild weather from a breakfast window.

"An early winter," I said.

"So it seems."

We got quiet. Last night, Roddy had agreed to hire Mattie, and we would notify Detective Finlay once the young woman settled in here. The grandfather clock sounded mournful, and irritation had flared, yet again, over my plan to follow Annie Flowers's suggestion. Roddy's fierce objections trailed into this morning's breakfast.

"I thought you'd abandoned notions of venturing into tenement slums to meet refugees from the Uptown Land."

"I don't plan to 'venture,'" I snapped. "I seek information." A tad pompous, I added, "Knowledge is power."

Roddy shot back, "*Scientia potentia est*," sipped his tea, and muttered about the philosopher Francis Bacon.

Our footman, Chalmers, promptly served a plate of bacon strips. We were too annoyed to laugh.

Roddy repeated his case against Annie Flowers. "The Lower East Side is a crime-infested breeding ground for disease, Val. You'd put your health and safety at serious risk."

"Like the young nurses from the Henry Street Settlement who make house calls? Are they at risk?"

"I assume they are trained."

"As I am not, so I'm supposed to settle for hearsay?" "'I can have you meet them.' Those were her exact words, Roddy."

"She was teasing you."

We each plucked a bacon strip that neither of us wanted.

Roddy said, "I have a better idea. I suggest that we schedule a meeting with the author of *How the Other Half Lives*."

"Jacob Riis," I said.

"Why not? He's the expert."

I sensed a trick in the foolproof logic. "He's in the city?" I asked.

"Editor at the *Evening Sun*, I believe."

"You'll go with me, Roddy? We'll go together, yes?"

"We will." He smiled. "Make a list of questions, Val. The newspaper business aims for the speed of sound."

The plan worked—at first. Roddy sent a telegram to the *Evening Sun*, *but* a reply zipped back: "regrets...unavailable." My husband scowled.

The weather worsened through the day with high winds and cold, and Mattie shivered at our back door in the afternoon with a pitiful bundle of belongings. A tight-mouthed Mrs. Thwaite inspected the new maid. ("A temporary arrangement, I trust, Mrs. DeVere …highly irregular"). The housekeeper demanded the young woman's full name, which she spoke in a hoarse whisper:

"Mattie Sue Joiner, ma'am."

A house maid was ordered to take "Joiner" to the kitchen for a meal and show her attic quarters. Mattie's bruises had yellowed, and her nose looked slightly crooked. Mrs. Thwaite would see to her uniforms.

I promised to look in this evening and spent the afternoon upstairs in my workroom with the Morocco leather and the yet-to-be-bound books. Keeping the glue tightly capped, I simply sat with Mark Twain's *Roughing It* and spent a few hours reading about Twain's antics in the West. Roddy probably had "escaped" into his "laboratory" to invent new cocktail concoctions. We did not speak until evening, when the sore subject of the Lower East Side surfaced like a garden weed.

"Not 'tramping,' Roddy," I said. "Fact finding."

"I won't have it."

What my husband would not "have" stoked fury every time. We fell silent while the wind howled and sleet ticked at the window panes. By five-thirty p.m., it was nearly pitch dark. A footman closed the drawing room drapery lighted a birch log fire. He asked, Would Mr. DeVere wish his wheeled cart this evening?

"I'll have Irish whiskey this evening, Bronson," said Roddy. "Please bring the decanter and glasses."

"And I'll join Mr. DeVere," I said.

The footman nodded without comment, and we uttered not a word while the flames crackled, firelight flashed, and each of us seethed in a frosty silo.

The footman returned with a tray, and Roddy poured an amber inch in two short glasses. "Shall I call for ice, Mrs. DeVere?"

"Straight up," I replied. "No dilution."

Roddy offered a taut toast. The whiskey streaked my throat, and both eyes watered. "Nice," I said.

We took opposite ends of a stiff leather sofa. A remark about Mrs. Thwaite died on my lips when our butler approached to ask, were we expecting Detective Colin Finlay?

"Mr. Finlay is at your front entrance, sir…ma'am. Are you at home to him?"

But the detective had barreled in on the heels of the butler.

"That will be all, Sands," Roddy said.

Dripping wet in his peacoat, Finlay loomed over us, clutching his hat. "I have come," he said, "from the Martendale house. The maid has been discharged, her whereabouts unknown."

Roddy and I exchanged glances. "Do have a seat, Mr. Finlay," I said. "We were going to notify you…Miss Joiner… Mattie…she is here with us…."

"With you?" He scanned the room, his gaze moving from the decanter to the glasses on the end tables as I explained that we had hired the discharged maid. If whiskey at my elbow surprised him, he showed no sign.

Roddy invited him to sit down.

My cheeks felt hot.

Peacoat buttoned, the detective perched on an antique chair while I rattled on about hiring Mattie until she got back on her feet. "An act of good will," I said.

Finlay looked like a man accustomed to excuses.

The room smelled like wet wool.

"Detective Finlay," Roddy said, "may I offer you a drink?"

"I am on duty, Mr. DeVere."

"Duty, of course," Roddy said. "But at sea, doesn't a sailor get his daily rum ration?"

The detective cracked a little smile.

"Jamaican rum, sir, or perhaps a drop of whiskey on this miserable night?" Roddy leapt up to signal Sands, and a second tray appeared in a flash.

Finlay refused the drink, but he opened his coat. "I will expect to interview the young woman without interference," he said. "And in privacy."

"She is probably at the servants' dinner," I said. "Give her half an hour? You will have a secure space."

Finlay's curt nod gave us a truce. "Mr. Finlay," I said, "Mr. DeVere and I were talking about the Central Park crimes of property."

"Yes?"

"A point to consider," I said, "that Clayton Philbrick might be indirectly involved... that the young man might conspire in the Central Park crimes...."

"—but hire others to commit the crimes, is that it?"

I nodded.

The detective spoke slowly, as if to a young child. "Mrs. DeVere, have you heard of the Lenox Avenue Gang? Or the Gophers?"

I had not.

"Is the name Kid Twist familiar to you? Or Big Jack Zelig? Or Pioggi's gang in the Bowery...the gambling?"

"No."

"They are gang leaders, Mrs. DeVere. The gangs of New York are very busy, and they offer a variety of services for a price." He fingered a coat button for long seconds, as if testing a suspect. "Are you interested in Jack Zelig's price list, Mrs. DeVere?"

Finlay did not wait for an answer. "For slashing a cheek," he said, "one to ten dollars, and a bomb will run as much as fifty, payable in gold."

The detective cupped his hands over his knees, his knuckles as white as his hair. "A murder," he said, "costs a good bit more. It will set you back as much as one hundred dollars."

I swallowed, cheeks hot.

"One of Zelig's henchman," he continued, "advised a police detective that these prices might go higher, depending on the risk.

My husband suddenly sat forward. "Detective Finlay," he said, "I trust that you have informants...that you are investigating the possibility that Clayton Philbrick is involved with a gang...a thug."

"I am indeed."

"And I assume you see officials in Mulberry Street?"

"Daily."

"So perhaps you hear the city's news before the papers report it?"

"Depending, Mr. DeVere." He paused. "Scuttlebutt, it that it?"

"...some talk about re-zoning Central Park," Roddy said. "If rezoning talk has filtered into police headquarters, it could be a useful clue."

"Clue? Like a shave from a barber named André who has not seen hide nor hair of his favorite client, Clayton Philbrick?" The detective snorted, but Roddy's face shut down all mirth. "Mr. DeVere," he said, "I will join you for a nip after all."

I sat back when my husband poured the drink and invited the detective to the *Fleur de Lis* room to see the map.

The clock chimed and chimed again, and the footman was asked to hold dinner. On return, Finlay eyed my glass to see the amber inch intact. Just as well.

"So you see," Roddy said, "that Real Estate ambition might be in play in property crimes and...."

"And murder," I said.

The men drained their glasses.

"This year," Finlay said, "the five boroughs have become one city, and so property is more costly than ever."

"Including tenement property?" I asked. "Slum property?"

Roddy slid forward. "I must ask a favor, Detective Finlay," he said. "It seems that Mrs. DeVere is eager to visit the tenement slums...so please warn her about the danger...."

"A charity visit?" asked Finlay. "In my days on patrol, I escorted parties to the Lower East Side for 'observation' on many evenings."

"That's different," Roddy said. "You mean slum tours."

"That I do. No offence, but sometimes the rich enjoy sight-seeing in the Lower East Side... These days, my uniformed shipmates man the detail."

"I don't mean entertainment, sir." Roddy's glass snapped down on the table. "Mrs. DeVere has the idea that New Yorkers from the old days were run off the land that's now Central Park. She imagines they were pushed into tenements."

"Could be...." The detective shrugged and looked my way. "But you mustn't plan to go by yourselves." His gaze shot to Roddy. "We'll provide you the escort. My old squad partner, Doyle, might be available, Sergeant Leo Doyle. Let me know." He put down his glass. "If I may speak to the young woman now...?"

"Of course," Roddy said. He suggested the ochre drawing room, and I nodded and picked up Velvet. We stood. Finlay took his hat, but lingered, tapping the brim against his leg.

"Something else," he said, "about Mulberry Street.... Saints preserve us, too much to do...the park up, down, and sideways, and all the rest...."

Was he tempted to spell out "the rest?" He bit his lip and ran a hand through his short whitening hair. "One thing about headquarters..." he said. "One thing that comes to mind...."

We were at the doorway, and Sands had stepped into view, ready for orders.

"Mulberry Street..." Roddy prompted.

"Good Catholic as I try to be," Finlay said, "you'd think I'd know a monk from a friar."

Roddy looked at me, I back at him.

"The talk in Mulberry Street," Finlay said. "These last days, it's about somebody that's stirring everybody up. No idea who it is, but they call him the Friar."

Chapter Twenty-nine

"THOSE INTERESTED IN THE 'Other Half' ought to spend an evening in a parlor viewing pictures in a stereopticon," Theo said. "But you 'volunteered' me, Roderick. Whatever urgent matter at the Waldorf Hotel outweighs the pleasure of the slums this afternoon…I can't imagine."

"A confidential matter, Theo, which in time will benefit the gentlemen of New York City and its visitors."

Roddy flashed a smile that revealed nothing. I had been told that "grave matters" in a certain men's café and its drink menu required my husband's immediate attention, and Theo Bulkeley stepped into the breach on an hour's notice, pledging to escort me door-to-door. The first freeze of the season delayed us until the sun melted the asphalt ice. It was nearly two p.m. when we set off for the facts of the Uptown Land.

Theo and I sat kitty-cornered on the opposite seat cushions, I passed him the new, short note from Annie Flowers:

Mrs. DeV—

Ludlow Street, in the rear, third floor—name
is Dougherty. Ask for Old Catherine. (Avoid
Bandits' Roost.) Fear not!

A. Flowers

Theo handed back the note. "Flowers? Is she the woman
from jail last summer?" I nodded. "And you keep up with
her? Valentine, whatever are you thinking? And who are
these people?"

"I don't exactly know. I tried to meet with Annie
Flowers—'A. Flowers'—but her message said 'Consumers
League, too busy,' and she sent this note."

"Do you suppose that 'Old Catherine' is a relative?"

"I don't know."

"And where is 'Bandits' Roost'?"

"A photograph in Riis's book shows men in an alley," I
said. "That's the 'Roost'...all ragged."

"As I recall," Theo said, "everybody is ragged in *How the
Other Half Lives*. And what is the meaning of 'fear not'?"

"Probably biblical."

My friend made a sour face and said, "Fool's errand."

"We'll find out."

We had dressed "down" for the Lower East Side. I wore a
rough cloak that my husband compared to an army blanket.
Theo's custom brown tweeds, woven in Scotland, might

pass for a cheap suit in poor light. No jewelry for either of us.

The cityscape unfolded through blocks of brownstones, apothecary shops, haberdashers, tobacconists, and saloons, until the cab stopped at the corner of Houston and Ludlow Streets, where a uniformed police officer met us.

"Sergeant Doyle?"

"Mrs. DeVere?"

I introduced "Mr. Bulkeley" to a stocky figure whose blue tunic pulled at the buttons. His helmet added inches to his height, but the chin strap disappeared into the folds of his neck, and his wide belt was tight. The sergeant's dark eyes scanned the scene in constant surveillance. His Colt police revolver, I guessed, was holstered under his coat, though a nightstick hung in full view from his belt.

"Detective Finlay tells me you have a name in Ludlow Street?"

"Dougherty," I said.

"Ah, from County Cork," he said, gazing down the walkway littered with paper, straw, fruit-peels, smashed vegetables. "The Doyles," he said, "are from County Wicklow. We'll see." He nudged us into a scene much like Henry Street, a maze of pushcarts and boys in tatters with cold eyes. The air smelled burnt, and the sidewalk felt gummy.

"Ground rules, Mrs. DeVere, Mr. Bulkeley...."

Theo took my arm.

"Keep your arms to your sides, and do not give out money. One penny, and you will be mobbed. Keep your eyes forward, no smiling. Look straight ahead."

Doyle's gaze was a searchlight onto the street.

We walked in front of him. Tenement buildings of six and seven stories loomed like canyon walls.

At midblock, Doyle beckoned a figure in a shoddy cloak. "English? Speak English?" She shook her head and sped off. He stopped at a pushcart and faced a thin man who cried out, "*Polizist*" and jerked off his knitted cap.

Doyle asked, "A little English...?"

"*Kein Englische*...no English." He trembled. "*Nein*."

"Please ask," I said, "if he knows Old Catherine."

"*Alta Katherine?*"

"*Ah, Gammelig Katherine, Ja.*"

Gestures followed, both arms sweeping wide as Doyle nodded while Theo whispered to me that *Gammelig* meant decrepit. We heard "*dritte Etage*," and Doyle said thanks, then led us into the narrowest, darkest alleyway that forced us into single file on slick paving stones. Theo yelped, "Slime!" He had skidded, grabbed at the brick wall, and fumbled for a handkerchief to wipe his fingers.

At a rickety back stairway, we climbed to the third floor and faced a row of doors along a dim hallway. "If we find your Catherine," Doyle said, "I will wait in the hall."

Gutteral sounds erupted when he rapped at the first three doors, but the fourth prompted a grudging "Yes, Grandma Catherine."

Doyle waved us in, and the stench could have knocked us down. Unwashed bodies, stale air, drainage…. And my déjà vu sense of dugouts and sod huts of the West.

A whiff of sweet-sour air, and Theo murmured, "Gasoline…."

"Gas…?" I held my breath. The room felt like a cave.

"Catherine? Are you Catherine?" Like a sickbed visitor, I spoke softly.

"I am Bridget," boomed the woman who opened the door. Like a pirate, a black bandana raked across her forehead, her shoulders draped in tattered shawls.

The room came into focus—a big dirty mattress on the floor where a small blanketed figure lay sleeping, surely a child. Beside the bedding, wood crates stacked like a work-table and stool, where, it seemed, Bridget had been busy moments earlier. An oversized man's jacket hung from a peg, the sleeves creased from use, the collar frayed. No rug or carpet lay on the bare floorboards, but a pile of clothing lay heaped on canvas in the middle of the room.

The child coughed, and Bridget looked fretful. Was she the mother? Was the child a girl or boy? From the shape and size, I guessed about little Charlie Forster's age.

Pressing thin lips together, Bridget pointed to a table and chair in a far corner, where a shrunken woman in a babushka scarf slumped to catch the sullen fading light from a tiny window. She sewed a cloth that draped from her lap to the floor.

"Grandmother Catherine," Bridget announced.

I squinted.

Old Catherine held a needle and thread mere inches from her eyes, and her veined fingers stabbed at the cloth.

"Grandma Catherine?" I asked, stepping closer. Finished sewing a button, she bit the thread, looked up with a milky glare, and pointed to Theo. "Sweater man," she said, her voice rasping like a file. "The lot will be ready tomorrow, and we need cleaning fluid...the gasoline...lots more of it. Where are the sequins?"

"And pearl buttons? We're needing ribbon too." Bridget sounded sharp.

Confused, I glanced at Theo, who had approached the heaped clothing, leaned down, and peered closely. "Dry goods," he said. "New clothes...all new." He stood. "You're finishers, that's what." He looked from Catherine to Bridget. "You sew the buttons and trimmings." His voice rose. "This is a sweatshop." He sounded triumphant.

The child wheezed.

Bridget said, "Croup."

"I'm sorry..." Theo said. "I didn't mean...."

"Bring rat poison too," Catherine added. "They eat anything."

"I apologize," Theo said. "I am not your 'sweater.'"

Sweater? I scrambled...not a garment...a job...yes, a contractor. He would come to retrieve the finished articles... the heap on the floor.

Theo repeated, "I am not your sweater."

The women had frozen. "Then what?" Bridget's fists opened and closed on her hips. "We're paid up," she said. "Rent's not due...."

"...last day of the month." Catherine sat like a cat about to spring. "Thirty-one days...thirty-one this month...."

"I come from Annie Flowers," I blurted. "Annie Flowers sent me."

The atmosphere changed at once.

"Annie?" A moment of confusion, then Catherine almost purred. "Annie...how is the girl?"

"...doing well," I said.

"No more family.... She got free...she moved out." Bridget sounded wistful.

Catherine punched her needle into the cloth. "You must sit for a cup of tea," she said. "I don't move so well, but Bridget—"

In minutes, I was seated on a wood crate with a cracked mug of lukewarm tea thrust into my hand. I was cushioned with a shawl lifted from Bridget's shoulders and folded for my comfort—on Old Catherine's order. Theo was left to stand.

"Annie's grandmamma and mine go back...granddaddies too," Catherine said. She let the cloth slip from her lap. "Our mamas heard about the air so fresh, the woods, the flowers...."

"The Uptown Land," I said.

"Our land." She stamped a foot, her voice like barbed wire. "Ours...stolen away from us." Her fingers curled like claws. "Shanties, they said...our own homes, 'shacks.' We had deeds...Bridget, fetch the deed. I want to show it...."

But the sick child stirred, coughed and wheezed. Bridget went to the mattress and hummed a soothing tune.

Catherine leaned my way. "'*Dens*,' they called the homes we built ourselves. '*Dens*,' and us '*squatters*.' I say, not one squatted. Hard work, that's what. You could starve in County Cork or try your luck in the Uptown Land. But grandpapa lost his tools when they burned him out, drove him off... carpenter's tools, and his chisel and mallet too...."

"—tools for a stone mason," Theo said. She ignored him.

"You learned sewing..." I said.

"Magic with a needle and thread, that was grand-mamma. She taught me, and I taught Bridget. And we all got along. The 'color line' is Harlem now, but we had Seneca Village in the Uptown Land. Teachers, tailors, carpenters... everybody.

"Nothing in earthly life goes perfect," Catherine contin-ued. "Poison ivy blistered Grandpa when he cut firewood, but Ireland has nettles, same difference." They say, 'Forgive and forget,' but we say, 'Never.' She looked ferocious. "One day...the reckoning will come."

Bridget turned from the mattress and hissed, "Not soon enough," then turned again to cuddle the blanketed child.

I sipped the tea. Rage blossomed in this place, the boiling anger...I felt the vehemence. Jacob Riis was so right about housing.

As for Clayton Philbrick, this venture seemed like another "blind lode," as Papa would say. "By chance," I said, "have you heard of a man named Clayton?"

"Clayton? From County Cork?" Catherine's eyes searched the ceiling.

"A name," I said. "It's Philbrick...Clayton Philbrick."

The women shook their heads. "Maybe Annie knows," Bridget said. "Maybe Mack knows...."

Who was Mack? I eyed Theo, who shifted his weight from foot to foot. Sergeant Doyle waited, and Theo would probably tip him. We had got a late start, the October light was dimming fast, and I would hear about the "fool's errand" in the cab.

A hallway scuffle just then, and men's voices outside the door, which burst open and slammed shut as a hulking man suddenly filled the room. His thick black beard, hair, and moustache were all one, and his eyebrows scalloped ink-dark eyes.

"You're early," Bridget said. She pointed to the coughing child. "He's no better," she said.

He grunted, eyed the mattress, and pointed at Theo and me. "Who's this?" Huge hands, thick fingers, black nails. "I said, 'Who's this?'" His voice was low, guttural.

Catherine pointed to me. "She knows Annie."

He grunted.

Bridget said, "You're early for supper...." She sounded strangely timid.

He ignored her.

"Working extra tomorrow, then?" Catherine asked. She looked my way. "Wood and stone," she said. "Night and day, our Mack works...takes after his granddaddy, handy with all the tools...night and day."

Mack stared hard at Theo and me. "You from the city?" He growled.

Theo nodded.

"Uptown?"

Another nod. Theo swallowed.

"The cop in the hall, he's yours?"

"The officer is not 'ours'" I said. "He helped us, and we'll be going."

But his body blocked the doorway. He peered closely at Theo's suit of Harris Tweed and sneered.

"Don't mind my Mack," Catherine said. "Work is where you get it, that's work…. Coal at ten cents a pound, meat at twelve…if it pays, our Mack goes to work day and night in that devil's circus."

"What circus?" I asked.

"The Uptown Land," she said. "The park…the devil's circus."

I stared at Mack. "You work in…Central Park?"

"So they say."

"What sort of work?"

"Everything. I do everything."

A standoff moment. I stood, handed Bridget her shawl, and set the mug down.

"Kind regards to Annie," Catherine said. "And may we meet again." She reached for her needle and spool of thread.

Theo took my arm, and Mack stood aside just far enough to let us out. At the door, he brushed against me and against Theo, who winced and held his breath.

"Are you all right?" I asked. We stood in the hall as Sergeant Doyle approached. Beside me, Theo gagged. "Are you—?"

He paused, counted aloud to five, swallowed and stood straight. "Valentine," he said, "if it's perspiration, or manure, or coal dust...all odors we must live with." He shuddered. "But gasoline and foul breath...." He pressed my arm. "I'm thankful you were spared.... It's assault. One simply cannot bear the stench of rotten teeth."

Chapter Thirty

THE NEXT MORNING, OUR private stable became a sanctuary after a ride in the cold, crisp air. The horses had run for a quarter-mile, both Comet and Justice in a full-on gallop, though Roddy's Justice reared, a rarity for the Arabian gelding. I knew from the West, never tug the reins when a horse rears, and Roddy "went" with Justice as he rose on his hind legs and sent him forward when he landed.

"Spooked," Roddy said as he hung a lighted kerosene lantern in the stable. We unbuckled the saddles and took off the bridles and reins. The leather and bass felt good to the touch. "I think something spooked him."

"We're all 'spooked' these days," I said. "Maybe the horses feel it too."

Roddy's jawline tightened. "For certain," he said, "Theo was 'spooked' yesterday."

On our return from the Lower East Side, Theo declared his tweed suit bound for charity, "nevermore" to occupy space in his bachelor's haven. Returning in the hansom cab, he had "borrowed" my cambric handkerchief to wipe his fingers. We barely spoke.

Roddy and I had little to say last evening. He was tight-lipped about his Waldorf Hotel venture, and I recounted the episode on Ludlow Street, including the link to Annie Flowers and the tenement fury over the Uptown Land. Roddy verified that I had not actually seen the deed. ("Alleged deed," he said, which meant my husband doubted the usefulness of details about Mack or my dark, vague feelings—the sort that Cassie best understands.) I had checked on Mattie, who spent the day "kissing" various surfaces with a feather duster. Fortunately, she felt better.

"Let the horses have forkfuls of hay," Roddy said. "No grain for the next hour." Walking Comet and Justice for the last ten minutes for cooling, we now watered them at the trough, and Roddy threw a light blanket over each warm broad back. We led them into their stalls, and I reached for a pitchfork. Two stalls away, Cassie and Dudley's horses, Bella and Venture, nickered to remind us that they, too, were at home and eager for morning hay. Noland and the groom had been sent off for breakfast, and Roddy had just reached for a hoof pick, when a sharp rapping sounded against the stable door.

"Mr. DeVere...Mrs. DeVere...."

A familiar voice. I looked at Roddy, he back at me. We both turned to see a figure in a peacoat and derby hat at the open stable door.

Finlay.

"I must speak with you...both of you."

Roddy's shoulders tensed, and I clutched the pitchfork handle. Such intrusion.

Roddy called, "Might this wait?"

"No, sir."

He came forward and stood before us. Roddy clutched the hoof pick, and I gripped the pitchfork.

"Yes, Mr. Finlay?" Roddy's voice chipped like flint.

"Can we sit for a bit?" His "can we" was no suggestion.

We led him into the tack room, where saddles, bridles, and horse blankets hung from brackets and hooks. Roddy put the pick aside, and I leaned the pitchfork against a wall. We sat on oak benches on opposite sides of the stable.

Roddy and I waited. No courtesies, no "please do begin."

Finlay put his hat on the bench beside him. "Your butler, Mr. Sands, thought that I might find you here."

"And here we are," Roddy said.

"A matter of some urgency...."

We waited.

"Late yesterday," Finlay began, "I received information..." He crossed his legs and raked at his hair. "At sea," he said, "a gale blows steady, but not a squall. Every squall is different." Roddy bit his lip, and I dreaded a quip about a sailor in the tack room.

"You may know, Mr. DeVere, about the city Coroner. As a gentleman of affairs, you keep up with such positions...."

Roddy nodded, but I knew he bluffed on this one.

"So, you know the Coroner oversees suspicious deaths. Homicide, of course, some accidents...suicides too. The current Coroner is Edward Fitzgerald."

"Mister—?" I asked. "Or Doctor Fitzgerald?"

Finlay colored. "If a doctor is needed, he would be called." He cleared his throat. "The job is on the mayor's list."

He meant a political appointment. A moment passed. A horse whinnied, not one of ours.

"What are you telling us, Mr. Finlay?" Roddy asked.

"—new information about the third murder in Central Park."

"The young actress..." I said. "Roxie LaRue."

"From Ohio." Finlay had taken a paper slip from his pocket and spoke the name most firmly. "Chagrin Falls," he said. "And her real name was...." He read from the slip. "Myra Keckenmeyer."

I kept quiet. If he had questioned Lola Taylor and learned of my visits to the Demple boarding house, he gave no sign.

The detective's next words hit like a hard slap. "The actress..." he said, "did not die from asphyxiation."

"What—?" Roddy lurched.

"Her windpipe was not crushed. She was not strangled to death."

"I don't understand," I said. "Her throat showed marks of choking, did it not?"

"Yes, bruises," Finlay said. "There were thumbprints in front, and fingers in back...against the trapezius muscle."

"Then she was strangled," Roddy said.

"We thought so." Finlay toed the tiled floor. "No need for an autopsy, we thought. The Coroner released the body."

I sucked my cheeks. The Coroner had charged eight dollars and fifty cents so that Roxie could go home to Chagrin Falls. So said Lola Taylor.

"Then...how did she die?" Roddy's defiant tone matched his ramrod posture.

Finlay cracked his knuckles and wet his lips. "We understand," he said, "that she died of a gunshot wound to the head."

The horses nickered. Otherwise, dead silence.

"You 'understand?'" I said. "What does that mean?"

He fidgeted. "Second-hand information."

"Whose information?" Roddy asked.

"From Ohio...." Finlay peered at the paper slip. "From Chagrin Falls...to our Coroner."

"Two Coroners?" I asked.

"No...from a funeral parlor. Fixing her hair for the funeral," Finlay said, "her scalp, her skull... somebody found a hole...."

"Under her hair..." I said.

He nodded, raking his own hair.

Sick to the pit of my stomach, I asked, "Is there proof... proof of a gunshot?"

Finlay studied the tile floor. "The bullet was extracted… from deep in the brain. It entered above the right ear."

The room whirled. "I don't understand," I said. "She was strangled and shot too? Is that it?"

Finlay hunched his shoulders. "Something like that." He pouted. "But her windpipe…her trachea…was not crushed."

Roddy looked indignant. "Detective Finlay, are you saying this information came from a funeral parlor? Not from a medical man?"

Finlay almost whispered, "The undertaker's wife."

Roddy looked confused.

My breath sucked in fast. "If she works with her husband," I said, "she would dress the hair. She would touch the scalp…." Mouth dry, I said, "She would discover the bullet hole."

Finlay nodded.

"And so, she notified the New York Coroner?" I sat forward.

"The undertaker wrote a letter to the Coroner, yes."

"When?" Roddy asked.

Finlay looked embarrassed. "I'm not sure. The letter came to the Coroner, and he notified Chief Devery, and…." His voice trailed. "Like I said, a squall, every single one is different. You never know."

"When did you learn all this?"

"Late last night. Chief Devery ordered me in, laid into me like I'd run the ship aground. Pounded me good. Keeps a log, and he uses it."

He clutched his knees. "If the newspapers get onto it, the Department looks bad, and the chief will lay it all to me...." He clawed at his knees. "The one that takes the blame... the goat...."

"—Scapegoat," Roddy snapped.

Finlay nodded, a portrait of misery. "So, I'm here about Clayton Philbrick," he said. "With me, the grandparents are tight-lipped, but they'll tell you if he had a pistol and practiced with it."

"You're asking us to question the Philbricks," Roddy said. "Yet again."

"As soon as possible. Today."

"But Mr. Finlay," I said, "we three talked about the likelihood that young Philbrick is not directly involved."

"A 'likelihood' isn't good enough, Mrs. Devere. I must cleat every line."

Roddy squinted. "You must satisfy 'Big' Bill Devery, isn't that it? To keep your job?"

Finlay sat bolt upright. "My job, Mr. DeVere—and the safety of your neighborhood. Three homicides so far, and your new housemaid could have been a fourth. I need not remind you, sir, that killer is loose, and he will strike again."

Chapter Thirty-one

FINLAY LEFT THE STABLE when our coachman returned from breakfast. Back home, we quickly changed clothes, had a bite, and I took Velvet for a short walk while Roddy went to the Philbricks. Tempted to visit Cassie, I feared blurting my confusion and fear that another attack in the park was due any night.

By two o'clock, Roddy and I ordered afternoon tea in the conservatory, the space that usually felt like the tropics when cold winds blew outdoors. At the moment, it felt clammy, our wicker chairs stiff, the fountain sluggish. The lemon trees looked dry, and the afternoon tea metallic on the tongue.

Or was it my mood?

"I could have predicted Gladys Philbrick's answer," Roddy said.

"Which was—?"

My husband's fish-eyed stare meant I need not ask. "Gladys clutched her throat and gasped, 'Our Clayton with firearms, Roderick? Heaven forbid! No such thing.'"

"And Victor? What about Victor?"

"He grunted 'no' when I asked about Clayton and guns. He looked unshaven. I suspect he's drinking heavily."

"Then you said nothing about the actress's cause of death?"

"—and inflict more misery? The Philbricks are unhinged, Val. Gladys is hysterical and Victor's in a stupor. I'll report 'no known guns' to Finlay, but I won't trouble the Philbricks again, not unless…."

I echoed, "Unless…."

Bothered and stuck, I said, "Roddy, why didn't we talk to Finlay about Eli Fryer this morning? Three of us in the stable, we had the chance. Why didn't we?"

"Because he shocked us with news about the bullet, that's why…and because he 'one-upped' us with his slick New York gang talk." Roddy sat forward. "The Lenox Avenue gang…and the price list for crimes…a dollar to slash a cheek. And something else."

"What?"

"You tell me."

I picked up a dead leaf fallen from a lemon tree. "To accuse Eli Fryer of masterminding crimes, we need a strong case." I twirled the leaf. "I suppose the police chief is out of the question?"

"'Big' Bill Devery—?" My husband snorted. "If there's money, he'll turn a blind eye and take his cut. He started out as a bartender and bought his way into the police. It's been pay-to-play for years. Finlay is right, the man is corrupt to the bone."

"Could you speak to City Hall?"

"Mayor Van Wyck's cronies?" Roddy snorted. "Did you see the *Herald*? His Honor is caught up in a scandal about ice."

"Ice? Like...cubes?"

"Cubes, blocks...the paper reports an "Ice Trust" scheme, and Robert Anderson Van Wyck in the thick of it. And here's another nasty tidbit...." Roddy reached into his jacket pocket and held up an envelope.

"What is that?"

"An invitation that came by messenger. Remember the Bicycle Tea when Eli promised a surprise for the club members?"

"Vaguely."

"Eli invites us to the Knickerbocker Theatre to his *'Behind the Footlights Un-Dress'* rehearsal of *The Black Crook*."

"I don't understand." I reached for my tea.

Roddy unfolded a sheet. "We will witness *'magic behind the scenes,'*" Roddy read, "'exclusive to the Cycling Club membership .... Demonstrations ...champagne with 'leading lights' of the show...welcome by renowned director David Drake.'"

"When is it?" I sipped.

"Thursday evening."

"Why is it?"

Roddy gazed out at the fountain and the plantings. "I'd guess for money. Eli will solicit us. The evening will conclude with a pitch for a new 'investment opportunity' exclusive to the cyclers. Probably to do with Real Estate. The man's a wizard at using other people's money."

The fountain splashed, and my gaze stopped at the stone goddesses at the door. "Real Estate…" I murmured, "Real Estate…Real….."

"Val, is something the matter?"

"I'm…not sure."

"What is it? Are you ill?"

Roddy's alarm rose as my fingers clutched the teacup. "No, not ill," I said, "and no…Roddy, it won't be Real Estate." My mouth was going dry. "It will be *The Black Crook*….and Eli Fryer. I should have guessed…."

"Guessed what, Val?"

"…the Knickerbocker Theatre…I should have known." I stood to pace in small circles, lemon tree to potted palm. Teacup clenched, I faced my husband. "The 'older man' who came for Roxie after rehearsals…his hair was pomaded…it had to be Eli Fryer."

"Val, a great many men use pomade….beards and side-burns as well as—"

"—and he fiddled with a watch chain 'gewgaw.' Lola Taylor said so. The rehearsals were closed, but investors had passes…and he waited for her in the wings. Roddy, don't you see?"

I met my husband's gaze. "It was Eli. Roddy, it had to be Eli Fryer. And that means…it means that Roxie was Eli Fryer's lover…Eli's lover and Clayton Philbrick's too. Lola Taylor said the older man was insanely jealous of 'Phil,' and she used his jealousy for diamonds."

My teacup smashed on the floor, and Roddy stood, ignoring the cup.

"His jealousy might have killed her," I said, "if he was that angry…. How much does a murder cost? Did Finlay say one hundred dollars?"

Roddy almost whispered, "Strangled and shot…. On Eli's order…?"

Teacup fragments crunched underfoot. "And Clayton… if Clayton Philbrick believed that he was Eli's partner…the young gambler that knew where to find a henchman…and hire him."

"—for his desperate need to clear his gambling debts," I said. "But only Eli knew that 'Phil' was his rival lover…."

Roddy blinked twice, three times. "Val," he said, "if you're right…then young Clayton Philbrick has been caught tight in Eli Fryer's trap."

My husband bit his lip. "Eli's schemes, Val…everybody knows, everybody has a story about him. Fraud, falsified papers, sour land deals…Eli Fryer is relentless, never gives an inch." He paused. "But to toy with a young man for murder…and then…."

"Then what?"

My husband's voice tightened. "Fryer won't let Clayton Philbrick go, Val. He's unforgiving. If Philbrick is still alive—"

"—if?"

"We don't know, do we? Let's say he's hiding, guilty of homicide. But when he's found, Eli will see to it that he is prosecuted for Roxie's murder, or else...."

My husband hesitated, but I have come from the far West where the words are frank. "I'll say it, Roddy." I looked my husband straight in the eye. "Or else Eli Fryer will have him killed. So, we will attend the 'un-dress' night at the Knickerbocker Theatre, knowing that our host is a very likely a murderous mastermind."

Chapter Thirty-two

"THIS TIME, WE'LL GO in the front door," said Cassie.

"We will indeed," I replied, my throat dry.

My friend and I entered the Knickerbocker Theatre on our husbands' arms and were ushered toward front rows marked off with decorative "bicycles" made of stiff red ribbons. Musicians tuned in the orchestra pit, and thumping behind the closed curtain. The theatre smelled of stale cigars and perfume.

"Reserved for ladies and gentlemen of the Cycling Club," cooed the usher, who bowed us into the third row. The empty balconies and boxes gave the space a deserted feeling.

Our 'host' was not in evidence.

Cassie and I shed cloaks and long gloves and nodded greetings to friends, several from the recent Bicycle Tea. The Bains were settled in front of us, and Colonel Jay with a lady I did not recognize. Theo gave a little salute as he slowly escorted Bertha Candler down the aisle. The elderly widow was his distant cousin.

"Look who else is here…" Roddy said quietly.

I turned. "The Martendales…."

"A sure sign of Eli Fryer's power," Roddy said.

Priscilla looked righteous, as if in church, and her husband nodded to everyone with a toothy smile.

Cassie touched my wrist. "Val, do you feel well?" she asked softly.

"Perfectly well," I said.

"But are *you* all right?" I asked. Cassie's beautifully manicured nails signaled yet another visit to Madame Riva. "The last time we were here, Cassie, you felt …well, faint," I said.

"Val," she said, "I am resolved to live in three dimensions this evening…three only. And we are here because… because social duty calls." She turned to her husband. "Am I right, Dudley?"

Dudley Forster gave his wife a sweet smile, though he had wished to spend the evening reading Darwin's treatise on coral reefs. "Mr. Fryer's "mercenary vaudeville," as he put it, left him cold.

Quite cold, we all agreed, promising to make the best of it. I hadn't known that my tension showed, but Cassie can be a weathervane.

"The orchestra has tuned," Roddy said, "and here comes you-know-who."

Eli Fryer took the stage in front of the curtain, clapped his hands and leered. "Welcome, Cyclers…" he boomed, gusting on about the premier event and his delight seeing friends together in the Knickerbocker Theatre, and all the while counting the house. Were three rows filled? Four? His shirtfront bulged, his watch chain ornament glittered, and his hair glistened as if waxed.

I fought rage.

"Val...?" Roddy touched my arm.

"I'm fine," I said.

Roddy took my hand.

Fryer hailed the "most special of a special evening—and without further ado, the acclaimed director of *The Black Crook* of 1898, Mr. David Drake!"

Polite applause as a tall, gangly figure in checkered trousers loped onto the stage, his red suspenders set off against a white shirt with rolled sleeves. A brief handshake sent Eli Fryer into the wings, and the director faced us, waiting for silence. With dark hair combed forward to meet his cheeks, his eyes became beacons, and his hands like two large blades ready to slice the air.

This was the "Simon Legree" that Lola described, and her words had weight in the next minutes as the director promised "samplings" of the show to "whet" appetites in this holiday season of "'naughty or nice.'"

"Big helpings of 'nice' for you dear ladies," he said in syrupy tones. His palms carved the air. "And for you gentlemen in the house...for you, my dear sirs...." A pause and downward chop of a hand before "naughty" cracked like a whip.

Drake's voice, I imagined, could sing a lullaby or shatter glass.

"So, Maestro, if you please—"

The orchestra struck up a bright tune, and the curtain rose on four stilt-walkers who juggled colored balls, while a troupe of women in spangled flesh-tone leggings danced onto the stage. Circling the stilt-walkers, they curved into a line, kicked high and tight all together, bare arms raised up, then down—all legs in constant motion.

Knowing that Lola Taylor was not among them, I looked for her anyway. All the powdered, rouged faces looked just alike. In a row behind ours, someone's lips smacked, and I heard "well, that's more like it..." and then a woman's "tsk tut" in seats to the left.

The dancers spun backward as trombones announced a muscular character in black leggings and a black cap with devil's horns—the Black Crook. He squatted and lunged and flailed while a quartet of bell ringers in scarlet ostrich plumes skipped onstage and chimed out "Jingle Bells." The Black Crook pranced and made a show of covering his ears.

The bell ringers skipped offstage after "a one-horse open sleigh," and the Black Crook saluted as the director stepped forward to announce "a very special scene...special indeed...a heart-stopping moment."

The lights dimmed as the Black Crook and dancers skipped to the rear, and a war whoop erupted when three brawny figures in loincloths and feather headdresses pounded onto the stage, howling and brandishing tomahawks in a circle of light. A drum roll began, and a second shaft of light beamed upwards to guide our view to the catwalk far above. Cymbals crashed, trumpets spoke, and a figure swung down, flashing with snow-white fringe, crystals, and boots, one hand holding a rope, the other with a pistol that smacked the air once, twice…. The shots rang…bang bang bang."

The Indians collapsed in a heap, and a triumphant Betty Bang-Bang landed on the stage and stepped over them…no, her white cowboy boot was planted on the buttocks of a "dead" Indian. With arms raised high and a smoking pistol held aloft, she turned in profile, smiling in triumph before one and all.

"Lola…" I murmured as applause rained, the curtain dropped, and behind it, sudden sounds of tinkling glasses and popping corks.

"—Ladies and gentlemen of the Cycling Club, hear ye, hear ye…."

Eli Fryer was back.

"Here it comes," Roddy said, "our 'investment opportunity.'"

"—a once-in-a-lifetime opportunity," Fryer went on, "to come onstage to meet the leading lights of *The Black Crook*. Mingle and explore the stage. And make acquaintance with David Drake, the premier cast members, and the stagehands who make magic happen behind the scenes. We welcome you with chilled champagne."

The curtain rose, and the lighted stage filled with performers and wheeled wagons with glasses and bottles of wine.

"Let's be off—" Dudley sprung up and smiled at Cassie and me. "We could be the first cyclers to exit."

"Not the first," Roddy said. "The Martendales are halfway out the door."

We glanced at the departing Martendales as others left their seats, hesitated, and followed ushers up the steps onto the stage.

"I wouldn't mind if we left now," Cassie said. Her eyes blurred with that faraway gaze I had come to recognize.

"I am curious," I said. "Perhaps a few more minutes? Look, Colonel Jay is shaking hands with the Black Crook."

"Val, we ought to slip out, all four of us," said Cassie. She took Dudley's arm. "Perhaps you're not quite yourself this evening? You and Roderick ought to come along with us. This is no place for me...or you."

On the stage, Eli Fryer touched his wine glass to Lola's. Her stiff smile reminded me that Fryer gave her gooseflesh.

"Apologies, Dudley," Roddy said, "but Valentine and I will stay just a bit longer. We wish you both a good evening...a good night."

Wrapped in her cloak and furs, Cassie was led to the door by her husband. A lingering, regretful glance in my direction, and she was gone.

I envied the Forsters as Roddy and I entered a scene like a carnival midway, as if the children of Society were let loose for an hour at the circus. The stilt-walkers sipped champagne, and the dancers in flesh-tone leggings twinkled amid ladies and gentlemen in evening dress. David Drake seemed to hold Mrs. Mills and her daughters spellbound as he snapped his red suspenders. The Indian warriors dispersed, their headdresses mixed with ladies' feathered hats.

Roddy took two glasses and handed one to me. We toasted one another, our eyes locked in a silent pledge to see what we could see, learn what we could learn. My husband began to subtly follow Eli Fryer, who made his way among club members, perhaps suggesting investments as he chatted. Maybe Fryer would rely on pressured tête-à-têtes instead of a speech.

"I had hoped to see acrobats," Sarah Jones murmured, voicing disappointment in soft southern tones. "Circus acrobats were special in Charleston years ago, but tonight it seems like the actress shooting Indians is the favorite. Who is she?"

"That's Miss Taylor," I said, "Miss Lola Taylor."

"Bless her heart, she's the belle of the ball," said Sarah Jones. "And my, what a dazzling smile...helped by dentifrice, Valentine. I'm sure of it."

The sparkling Betty Bang-Bang stood surrounded by club members, men and women alike. The pistol was holstered at her side, and she held a champagne flute in each hand, sipping left, sipping right.

Sarah Jones stepped closer for a better look, and her husband, Pembroke, moved just behind her, looking intrigued.

A clean-shaven man at the farthest "stage left" caught my eye. He wore corduroy pants and vest, boots, and a twill shirt open at the neck, something like a western sheriff. He held his wine glass as if it were a foreign object.

I stepped closer. "Good evening, sir."

"Good evening." He kept a lookout on the stage.

"So many acts in *The Black Crook*," I said.

"Not many tonight," he said. "You've got the stilts and Indian feathers and tomahawks—and Betty's pistol. That's about it. And the Crook's horns, but he takes care of them."

"Are you...in charge of costumes?"

He chuckled. "Helping the costume designer tonight," he said. "She's got the grippe. Me, I'm the properties master."

"So you are in charge of...."

"The props, stuff you see onstage...furniture, curtains, pictures on a fake wall...cannon if it's a fort...swords, skulls, whatever...."

"Interesting," I said. "I understand a ventriloquist will appear in the final production."

"Good thing," he said, "that Drake nixed the ventriloquist and dummy tonight. They're a big pain. Too many props for the bang."

"Bang?"

"Not like her—" He pointed to Lola, basking in her spotlight. "What I mean, the ventriloquist set is fussy. He needs a table with two big candleholders, both the same, and the dummy doll needs a big hand mirror for a short bit called 'Seeing Is Believing.'"

He kept his lookout on the stage. I sipped my wine and started to move away—and a good thing I did not, for the next words soon set my world tilting on its axis.

"My job would be easier," he said, "if props didn't disappear. The jugglers' balls, I've replaced them twice. A dance number needs a throne, but where's the throne?"

"Stolen?" I asked.

"Drake says, 'pilfered,' but it's thieving. The ventrilo-quist's two big brass candlesticks, I'm down to one. The big hand-mirror, nowhere. At rehearsal, they're on the prop table near the actors' entrance. Otherwise, they're locked up."

I sipped wine to moisten my mouth. "Who steals?" I asked, suspecting his answer.

He gestured to the stage. "Dancers," he said, "actors, anybody in the cast. I tell Drake, if the pay was decent, the props wouldn't disappear. He says he pays what the market allows, but I tell him, cheap can be dangerous. The rigging ropes…like a trapeze…ropes broke, and the first Betty came down, broke her arms and legs, lucky she's alive."

"It was in the papers," I said. "…and something about a frayed rope?"

"Something…" he said, as if tempted to say more. A moment passed before he said, "We lost a gun."

"A gun…a theatre gun," I said.

"Supposed to be. Not that one."

"What kind of gun?" I asked, my voice thin.

"The rules are strict," he said. "Never point it at anybody, check the chamber, and never take it out of the theatre."

"But it disappeared?"

"We replaced it," he said. "What you saw tonight, it fires blanks. The gun in her holster, these days I personally store it after every rehearsal."

"These days…" I echoed, sipping the warming cham-pagne. "I don't suppose you know what happened to the gun you lost."

"Lost it earlier this month," he said. "Disappeared from the prop table after a rehearsal." He turned to me. "Lady, are you feeling all right? You look like you've seen a ghost."

Chapter Thirty-three

"MAYBE HE MEANT HALLOWE'EN?

I met my husband's gaze across our breakfast table. "No, Roddy, he saw my reaction to the gun...." I fingered my napkin. "I think the gun might change...everything."

"Val, please...the servants." Roddy put a finger to his lips to signal "hush." He suggested toast. Was my voice that loud?

Maybe so. I hadn't slept a wink, staring at the ceiling and turning *The Black Crook* scene over and over, the prop master's words, thoughts of Lola, the boardinghouse...and back to the stage, the props, on and on until dawn, when I tiptoed downstairs, saw to Velvet's food and water, then handed her over to Bronson while I waited for breakfast with my husband.

If only Roddy and I had talked last night when we got home, but Sands waylaid him about a mix-up over the footmen's uniforms. It grew late, and I needed Calista's help with the confounded hooks in my underthings. My maid needed her sleep.

So here we were, first thing Friday morning at breakfast, and my jumbled thoughts fell on deaf ears because Roddy wanted to talk about Fryer's tête-à-têtes.

"I overheard his sales pitch for the *Black Crook* investment scheme, Val. He circulated among the club members one by one, halfway strong-arming and sounded like a snake-oil salesman. The man is slick. Colonel Jay and Lucius Graham fell hard, and others might do so, as well."

Roddy lowered his voice. "There's a novel titled *The Confidence-Man*, and it suits Fryer. The character in the book stops short of homicide, but he's forceful and suave." My husband paused. "It won't be easy to bring a case against Fryer, even with strong evidence."

"Roddy," I said, "I'm rethinking Eli Fryer...."

"You're...did you say 'rethinking?'"

"...beginning to go back over things..." I murmured.

My husband's brow creased, and he gripped my hand as if to bind me tight. "Val, did you sleep well last night?"

"How could I?"

"I regret exposing you to that bazaar...champagne and jugglers. And Fryer just a few feet away, breathing the same air."

"I'm thinking somewhat differently...."

My husband did not hear me. "I didn't sleep well myself," he said. "In fact, I am changing my mind about talking to Finlay. We agreed to help him, and I'll seek him out to talk frankly about our suspicions about Fryer. I hope you approve."

Roddy paused. "If he's half the detective he thinks he is, he'll listen." Before I could speak, I heard, "Let's eat these eggs, Val. We need our strength."

That was that. Within the hour, my husband was out the door.

๑๑

Maybe I should have spilled all my garbled thoughts at breakfast, strewn them in front of Roddy as we forked the eggs and sipped from the Royal Doulton cups, Roddy's tea and my hopeless coffee.

Then again, maybe Roddy's "mission" of the day was just as well. It would give me time to gather my wits...and perhaps allay dark suspicions.

Or open a glaring light?

I lingered at the breakfast nook, pretending to read the morning papers, my thoughts like western rushing rapids.

The furnishings in Lola Taylor's rooms included one big brass candlestick and an oversized hand mirror. They were in the suite she shared with Roxie LaRue, and they turned up in the single room too, memorable among the suitcases, the bottles and jars, the steamer trunk.

Were both pilfered stage props? Swiped? A burned-down candle and dribbled wax suggested the candlestick helped to brighten drab spaces, and perhaps Lola and Roxie both agreed they deserved to "have" it.

And a hand mirror for young women in show business—a necessity. Maybe one of them had broken a mirror, so why not help themselves? Both women needed to watch every penny. Those items did not make Lola or Roxie lifetime thieves. For Lola, both were now keepsakes in memory of her deceased friend.

The gun, however....

As the prop master hinted, the firearm was another matter. The gun that Lola fired last night was a stage prop loaded with blanks. Even so, the rules for safety applied, the same rules we followed with handguns out West. Check the chamber, never point the barrel at a living thing—unless necessary.

My papa was strict with guns, rifles, shotguns, pistols, and "safety first" his motto, drummed hard every time he took me shooting or hunting. In Virginia City. His long guns were locked up, and so were the pistols, except for the one holstered at his side.

His Colt revolver—the "Peacemaker" with hand-carved grips that were inlaid with his initials in silver—it was my memento, along with the Barlow knife and a few photographs of Papa at the silver mines. And the cartridges, the dozen bullets that nestled in a drawer of my dressing table.

Who would lift a gun from the prop table at a *Black Crook* rehearsal?

And why?

The prop master said that petty theft was not unusual, that cast members made off with various items, the jugglers' balls and a "throne" of some sort....

But a pistol?

What sort of pistol? For the theatre, like all props, it must be large. The audience in furthest rows must see it. The candlestick was large, the mirror over-sized. The gun? No purse nor pocket pistol would do, no Derringer. It would be…most likely, a Colt revolver.

Just like mine.

Stepping upstairs into my boudoir, I slid open the bureau drawer to look under the camisoles and corsets, and there it lay—the hand-carved grips with the silver initials P M, the steel cylinder, the barrel, the trigger. In one brilliant piece, an elegant and cold machine.

For protection, for death.

I had not fired it since I left the West.

Closing the drawer, I called to Calista. "Please get ready," I said, "to go with me on a downtown errand."

"Right away, ma'am. Let's dress warmly."

"Warm or not, Calista, I'll need my navy blue suit and high-necked shirtwaist…the same one I wore several days ago. And the silver brooch that looks like a leaf…no, don't polish it. No other jewelry, and please pull my hair into a tight bun."

My maid kept her questions to herself. "We'll take a hansom cab," I said. "We're going to West Thirty-fifth Street. The errand…let's say it's a clerical matter."

Slowed by late morning traffic, the hansom reached Mrs. Demple's boardinghouse before noon and stopped midblock at the curb. Calista would wait in the cab. The driver tipped his hat. "Less than an hour," I said, and hastened to number 641, hugging Roddy's leather portfolio in order to appear exactly as I did on the last visit—all business.

Once again, the landlady skulked at the site of the "professional" woman at her door when I asked for a few minutes of Mrs. Demple's time. "I am here today," I said, "on a matter of inspection."

We stood in the foyer by the table that had held the leather-bound register for tenants' signatures upon leaving and returning.

Except the tabletop was bare—no book nor inkstand, pen nor pencil. Nothing.

"If it's about my kitchen," said the landlady, "the Demple kitchen gets cleaned in the afternoons, floor and stovetop... different wash waters...."

"I am not here about the kitchen," I said. The odor of cooking cabbage combined with fresh paint. A sticky sheen glistened on the tabletop.

"You were here before, weren't you? You went upstairs."

"I did," I said in my strictest voice. "And I have come to you because the City of New York is considering new rules for boardinghouse lodgers. I understood from you, Mrs. Demple, that tenants are required to sign their names when they depart the premises, and to sign their names once again when they return...am I correct?"

She nodded, warily.

"The city," I said, "is considering such a rule for other boardinghouses, and I plan to bring your fine example to the attention of our committee."

She nearly preened. "Then you came for permission," she said. "I suppose you need my name on some sort of paper? Would I get a premium?"

I unclasped Roddy's portfolio, thoughts jumping. "... signature, yes, and a premium if the idea is adopted. So, might I have a look at the registry? I'd like to describe it to the committee. As I recall, it was on this table—?"

"—until one of them spilled a whole bottle of ink, so it's painted over. They're careless...it's not theirs, so they don't bother." She sniffed. "It'll dry by tomorrow, if you want to come back, you can see the book and the inkstand too, and the pencils, all arranged like a nice table setting."

"Actually," I said, "I'd like a quick look if the book is available." She looked dubious until I promised a document for a signature and the possibility of her 'premium.'"

In the parlor, minutes later, I perched on a stiff horse-hair settee, clasped the oversized book, and opened it to this month, October, 1898, my index finger ranging up and down the columns of names, the hasty signatures—Susan and Trixie, Laurette and Ethel, *out* to the left, *in* to the right. Small suns and moons for *a.m.* and *p.m.* The second week of the month, and they were—Roxie and Lola *out* and *in*, out once again, and back inside over and over again.

Until the night of October eleventh. Under *p.m.*, the two distinct signatures, both Roxie LaRue and Lola Taylor had signed out.

Only one name, however, had signed back in: Lola T.

There was no returning signature for Roxie LaRue on the night of her death nor in the wee hours of the following morning.

Chapter Thirty-four

"SHE SIGNED A DOCUMENT? What document?"

"I snatched a paper from your portfolio, Roddy, and Mrs. Demple signed it without her eyeglasses. Luckily."

I had returned home, changed into a woolen skirt and shirtwaist, and waited for Roddy's return. He arrived just after two p.m., and I sat with him in a small drawing room while he spooned a bowl of bean soup.

"And what document did you unearth, Val?"

"A receipt," I said, "for seven sterling silver stirrup cups from Black, Starr, and Frost. Don't laugh. The signature of Mrs. Clara G. Demple appears under 'Paid in Full.'"

Roddy smiled. Or did he smirk? My thoughts swirled. "Roddy, the tenants' names were clearly entered into the book. All must sign-out and sign-in. It's a house rule, and the landlady is proud of it, and strict."

My husband nodded and signaled the footman for more soup.

Was he listening to me? "Roddy, did you hear me? On the night she died, October eleventh, the space for Roxie LaRue's 'sign-in' was blank."

"Of course it was blank, Val...because she was killed." Slight exasperation narrowed his eyes.

"...but Lola did sign in."

"Val, let's think straight." He put down his spoon. "After the rehearsals, the two women probably went separate ways for nightlife into the wee hours. They would each return to their suite of rooms at different times."

"On most nights, yes," I said, "but—"

"—but let's assume that Lola came back, signed her name, and went to their shared rooms. She probably fell asleep and learned the horrible news the next day when the whole city found out that her roommate was murdered."

The footman brought a tureen, ladled more soup, and withdrew. My husband reached for the pepper.

"Roddy, let me start at the beginning. At the theatre, you overheard Eli's sales talk, but I learned about stolen props. Two particular items perfectly match those I saw in the boardinghouse rooms."

"A few things snitched by Lola and Roxie?" Roddy said.

"Yes, but another prop also went missing—a gun."

Roddy held his spoon in midair. "A stage prop, yes?"

"Meant to be a stage weapon, but a real gun." My husband frowned. "The first gun used in the *Black Crook* rehearsals," I said, "was probably a Colt revolver, like my papa's 'Peacemaker.'"

Roddy looked doubtful. "The pistol that Lola fired when she swung down on ropes," he said, "...those shots were blanks, and the gun was—"

"—a stage gun. A fake. The prop master told me that Betty Bang-Bang is now firing blanks." I paused. "But the first rehearsal gun—the one that went missing—was real. It was probably used during rehearsals, not fired."

"Unloaded, I should think." Roddy rested his spoon.

"But suppose," I said, "that bullets were in the chamber?"

"Val, why should I 'suppose' any such thing?"

"Because both Roxie and Lola were auditioning for the role of Betty Bang-Bang. Both wanted the starring role, and both competed for it. The rivalry was friendly, but intense. Lola said that four dancers were finalists, she and Roxie and two others."

"So you think the two snitched the gun for...for practice?"

"Practice...and then something happened—in Central Park."

My husband's "lawyer" look could be irksome. "What do you suppose happened?"

"Let's remember," I said, "that both women earned extra money soliciting men in the park. Lola said so."

"Said so directly?"

"In so many words, Roddy."

"Val, what are you telling me?"

I faced him at eye level. "I'm telling you that our ideas about the Central Park crimes could unravel...could be very wrong. Don't 'Val' me, Roddy. I need you to listen." I added, "Just listen...."

"All ears, Mrs. DeVere."

"Suppose," I said, "that after a *Black Crook* rehearsal, the two women took a Night Hawk to Central Park in the late night hours. The weather was cool but pleasant, and they intended to solicit men."

"Go on."

"And they had stolen the pistol from the prop table and took it along to the park with them. Walking along, smoking cigarettes, they handed it back and forth, holding it, pointing it...almost playing with it."

"And—?"

"And Lola Taylor pointed it at Roxie, just for fun. She pointed it at Roxie's head...."

"And the gun fired?"

"Yes."

Roddy turned somber, then shook his head. "But Roxie LaRue was strangled."

"—by two hands clasping her neck, Roddy. Two thumbs pressing the front of her throat. Picture it—the gun fires, Roxie collapses, and her friend tries to revive her...shakes her, presses her throat, rips her clothes in panic."

"And the gun—?"

"She drops the gun, grabs her friend's throat, and tries to shake her back to life. When Roxie didn't move, Lola grabbed the gun and scrambled out of the park. She hailed a cab, went to the boardinghouse, and signed herself in. Maybe she thought about signing Roxie's name, maybe not. The space was left blank.

Roddy pushed his soup aside. "And we know the rest...." He folded his hands on the table. "—but the cigarette case... Clayton Philbrick's cigarette case...."

"Accidental...or incidental...a trinket Philbrick gave Roxie, or maybe she swiped it. Both women smoked, and they probably lighted up in the park."

"Then the cigarette case would have nothing to do with the actress's death."

"Nothing," I said.

Roddy tapped his thumbs together. "If you're right," he said, "Lola Taylor could clear Clayton Philbrick of Roxie's murder."

"In a heartbeat, which she knows full well, Roddy. The woman's ambition overrides everything."

We sat still for a moment. A clock struck the half-hour. Roddy said, "You'll tell all this to Finlay."

"I will."

"But Val, if one young woman's death is accounted for, the two others are not—the laundry worker and the woman from the ladies' hat workshop. And the attack on our new maid...."

"Mattie Joiner," I said. "I spoke to her again, Roddy. She remembers a man's hands and fists, but nothing like a gun...no metal. I wanted to be more certain about the gun."

"But the arson crimes," Roddy said, "and the stone bridges blasted with dynamite.... Finlay was very interested when I met with him this morning. He has heard rumors about rezoning the park. He's up to his neck investigating gambling and gangs, but Fryer is on his list, thanks to us. Our suspicions about Eli Fryer are merited."

"For the moment, Roddy," I said. "But I have another thought."

"Oh?"

"Not now," I said. "I'll first pay a call on Cassie. I've ordered Nolan to drive, and you'll see me go out the door with a valise containing the cloak that amused you and Theo."

"That brown 'army blanket?'"

"The very one," I said. "And when I return, we might have another talk about crime in Central Park."

Chapter Thirty-five

THE FORSTER HOUSEHOLD RANG with children's cries when the butler, Hayes, ushered me into the carpeted foyer.

"Auntie Val, did you bring Velvet?"

"Not today, Charlie, but soon."

"What's in the suitcase, Auntie Val? Did you bring us presents?"

"Children, please...." Cassie rushed forward. "Remember your manners. We must be polite."

"We want to know what's inside," said Charlie, who stamped his foot. "Daddy says scientists have to be curious, and I am going to be a scientist."

"Aren't scientists polite?" Little Bea looked perplexed. "Daddy is polite."

Cassie shook her head, shrugged, and laughed all at once. "You see, Auntie Val, how it goes in the Forster house."

She beckoned the children's nanny, Cara, who stood in the hallway trying not to laugh aloud. "Children, Cara is ready to give you tea."

"And ginger cookies," Charlie said.

"Lady fingers," his sister replied. "Ginger burns my tongue."

The tea party went to the nursery, and Cassie asked whether I wished to leave the valise with the butler.

"I'll keep it with me, Cassie…it's the reason I'm here. And could we please speak privately—?"

My friend led me to a small reception room in the Forsters' Italian Renaissance home, where Florentine figures mixed with Dudley's souvenir seashell wall sconces and calabash candy dishes.

The verbena scent is pleasant, and it's quiet here," Cassie said, trying not to stare at the valise. "Shall we have tea?" She saw my face. Val, is everything all right?"

"Not really, Cassie. Inside this bag…. It's about the park."

My friend wrung her hands. "Everything is about the park," she said. "What else could it be? The children are kept indoors, and the adults…." She gazed at a window. "Dudley crossed the park this afternoon to help the Museum of Natural History with a South Seas exhibit. He ought to be back any minute. I promised not to be nervous." She closed he eyes. "How can I help?"

"Cassie, I need a favor…from your 'second' sight…when we talked to the 'chalk' man at the theatre and then saw Lola Taylor at the boardinghouse, both times you felt… sensations."

"I did. Val, don't remind me. And that *Black Crook* evening…I was nearly overcome…I tried my best…but the actress swinging down—"

"—Lola."

"It became so very difficult."

I glanced at the valise, which would raise "difficult" to a stratosphere. How much could be asked of a friend? This much, when ordinary became extraordinary, when lives hovered….

"Cassie," I said, "I shouldn't ask this of you…but I must. Inside this valise…is a cloak and a cambric handkerchief. When you see them…touch them, you might experience something. I don't know what, but would you please…?"

Without a word, my friend leaned down, drew the bag toward her, and released the catch. The valise opened, and we stared at a bulge of rough brown wool.

"And the cambric square too…."

We peered at the linen across the top, stained from Theo's fingers.

Cassie made a face.

"Should you put on gloves?" I asked.

"I'll do this bare-handed." Cassie took the handkerchief in one hand and tugged at the cloak.

"Are you all right?" I asked.

She had suddenly stopped, the cambric in one hand, the brown wool clutched in the other, half in her lap, half in the valise.

"Cassie—"

Did she swoon? I gripped my chair arms as my friend's eyes squinted tight and her hands quivered.

"Cassie—"

Her fingers gouged the cambric, the wool, as if trying to escape the touch. "Do you smell it, Val?"

"The verbena?"

"The decay...the rot. Don't you smell it?"

I shook my head, but Cassie's eyes had closed.

She turned her head. "Do you see it? Do you?"

"What, Cassie? What do you see?"

The blue veins of Cassie's throat stood out against her pale, slender neck as she twisted her head again and again.

"What do you see?"

"It's...like a battlefield," she said. "...smoke, heat...furious." She opened her eyes, and tears streaked her cheeks. "I felt it, Val...it was something like...like a war."

Chapter Thirty-six

I EXPECTED THE DOOR to be opened by the butler. Instead, Roddy met me with a finger pressed against his lips to signal, "hush."

"What's the matter—?"

"Finlay is here. He's downstairs in the servants' hall."

"What for?"

"A signature," he said, "from the maid who was attacked. She needs to sign a statement for the police."

"Mattie," I said, "Mattie Joiner."

"I'm glad he's here. I need to speak to him."

"About Eli Fryer? You needn't. I already talked with him about Fryer's schemes and our *Black Crook* escapade and Lola Taylor too...so you needn't...."

"Roddy," I said, "I have new ideas...and my papa's slogan, 'Nobody ever drowns in sweat.' He meant hard thinking, but feelings matter too, and I wanted Cassie's 'touch.' My fears about the brown cloak rang true. And the handkerchief too...."

Roddy frowned at the valise at my feet. "Val," he said, "do not talk to Finlay about Cassandra's spells."

"I will speak my mind," I said. Roddy cleared his throat just as Detective Finlay appeared, escorted by Sands. My husband half-heartedly invited the detective into a drawing room.

"You secured the signature from our maid?" Roddy asked.

"At Chief Devery's request, yes. Thank you."

"Mrs. DeVere wishes to have a word with you, Mr. Finlay."

The detective unbuttoned his peacoat, bent a knee on a chair cushion, and cocked an ear.

"Detective Finlay," I said, "the police must have many tips about the deaths in the park."

"We do, and they are many."

If he merely humored me, I was lost. "So then, Mr. Finlay, you are about to get a tip from me...starting with a young woman named Annie Flowers...and could we all sit down...?"

We perched like creatures about to take flight. "... Central Park in years past," I began, "was an area called the Uptown Land...."

My tone held steady, the words spaced as I had learned in speech class at the Fourth Ward School in Virginia City. I bypassed western slang, no "wrangle" or "bushwack." I merely mentioned a dear friend whose extreme sensitivity became useful but stressed revenge over the Uptown Land and my visit to Ludlow Street.

"...a Central Park laborer," I concluded, "named Mack Dougherty, and Sergeant Doyle can verify the tenement address." Finlay had taken out his notebook and pencil.

"Dougherty," I said, "knows the park like the back of his hand, and his tenement family gets gasoline to clean stains from clothing. They were immigrants and outcasts from the Uptown Land. They call Central Park the 'Devil's Circus,' and the park...." I swallowed hard. "The park is their killing ground."

I took a deep breath. "Detective Finlay," I continued, "the laborer, Mack Dougherty, does the filthy work of sabotage that benefits Mr. Eli Fryer's real estate scheme, but Dougherty is the arsonist and killer. I believe he strangled two young women and attacked Mattie Joiner, intending to kill her as well. He is enraged, and he will kill again."

Finlay jotted furiously in the same notebook that I recalled from his first visit to this house, when he suspected us of arson.

"How all this relates to Clayton Philbrick's disappearance," I said, "I have no idea. Perhaps the actress Lola Taylor has information, so when you investigate her...."

The detective nodded, abruptly lifted his pencil, faced Roddy, and looked at me with an odd glint in his eye. "As to the Philbrick case, Mrs. DeVere...Mr. DeVere...we may soon have something to say."

"What?" Roddy asked. I had seldom heard him sound so truculent as when he asked, "What?" And "When?"

"Mr. DeVere, we have to be full to the gunwales before we can pipe up. That means full to the brim, sir...packed tight, you might say."

Roddy sat ramrod straight. "I would say to you, Detective Sergeant Finlay," he said, "that two elderly people—a fine lady and a gentleman of this city—are at their wits' end. Mr. and Mrs. Victor Philbrick are desperate for news about their grandson...desperate to know whether he is alive, or—"

"—Mr. Devere, please...I must tack against the wind on this matter. You understand me? Hard winds blow from Mulberry Street, Mr. DeVere, when the Chief issues orders."

"Chief Devery—" Roddy said.

"...whose very first act as chief was firing a captain." Finlay pocketed the pencil and notebook. "The captain, you see, had raided certain 'establishments' that were under the chief's protection. Gambling and...and...." He glanced my way.

"And prostitution?" I asked.

"A detective needs to know the tides of the city," he said quickly. "For Chief Devery, the tide is high when the newspapers print his picture and the story shines him up like brass brightwork."

He paused. "So, I can talk when...when the chief gives his order. One thing I can say, it will be soon."

Finlay took his hat, and we stood to see him out. Roddy began to open the door when the detective held up a hand. "One last thing, Mr. DeVere...Mrs. DeVere...." He cleared his throat. "Your cooperation has meant a great deal, but from now on, you'll leave the work entirely to us. The police will take full charge. The Central Park case is police work. It's far too dangerous for people like you."

Chapter Thirty-seven

FINLAY LEFT US AT loose ends and irritable.

"What now?" I asked.

"Now we secure our property." Roddy went to a window. "We must make certain of our safety. That crazed park laborer… near this house. Suppose he glimpsed you in the park, Val… on horseback on Comet or entering a carriage. Or at our front entrance…or recalling your face from the tenement."

"I don't think he'd remember, Roddy."

"I will send word to Noland and the grooms to guard the stable. My parents must take precautions…. I'll have Sands and Mrs. Thwaite summon the entire household staff this evening." I won't have my wife endangered in our home."

And so it went. After the servants' evening meal, Roddy asked the butler and housekeeper to gather everyone in our front hall. The footmen stood against the wall, and Calista joined Roddy's valet, Norbert. The maids lined up in sight

335

of Mrs. Thwaite, with Mattie Joiner in their midst. Sands, as Roddy's first lieutenant, stood close by his side. Our cook, her assistant, and the sculleries assembled at the rear.

I took my place with Velvet at the front as Roddy warned our servants to lock all doors and be extra vigilant about deliveries. "…familiar deliverymen only…the greengrocer, the fish monger, butcher…the florist, the dairyman." He added "…especially the coal deliveries…men manning the coal shovels…report all unfamiliar or suspicious persons."

With a general thank-you, Roddy wished everyone a good evening, waited until the hall emptied, and took my arm for our meal. The dog came with us to the dining room, gnawing a bone at our feet as we soldiered through the courses and made polite conversation.

"And will you return to your work-room, Val?"

"Book binding…" I said. "I'm not sure. And you?"

"The Dewey Committee meets tomorrow afternoon," he said. "I will propose a cocktail with Plymouth gin to be named for the Admiral."

"Nice," I replied. The meal ended at last, as did the frosty, silent evening in armchairs with open books on our laps and Velvet between us. The clocks finally struck the hour to let us say, "Good night."

છ⊚

At first, the message that drew me into the park the following afternoon looked like "low grade ore," as papa would say.

The day had dawned raw cold and very foggy, and Roddy left at midmorning to visit his parents and inspect their locks before his committee meeting.

With Calista, I took Velvet for a short walk up the Avenue, scanning side to side and glancing over my shoulder in the fog. My husband was no alarmist, but I couldn't shake his warning, although I refused to be housebound and went outdoors to prove I could come and go.

Teams of horses' hooves and carriage wheels sounded in the thick mist, but no footsteps on the sidewalk. The temperature was dropping, and it felt good to get back inside with a mug of cocoa. I ordered a cup sent up to my maid, when Sands approached to say, "A message for you, ma'am."

The tray, held at arm's length, signaled the butler's distaste for the envelope of cheap pulp paper on sterling silver.

"Who sent this?"

"Delivered by a hack driver, ma'am...not the sort of cab one usually sees on Fifth Avenue. Mr. DeVere would wish to know of such a messenger."

I looked for the signature on the sheet inside: Mrs. Clara Demple.

"Sands, is the person who sent this waiting for an answer?"

"No, ma'am. The hack drove on."

I went to the front windows but saw neither horse nor cab in the fog, which was thickening to a milky white. Across the avenue, the bare outlines of the stone wall along the park border, and further off, the faintest trees.

"Would you wish to send a reply, ma'am?"

He waited while I read, silently, "...Greetings to Mrs. Roderick Windham DeVere in hope this correspondence finds you in good health and recollection of your visit to 641 West Thirty-fifth Street with your friend...."

The butler waited.

In inky, labored handwriting, Mrs. Demple offered "very useful" information about a certain tenant with the initials L.T. ("and your further generosity would be much appreciated....")

She meant the boardinghouse visit with Cassie, I realized, not my "disguise" with Roddy's portfolio. The landlady remembered the silver dollar, and she knew this address from my calling card.

"...information this afternoon at noon to one o'clock when I will be in Central Park nearby your home at your convenience...on the walk in Central Park...nearest to your residence. Every courtesy is appreciated."

"A reply, ma'am...?"

"No, Sands. I'll see about this."

I postponed lunch. In little more than an hour, Clara Demple would hope to meet me on the walk from the park entrance nearest to the Arsenal, about twenty-minutes on foot. What might she tell me? That Lola skipped out owing rent? That certain belongings were left behind?

Why would she think I cared? She knew nothing about me. Clara Demple had once opened her front door to two well-dressed ladies who presented cards and asked to visit a young actress and dancer living in her boardinghouse. One of the ladies paid her a silver dollar for the visit.

Why pursue me now? The letter gave no reason.

I finished my cocoa as a clock struck the quarter hour. Perhaps, I thought, the landlady followed publicity for *The Black Crook* and saw the newspaper headline on Lola Taylor playing Betty Bang-Bang. Perhaps she suspected that her tenant, Lola Taylor, was involved with a gentleman in Society, a lady's husband or a son…a young man like Clayton Philbrick.

Was that it?

I had not inquired about Lola's own lovers, who surely took her for late night champagne suppers…special men, not those she "met" casually "off the paths" in Central Park. If Mrs. Demple knew something about Lola's stage door Johnny in New York Society, she might wager the information to be worth several silver dollars.

Was it worth it to me? I could suggest that Finlay question Mrs. Demple. The landlady, however, might deny all knowledge.

I glanced out the nearest window…fog, foggier, foggiest.

To go, or not to go? Roddy's warning about Mack Dougherty had weight. Did park crews labor in thick fog? To go?…or not? The note was open beside me, a lure and a dare on the seat cushion where I let it lie.

Another quarter hour, a clock chime, and I was upstairs calling for Calista. "My bonnet and heavy cloak once again, please…no, you stay inside. I'm going a very short distance… yes, I'm sure…just two more things…."

To a purse that held silver dollars, I picked five for a pocket in my cloak. Then to a certain drawer in my dressing table, I fingered cartridges, then felt under the camisoles and corsets in my bureau. My hand wrapped around the grips, and I pulled papa's Colt and flicked the cylinder to insert one, two...six. The cylinder locked in place, I called to Calista, "—and my muff, if you please. The weather so cold, Calista. A lady's hands are best warmed inside a fur muff...for her own protection."

Chapter Thirty-eight

WITH A CLOAK WRAPPED tight and bonnet tied, I marched south into the fog, a lady alone on a public street. The cold smacked my face and stung. Street sounds were muffled and visibility just a few feet ahead, but the brief clip-clop of a horse on the avenue felt reassuring.

Just three blocks to the park entrance.

"I'm only stepping around the corner," I had said to a fretful Sands, who assumed that I meant to pay a call on my in-laws. It struck me that no one knew my whereabouts.

No one.

Was it liberating? Isolating? Don't think too much, I told myself. Focus on the task. Close by, a dog barked, and a man's sharp command, "No...no...down, boy, I said, no!"

I saw neither dog nor man.

A street sign loomed...*61st Street*. I crossed. The cold was a presence that bit through my cloak, but my hands were warm, and so was the hard steel inside the muff. Suddenly, a figure brushed close...a man.

Fear surged, and I gripped the pistol tight.

"Excuse...'scuse me...."

It was someone's servant...a footman, going...going...vanished.

At *60th Street*, I listened for a horse or carriage, then crossed to the next block. This fog could set a record, a New York match for London's famous fogs.

The fog of Jack-the-Ripper?

"Ridiculous," I said aloud, my voice like cotton. I relaxed my grip inside the muff.

At last, *59th Street*, a commercial roadway with carts and wagons, all moving slowly. An ice wagon rattled past, and I recalled that Roddy had forgotten the ice man in his warning to our staff. Surely, they would pay attention to whoever held the ice tongs when the frozen big blocks were delivered to the back door. Surely....

Two uniformed policemen guarded the busy corner, one directing traffic, the other on street patrol. The patrolman eyed my cloak, my muff.

"Morning, ma'am."

"Officer..." I said, looking directly into his twinkling eyes, as reassured by his presence as he was obviously puzzled by a lady walking alone.

"May I offer assistance, ma'am?"

"Thank you, officer, but I plan to meet a lady on the park path ahead." I pointed to the right of the main gate.

"Perhaps you saw a lady walk in that direction a little while ago?"

"Just came on duty, ma'am. Sorry."

Maybe he saw my disappointment.

"Anything you need," he said, "I'm here the next four hours."

He saluted, and I walked to the footpath that wound just beyond a grove of oak trees. Charming in season, the branches and stark trunks now braced for winter. My boots crunched on fallen, frozen leaves.

Fresh footprints on the path—a woman's. The time of day, I guessed, was shortly after noon. Up ahead, Mrs. Demple was supposed to wait for me...for silver dollars. Around a curve, her back to me, the cloaked and bonneted landlady appeared ahead, walking slowly. I quickened my pace.

"Mrs. Demple? Mrs. Dem—"

She turned and stopped. Yellow curls curled from her bonnet brim, and her mouth was bright scarlet. "Hello, Mrs. DeVere."

It was Lola Taylor.

"Surprised?"

"I don't...yes, surprised."

She laughed. "I knew the odds were better if the letter came from Mrs. Demple."

"You wrote the letter...to propose this meeting?"

"I did."

We faced one another, our breath visible in little clouds. A bright red bird flew close just then...a male cardinal that chirped twice and flew off.

"Nice muff you have," said Lola. "Mink, is it?"

"Mink," I said.

She sneered. "Shall we stroll together? Us two ladies?"

We fell into step. Her gloved left hand brushed at a curl, and her right was snug inside her cloak.

"It's a different park at mid-day in the fog," I said.

Her short laugh cackled. "I wouldn't know about the day. You could ask about the nights."

We walked in taut silence, nearly in sight of the Armory. But Lola abruptly turned us back. "Back and forth," she said, "...like a promenade. Two strolling ladies, isn't it a promenade?"

I stopped. "Miss Taylor, why are we here?"

"I thought you'd never ask," she said. Her gloved hand opened and closed in a fist. Something poked from inside her cloak...an umbrella? "Can't you guess, Mrs. DeVere?"

"You tell me."

She laughed again. "You're a wily one, lady. In my line of work, a girl learns to spot the wily ones...gents and women, all kinds...."

I stood still, feeling the cold. Ice bits stung my cheeks.

"You came with your friend to ask about Roxie," Lola said. "Two nice ladies at Demple's...and you came back again by yourself, not so fancy that time, all about 'Phil' and the other gent...and we know that gent, don't we?—he paid for the big doings at the theatre, very exclusive, and you were there. I saw you."

I nodded.

"You with your handful of silver dollars. Got dollars today?"

I nodded again, puzzled. Waiting.

"But you came to Demple's one more time, didn't you? To look at the old woman's in-and-out book. It was you, wasn't it?"

I did not answer. She did not expect an answer.

"The old fool can't see so good, but that was you nosing in."

In the cold, I felt heat climb my neck to my face. Lola's gloved fingers pointed at my throat. Inside her cloak, her right hand looked busy.

"So, you saw me at the *Black Crook* night...I swung down...bang bang bang...."

"You did," I said. My mouth had gone dry.

"—but you had to go talk to Jake...."

"Jake?"

"The prop master. We're pals."

"All right...."

"And he told you about the gun...the first one...the mistake...."

I shrugged. Lola's right hand stirred inside her cloak.

"And you put two and two together, didn't you, Mrs. DeVere?"

"I don't know what you mean."

She laughed like a wild creature. "Yes, you do. You know what happened...the mistake...Roxie...my best friend...."

Her words flew, and spittle from her lips hung in the air. Inside her cloak, her hand shifted and poked. The umbrella?

"It could have been me," she said, "and you know it. It could be Roxie you're talking to here, and me, Dolores Fleck, six feet under in some Youngstown graveyard...and Roxie swinging down every night. Roxie could have been Betty Bang-Bang...but I had the gun...."

"An accident," I said. "It was accidental death."

"—cried my eyes out," she said, "every last tear. But a person goes on...like I go on. 'Harden your heart,' I told myself. When Irina James got the Betty part, well then, I told myself, 'two wrongs can make a right.' They can. They must."

"—the frayed trapeze rope..." I murmured.

"Wily one.... You know way too much...much too much...."

She looked around. No one was in sight. Her hand inside the cloak was moving, the shape under the cloth growing familiar...steadily too familiar. It was no umbrella. It was—

"Lola, put down the gun."

The barrel pointed at my chest. "You know too much," she said.

"Lola, put it down. There's no need...."

The pistol wavered, as if to drop down.

"No need at all..." I said.

An uncertain moment hung, indecision in her eyes. But she blinked, and her left hand rose to brace her right arm—the pose of a shooter.

"Lola, don't—"

My gun hand gripped tight inside the muff, thumb and trigger finger ready, my left hand dropped to my side.

She had shut her eyes.

"Please, Lola, don't—"

Her eyes shut, but that barrel waved at my face, my heart.

Her thumb nudged the hammer.

Through the muff, I took aim at her shoulder.

She pulled her hammer back and cocked her gun.

I cocked mine.

And squeezed the trigger.

That second shot was not my Colt .44.... The second one split the sky as Lola hit the path, writhing, screeching as blood seeped into her cloak...blood steaming in the cold fog. And the gun clutched in her hand, smoking.

A tableau...weird tableau. My ears rang, gunpowder prickled my nose, and papa's "Peacemaker" felt hot to the touch. The next seconds—minutes?—pounded from my heartbeat, and boots on the path...blue tunics, high helmets, nightsticks raised and ready.

The traffic cop and the "Morning" officer.

Anything I needed, he had said.

Both men stunned, then to duty. Lola writhed on the path, her hat askew. Dead leaves stuck in her yellow hair when the traffic officer bent to help, cradling her head and shoulder. I heard, "flesh wound...flesh wound...."

He pried the gun from her hand, and the "Morning" officer took my papa's .44 and marched us to 59th Street— one partner with Lola in his arms, the other clutching two pistols in one hand, his other hand clamped to my elbow as if I might take flight.

"Arrest," the partner said, "both of you...under arrest."

A public spectacle in the fog at the busy 59th Street corner, where passersby stopped to gawk at a policeman tending an injured woman, and teamsters reined their draft horses to stare at the second officer who restrained me, the lady with a muff.

I, too, gawked when the police patrol wagon (the "paddy" wagon) took the wounded woman away, and I blinked when two men suddenly came running around the corner from Fifth Avenue, both breathless. My husband's greatcoat flapped as he ran, knees pumping, hands clenched into fists. Our butler ran close behind, the tails of his morning coat like big bat wings. Close-up, Roddy's face mixed fear and confusion, relief and...was it a trace of a smile?

He took my arm, but the policeman held my elbow in a tug-o-war—until I broke free of both men, like a western showdown...two ruffians on dusty streets. I stood tall and took a breath. "Officer, let me introduce my husband...."

In moments, I agreed to accompany the policeman to the nearest precinct office at the Central Park Arsenal. The gawkers saw us go, the officer, the lady, and the gentleman in the greatcoat. Perhaps they thought he was the lady's attorney, and very much needed, since I was now in police custody.

Chapter Thirty-nine

"YOU SHOT FIRST, MRS. DeVere?"

"In self-defense, officer."

"And why were you armed, ma'am? Can you tell us why you carried a concealed weapon into Central Park?"

I blurted answers to endless police questions in the overheated precinct office. My muff became an object of curiosity, relayed from hand to hand as the questions flew. All the while, Roddy spoke calmly and caring as a lawyer and my husband. He had read the note given to him by our butler and hastened to the park. Further questioning would take place in the days ahead, perhaps by Detective Sergeant Colin Finlay. I promised to be available. At long last, we were free to go home.

Wide-eyed from whatever Sands had told them, our servants tiptoed as though the house were an infirmary. Calista drew me a hot bath and urged a long soak. The Greek

Isles, she said, had earthquakes. "Then," she said, "came the afterward shocks."

How true. All night long, I relived the sight of Lola's eyes shut tight, the gun in her hand and thumb on the hammer. My .44 had kicked when it fired, and my right hand jerked under the covers at midnight. With every breath, the scent of gunpowder in the air, on my pillow, until finally, at long last, came the dawn. The morning saw me sipping hot broth prescribed to "steady" the nerves. Whether ordered by Roddy or a servant, I never knew, but all the household felt agitated, including our dog.

In the Corinthian reception room this early afternoon, Roddy and I waited for Finlay, who was coming for the pulpy letter from "Clara Demple" that had lured me to the park. Lola Taylor had committed the crime of criminal impersonation by writing as the landlady, and the letter was evidence. Of course, yesterday's attempted homicide was the major charge. And the police agreed to investigate the matter of tampered "trapeze" ropes at the theatre.

In the precinct house, I had kept quiet about Roxie LaRue's death. Finlay ought to take charge of that investigation as soon as Lola recovered. I would talk to him, urge him to interview the *Black Crook* prop manager and put two and two together about the missing pistol. The monogrammed cigarette case was most probably dropped when Roxie fell dead, and Finlay could account for it lying by her body. He deserved respect on the force, a promotion and a raise. He needed a new suit.

"We ought to reward Sands," Roddy said. "If our butler hadn't read that message and tracked me down...."

"Roddy, I am fine. Just fine. Let's not...."

"You almost got killed, Val. Suppose the tenement criminal had lurked nearby."

"Mack," I said. "Mack Dougherty."

He nodded.

"I would have been ready," I said, "...locked and loaded in the mink muff. And Roddy, as my papa would say, 'Let's not chew it finer'...I mean, let's leave it at that."

A moment passed. My husband lifted Velvet onto his lap.

"Roddy," I said, "I want my 'Peacemaker' back."

"For now, Val, the gun is evidence in a crime."

"Not my crime." I spoke too loudly, and our dog startled. "The police know that I fired in self-defense," I almost whispered. "I 'neutralized' the threat to my life. I won't rest until papa's gun is back...."

"I understand, Val, but let's give it some time. Let's enjoy the sunlight."

Yesterday's fog had turned to sullen rain, but the late October sun now glared from the West.

I guessed the rustling in the hallway meant Sands with Detective Finlay, but the butler appeared alone with a small tray. "—a card from a man who is accompanying Mr. Finlay," he said, "a man wearing a uniform, and also a badge." Anxious disapproval showed in our butler's white knuckles. "His card, sir...."

I took Velvet as Roddy lifted a card from the tray to read aloud, "William S. Devery," Chief of Police, New York City." Roddy stood, touched his cravat, and requested that both men be shown into the Corinthian Room.

Finlay entered with a deferential half-step behind his chief, "Big Bill" Devery who swaggered, half-bowed to me and accepted Roddy's handshake. Thickset with a fleshy face and a dark broad brush of a moustache, Devery surveilled the room without expression, while Finlay shifted his weight from foot to foot, hugging a dark leather bag tucked under one arm. He unbuttoned the familiar peacoat, and underneath the shiny business suit with celluloid shirt collar and cuffs. I handed him Lola's letter from "Mrs. Demple," which he jammed into a pocket, his eyes darting from us to the chief. I had never seen him so nervous.

"Do sit down, Chief Devery...detective," said Roddy.

Finlay approached a spindly side chair, standing still until Devery claimed an entire loveseat across from us and set his cap on one knee. A double row of brass buttons gleamed on the dark blue tunic of his barrel chest, and "CHIEF" blazoned on the cap that faced Roddy and me.

"Chief Devery has brought news," Finlay said. His voice croaked.

"Good news, we hope," said Roddy.

"I warrant you, 'yes' to that," said Devery. His voice rasped. "The New York police are fierce on vice. Gambling rings go to smash—on my order."

I tried to appear impressed.

"Overhead, underground, wherever there's gangs...." He eyed Roddy. "This one in particular, deep underground, but we got the skinny on the slavers. Busted them Wops but good, every last Guido. No picnic, sir, but we got it done."

Roddy nodded, as if he understood the argot. Did he? An Italian gang, it seemed, but what "slavers?" It felt impossible to ask.

"Word always gets out," Devery continued. "Such as...a certain young fellow that owed Pioggi a bundle, couldn't pay it off, and so Pioggi put him to work. Like I say, word always gets out. The question is, 'Who hears it?' Bigger question, 'Who acts on it?'"

He glanced at me, then narrowed his gaze on Roddy. "We got dirt on Pioggi's dealer with the fancy card tricks," he said, "...he faked the shuffles for out-of-town rubes and cleaned them out. The flashy dealer...my Eighth Precinct got wind of this guy...high-toned gent. They called him 'Yellow Whiskers.'"

"Oh? Yellow—?" My fingers clutched at Velvet's fur. She whimpered. Devery paid no attention.

"—working off the debt to Pioggi all night, every night, dealing from the bottom of the deck in the Bowery. The rubes go on a spree, lose, get steamed, and bet more and more till they're cleaned out and it's all over." He leaned toward Roddy. "You get my drift?"

Roddy said, "Do you mean the dealer is a man named Philbrick? Clayton Philbrick? And he has been kept in confinement?"

"—not the first time Pioggi's slavers bagged a man." Devery nodded. "They run a cat house, they grab a johnny when it suits. He was theirs, all theirs."

Roddy said, "Then Mr. Philbrick has been...held prisoner by a gang?"

The chief nodded. "—all this month."

"But he's now freed?" asked Roddy.

"Free as a bird. You'll read all about it in the papers, big raid, how Pioggi's ring got busted. Weapons were emptied in the effort, but 'Yellow Whiskers' is on his way home, unharmed...a few blocks from your own place, Mr. DeVere...and Mrs...." He smiled. "Busted but good, and the Force will gladly take a donation when that young man's family welcomes him home."

Roddy gave me the look that said the Philbricks' generosity would be as boundless as police extortion required.

Devery turned to me. "Big city, our New York," he said. "All the boroughs at my command...three hundred square miles, and then some."

"You must be very busy, Mr. Devery," I said.

"Night and day. Not to waste my time or yours, ma'am, all five boroughs ...but hats off to you. And Finlay here...."

He neither glanced toward the detective, nor looked me in the eye.

"Here in Manhattan, Central Park can burn a chief," he said, "scald him good, like 'Clubber' Williams before me. Forced out, he was, and Tommy Byrnes too."

He licked his lips, fingered his moustache. "But here and there, a citizen helps us out. We got the skinny on that maniac from you, ma'am, and caught him with a gasoline can...."

"You caught Dougherty?" I asked, almost gasping.

"...said it was cleaning fluid, he did...all ready to pour it on a brand new boat at the boathouse, wee hours this morning. And tried to set fire to the officer that nabbed him...splashed him with gas and grabbed his throat to choke our man. Three officers heard the commotion, and all three held him down, him cursing the park like a demon, like the park belongs to him...like he owns it all."

Devery fingered his badge. "Bet my bottom dollar he's the strangler. He's in the slammer on Mulberry Street... gagged with a rag to shut him up."

Weak with relief, I held Velvet close.

"—and your maid that got attacked?"

"Mattie Joiner," I said.

"You keep her on the payroll here, so when the time comes, she'll testify?"

"We will," I said.

"Excellent news on two fronts, Chief Devery," said Roddy. "And we understand that all credit for the capture of the Central Park strangler will go to the Chief of Police... to you, sir, and you alone. And we appreciate you coming personally...with Detective Finlay," Roddy added.

I expected murmurs of farewell, but Devery sat back, expansive on the loveseat. "One other thing," he said, "so we're all clear." He swiveled slowly as if to view every painting on our walls, every stick of furniture, and all five ornate

Corinthian columns set in a row. "One last thing…" he said, pointing to Finlay with a sly smile. "Detective, if you will…."

Finlay slowly opened the leather bag, reached in, and took out…a pistol.

"I believe that might be—" I said.

"—a certain Colt .44." Devery sounded like an auctioneer. Finlay held the gun on the flat of his palm.

I fought the urge to jump up and grab it. "The grips of that pistol, Mr. Devery," I said, "are inscribed with the initials 'P M,' inlaid in silver. Am I right?"

Again, the chief's sly smile. "Excellent eyesight, Mrs. DeVere."

"Then I trust the pistol can be returned to my wife," said Roddy. "It belonged to her late father, Patrick Mackle…a keepsake."

"It is crime scene evidence, Mr. DeVere…ask the detective."

Finlay silently displayed the pistol, his face flushed.

"I trust you are here to bargain for the pistol," Roddy said.

"No such thing, Mr. DeVere, but the Force counts on good will. I recollect a private reward for the capture of the Central Park strangler. Five thousand dollars. Isn't that right?"

"A private donation," Roddy said.

"—announced in all the newspapers," said Devery. "If that sum could go to the New York Police…after all, we caught him, didn't we? And I, Chief of Police, oversaw the capture and will see to the conviction."

The muscles at my husband's jawline knotted. He put his hand on my arm.

"That pistol," he said, "is beyond price."

Finlay looked miserable. Too miserable. A silent moment passed. A clock chimed. Which of us would speak next?

Which one to speak up?

I sat forward and cleared my throat. "—the donation for the pistol, Chief Devery," I said, "can easily be arranged. I guarantee it."

The chief looked wary, Roddy confused.

"But something else must also be agreed on...."

The chief looked suspicious, Roddy bewildered.

"You see," I said, "I grew up in the far West, where a handshake seals a deal."

Devery's moustache twitched. "What deal?"

"Five thousand for the pistol," I said, "and Detective Finlay stays on the payroll, no risk to his rank, no transfer unless he wants it. And a promotion. And that, Chief Devery, is the deal."

A silent, thunderous moment passed. Roddy looked taken aback, and Devery's cheeks flushed a deep scarlet until, at length, he said, "Detective Finlay, if you please, give the pistol to Mrs. DeVere." He swallowed. "And let us be on our way."

Finlay bowed his thanks as he put Papa's "Peacemaker" in my hand. The men stared as I checked the chambers—all emptied, meaning the police had removed five bullets and one .44 brass shell.

Laying the gun on a table, I stood, stretched out my arm, and waited for Devery to collect his cap, stand, and tug the hem of his tunic. Roddy stood at my side as I shook the beefy, soft hand of the Chief of Police of New York City.

Our dog followed them to the door. "They're gone," Roddy said. "Let's have a drink." My husband suggested the New York namesake cocktail that had become popular. "The Manhattan," he said, "Irish whiskey, vermouth, orange bitters, ice…I'll mix them right now. And we'll toast…."

The bar cart wheels squeaked and bottles clinked as the footman pushed the cart to the room. Roddy set to work, and in minutes we toasted and sipped.

The Manhattan
Ingredients
- ½ ounce Irish whiskey
- ½ ounce Italian vermouth
- 2 dashes orange bitters
- 2 pinches refined sugar or teaspoon simple syrup.
- Ice

Directions:
1. Add whiskey and vermouth to ice-filled tall glass or shaker.
2. Add sugar
3. Add bitters
4. Stir and strain into martini glass.

"To Central Park!" I said.

"To Central Park," Roddy answered. "And to next month's Horse Show at Madison Square Garden."

COMING SOON

A Fatal Gilded High Note
By
Cecelia Tichi

New York's "Diamond Horseshoe" balcony in the Metropolitan Opera House glittered with ladies' jewels in January 1899, and Society seated in private boxes heard Mozart's murder victim sing his song of death—unaware that the sudden death of a "Coal King" in Box 18 will be ruled a homicide.

When opera-goers Val and Roddy DeVere are asked to investigate ("on the q.t."), Val finds herself suspected of complicity in the murder. The police have "material evidence" against her. Before a jury, Val's lawyer husband reminds her, "'material' evidence can be the bright, shiny object that overrides all reason and fact."

(The Second Val and Roddy DeVere "Gilded" Mystery)

Follow Cecelia on website
https://www.cecebooks.com